DOUBLE HAPPINESS
By RW Richard

WEB
Press

Published by WEB Press, Carlsbad, San Diego, California
© Copyright for *Double Happiness* is TXu 1-803-218 (text and artwork).
Published first in November 2014. ISBN is 9780980080476. Artwork by
RW Richard & Stephanie Knautz. Edited by Annie Seaton. All rights
reserved, including the right to reproduce this book without written
permission of the author.

The author thanks you for purchasing *Double Happiness* and wants to hear from you, either by email, review or blog comment.

E-mail to rwrichard@ymail.com.

Author's blog: http://romancetheguyspov.blogspot.com.

The author thanks the Writers Bloc critique group and the local RWA Chapter (San Diego) for their support and dedicates this double romantic comedy to identical twins everywhere and would especially love to hear their stories or comments.

Novels and novellas by RW Richard

The Carlos series - each book stands on its own and is a complete story:

1st - *Autumn Breeze: I am a New Yorker* - a novel in e-book and paperback - **Amazon's editors' pick for best books of 2015.**

2nd - *Angel's Eyes* will be out early 2016.

3rd - *A More Perfect Union* - **Finalist: San Diego Book Awards.**

Expect more in the Carlos series.

Stand-alone titles:

The Wolves of Sherwood Forest - a novella in e-book format only.

Double Happiness - a novel in e-book and paperback.

Neanderthals and the Garden of Eden: Running with Wolves - a novel in e-book and paperback.

Double Happiness
by RW Richard

Act One
Chapter 1

Once upon a childhood, adolescence, and college life, swapping places with his identical twin had been more fun than dropping frogs down girls' blouses, acing high school exams and then dating un-frogged coeds. But today there was no joy in Medford, New Jersey.

At twenty-seven, they were getting too old for this nonsense.

This will be our last swap, brother.

Raphael Chariote parked in the municipal lot and stayed in the car, safe and free. Safe—because the moment he stepped out, the darkening clouds would notice and soak him. Free for the moment—because he had promised to take his brother's place in jail.

He stuck a to-do list on the dashboard:

1.   Keep my art studio pristine. I couldn't re-schedule one client. She'll be easy. Just wing it.

2.   Go to my AA meeting. Resist the temptation to do a stand-up routine.

3.   Be a better me, please. Do not touch Stella.

Love always, Raphael

Stella, Raphael's fiancée, had kicked him out of his own home the week before. She told him to join AA, figure out what made him an alcoholic and to stay in his art studio and away from her until he stopped drinking. Raphael couldn't even take the first step of AA's twelve, because he enjoyed the taste and high of alcohol and found nothing wrong with doing so. At least he'd now have time to reflect once he sat behind bars. Maybe he'd slow his drinking down a little, just to placate Mom and Dad, Stella, and his brother. He really wasn't an alcoholic though.

Not. Not. Not.

His brother, Troy, didn't drink much and could go weeks without as much as a beer. Switching places, Troy, playing the part of Raphael, would look and act cured to Stella. *A regular miracle.* What could go wrong? Was there a better way to demonstrate brotherly love than to trade places and carry on for each other? They were each other's keepers. In short, he'd do anything for his twin, and vice versa.

Although a hopeless womanizer, Troy had never let his bro down and never touched Stella.

And he never will.

Troy always did things his own way and somehow it worked for both of them. Raphael smiled, crumpled the useless list his brother wouldn't need or read, spotted a kicked-in trashcan at a crosswalk, and stepped out of the car.

No rain yet. The gods were smiling. Sweet spring blossoms plumped by humidity would have to be his last taste of freedom for hopefully no more than two weeks. Squirrels chased each other's tails around the base of a fat oak that hugged the chipped red, white and blue brick jail. Irony struck, not lightning: he and his brother were doing the same thing as these two furry critters. A doubly foolish errand awaited them. That never stopped them before, so he'd carry on.

He straightened a fake mustache and tightened his Phillies' baseball cap over thick curly black hair. The more the police noticed about how different the identical twins appeared, the less likely they'd catch on to the switch. Right?

2

Stopping before the main entrance, he peered at his likeness in the silvered glass, grinned and whispered to his image their secret saying from many a classic Laurel and Hardy movie. "Well, here's another nice mess you've got me into." Cocky and laughing, he pulled open the door.

"Yo, Raphael, how the hell are you?" Deputy Max Brunkowski greeted him with his signature bone-crunching handshake. The three of them had played on the Medford High School football team with his brother Troy playing quarterback, Raphael halfback and supersized-Max center.

Max was used to looking at the twins upside down from the center of the football line, and being a follower, so odds were they would not be caught today.

"How's your fiancée?" Max asked. Although Max wasn't fat, his bulky size and height had scared off most girls. *Maybe he should date a lady wrestler.*

"Stella is fine. Got anybody special, big guy?"

"Well, it's easy for you two to get dates, although I worry about your brother."

"Oh, he's just waiting for somebody to love him and believe in his career. Most stand-up comedians don't make big bucks." Raphael lied by inference. He wouldn't share his brother's private financial information. Troy held down first billing at the Comic Freak in Philadelphia and had lucrative investments. Troy had talked about going national but at this point, today, all he needed to do was consider love.

"Your kind of artist does worse," Max said. For some reason people assumed the bigger the man, the dumber. At any time and for little reason, Max was liable to spout poetry.

Raphael put on gallery shows, entertained a following. "Doing fine, thank you."

"He'll be cleared of the attempted murder charge in no time. Pick up his spirits, will ya?" Max asked.

"Stupid charges."

"Yep. I'm just doing my job."

Max opened the steel door, which squeaked like a crypt gate in a scary movie. The dusty gray box his brother was dying to leave would be Raphael's resurrection.

3

"You two have ten minutes. Just call or I'll get you."

"Your accommodations are delightful, Troy." Raphael wrinkled his nose. At least, the place was simple, neat and everything in its place. He pictured his art studio after Troy finished abusing it, brushes at chaotic angles, improperly mixed paints, general disarray, like any other room his brother had claimed as his own.

The door squeaked, the lock turned, and very close to the jail, lightning struck. The sun was losing its battle with the clouds.

Max walked off, oblivious to the brothers' nefarious plot. They were alone.

"It kinda smells like a stuffed vacuum cleaner in here." Troy dropped his nose and sniffed his armpits. "Unfortunately for you, it's not my manly odor." Raphael had always read his brother—so when Troy shrugged and displayed a crooked smile—Raphael felt the love.

"Sorry about this piece of crap, cell," Troy said.

Triangular shadows cutting through light and dark slanted through the small cell window. Dust slid down a sunbeam into a bare toilet bowl in the middle of the cell, highlighting the main feature like a Norman Rockwell painting gone horribly wrong.

The brothers shook hands and his fake mustache and cap transferred to Troy. They had practiced changing clothes in their separate abodes.

Somewhat nervous, pants half-down, Raphael danced on one leg and fell against the bars.

"Troy, your shoes, damn it, don't fit." He tried jamming them on one more time.

"Everything all right?" Max shouted down the corridor.

"Yep, just lost my balance for a moment."

"And you Chariotes played football. Geez," Max said.

"Shh. Lower your voice," Troy said. "I'm not the one with fat feet. I'm not the drunk."

"Let's just keep our shoes," Raphael whispered back. "Max wasn't an A student, anyway. He won't notice." Max like Raphael, was a keen observer of nature—but hopefully not men's shoes.

In spite of being stuck in jail these past five days, Troy appeared much healthier than his brother. Both held the magical power to make women faint on sight, probably due to dimpled chins, hazel-going-blue eyes and puppy dog accessibility. Raphael's machismo was temporarily out of order, with an alcohol-blotched face. Vanity over his appearance also influenced him to switch with Troy. Raphael would be forced to detox in this cage and with a little bit of luck, get his looks back.

Personas exchanged, Raphael slouched onto the yellow stained mattress. Troy leaned against a cracked wall with obscene graffiti surrounding him like a halo.

"We don't have time for small talk. And try not to speak too close to the toilet," Troy said, reinforcing his words with hand signals meaning that people listen through the plumbing. He raised his hands, palms out, to show he guessed sound transmitted through the pipes from another cell.

Raphael nodded. "Before you leave, tell me something else I don't know." Due to the jail's liberal phone policy, they had already discussed the absurd charges and didn't need to do much else but switch places.

Almost imperceptibly, Troy flashed his mischievous look, a quick crooked grin, one raised eyebrow. He lowered his voice. "Well...my incompetent attorney is a pain in the ass, with a painful ass to boot. She's so ugly..."

"How ugly is she?"

"You'll beg for the death penalty. What about you?"

"Stella isn't ugly."

"No, tell me something I don't know, something we haven't already discussed," Troy said.

Raphael had also always known when Troy was joking. Perhaps, the likely very competent attorney, Ms. Hai Lo, would end Troy's fun— at pretending to be his brother—by getting the charges dropped quickly. Raphael had a strong suspicion she'd be damn good at her job and very easy on the eyes. He now looked forward to meeting this so-called abomination. Troy, forever after a joke, was, little doubt, setting his bro up for a huge jolt. Yep, Ms. Hai Lo would be a knockout to knock out all knockouts.

Raphael bent over the bed to scratch his ankle wondering if the place had bugs.

This will not do. He glanced up at Troy and frowned. "You'll be staying in my studio and not the main house. I was kicked out, but you'll still see Stella. We're still friendly. No matter what happens, don't touch her. Just be a sober me. She forced me to commit to AA. I don't remember when the meeting is. She'll prompt you, and oh yeah, if you have time, prove your innocence."

"Funny, bro. Consider your own innocence. People don't start drinking for *no* reason. You are guilty of something. If there's anything wrong with your relationship with Stella, it emanates from you, because that girl is an angel."

Raphael quieted. Nothing in his environment had changed. Troy was off base.

"I've got nothing but time. I'll think on it." Raphael didn't say he'd promise, which wasn't lost on his shadow, his other self, his...

"You're going to lose that girl. Promise me you'll give it some thought."

"Okay. Oo-kay, I promise to look within myself for answers." Now he was stuck. He'd have to give it a moment at least.

They did the man hug, not too affectionate, but really, neither would know what to do if the other died.

The stakes were high for this proposed last swap. But, being all grown up, this would definitely have to be the last of countless adventures.

Troy moved to the bars. "No problem. Get well, kiddo. Love you back." He called out. "Yo, Max."

Over the last five days, using the jail's liberal phone and stingy email policy, the brothers had worked out the broad strokes of a plan speaking in secret brother gibberish invented from being each other's shadows since birth. Shortly, if all went well, like all of their other triumphant and brilliant swaps, they'd get what they wanted.

Troy, pretending to be his brother, would plead try to get the mobster's girlfriend to change her story. She had lied for some reason about what was only an accident, not as she had said attempted murder. Troy would also play the part of a reformed Raphael to try to get his brother back together with Stella, while all Raphael had to do was get— and stay sober.

Troy smiled broadly. "Piece of cake, no file in cake necessary."

Raphael worried for his brother's safety and their success. "Two weeks tops?"

"Sure, what could go wrong?" Troy said in front of Max. Outside, lightning struck again. Maybe since Troy was playing Raphael, a loser, the clouds were waiting for him to emerge from the jail, and then he'd get drenched. As long as Raphael didn't have the love and affection of Stella, he was a loser.

The door squeaked open and then closed leaving Raphael with instant regrets. A little Wild Turkey bourbon would have been nice and would match some of the stains on the bare mattress.

Max addressed the guy he thought was Troy, while the real Troy on the outside of the jail bars beamed. Troy caught his brother's attention pulling on his silly mustache like Snidely Whiplash. "See you later…Troy."

That mustache had better not fall off, clown.

Troy left, but Raphael paced the cell, worried about his brother and his new environment. After a while, he glanced at the suggestive graffiti on the wall and bent toward the toilet. "Anybody who comes near me will get his ass kicked." He was more than strong enough from daily gym workouts and kickboxing to back up his words.

"No problem, man," the toilet said flatly.

Chapter 2

"Girls, girls, look at this," Janine said. Ms. Hai Lo's paralegal and confidante held up and fanned the lunchroom with the *Courier Post's* front-page story about Troy Chariote. She put the paper on the table and settled back down into her chair, and then turned her laptop around to show off more pictures of hunky Troy Chariote to a couple gawkers.

Sitting next to Janine, Hai stirred her noodles. "He's not all that." Hai turned up her nose. Most Jersey girls would spit out an expletive either positive or negative, but Hai being Chinese-American was a tad more conservative. Besides, Troy didn't merit an expletive.

Troy was the ultimate playboy. Although she didn't want marriage, she also did not want frivolous, meaningless sex. Whatever that was. She had never had any. Of any kind.

Bull-headed Troy Chariote had landed in jail because he refused bail, which in turn made her look bad in the eyes of her boss. Troy or his brother, Raphael, could have covered bail easily with their assets. Troy was part owner of the Comic Freak Comedy Club and his brother a famous and rich artist. Troy had claimed he wanted to take stock of his life, maybe freshen up his act. He was probably afraid of being bumped off by the mafia. She had told him that jail was no place to hide from the long arm of the mob. But he shushed and dismissed her. Arrogant so-n-so.

She'd find a way to get him out of jail and free of all charges. After all, the case was simple. A drunken mobster had fallen and knocked himself out after taking a swing at Troy for no rational reason. The only witness was the mobster's girlfriend and she'd lied. Hai, with the help of her investigator and medical trauma experts, would shred the girlfriend's testimony in court if it got that far.

"Honey, this boy was all star quarterback with more beef than a foot long Nathans," Janine said, as if she had done a personal inspection. Others in the lunchroom picked up Janine's vibe, probably, and pestered her as well.

"He's insufferable," Hai said to all, and then realized she really needed to cut this short. Was she running away from men? No. Hai and Janine had a full docket to work on.

"All I'm saying is—give him a chance," Janine said, pushing her luck. Hai knew that married attorneys made partner and unmarried ones did not in this firm. Janine was just looking out for her boss. If Hai had wanted to get married, she could do a lot better than Troy Chariote.

Hai peeked at his pictures again, as if staring at a box of forbidden fruit. Troy had a square dimpled jaw, rugged eyebrows over blue mixed with what…hazel-ish eyes, chiseled nose, thick curly black hair. Of course, he was cute, if you liked football quarterback brutes.

The head of the firm stuck his face through the doorway. "Yeah, Hai, we encourage everybody here to let their hair down, have a little fun once in a while."

Mr. Furgensen's idea of a little fun included joking with clients on their nickel. Was his hearing that acute? She looked up for hidden speakers.

"I mean all work and no purposeful play isn't good. I've noticed married associates are happier associates and seem to become partners more quickly, and therefore, quid pro quo, more productive." Furgensen had forgotten that he wrote the rules and failed to mention there were no unmarried partners.

Men had done nothing but mess with her head her whole life. In grammar school, they stole her crayons. In high school, they saw her as a study mentor, a pretty computer. In college with her a star on the figure skating team, they wanted her panties *off*. Not for being pretty but because they fantasized, she'd be the next Kristi Yamaguchi, the greatest twentieth century figure skater. They didn't even get her heritage right.

9

In her working years, men hit on her because she was a pretty meal ticket. Give her an honest man, and she'd have a *little* fun, but only after she cleared her current portfolio and made partner. At twenty-six, she didn't need to rush.

Furgensen, who always lost quarters in the soda machine, came up to her holding his cola and then bent over, practically dipping his ugly yellow tie in her noodles. In a low voice he said, "When you get engaged, see me and we'll talk about you making partner." He patted her on her back as if burping an infant. Here again, he had conveniently forgotten their scheduled meeting for next Tuesday in which becoming a partner was the only item on the agenda. *Oh, fudge.* That was the best she could do with expletives.

Her cell phone buzzed. It was her grand mom.

"Excuse me, sir." Furgensen popped his drink, waved and left the room with his cola fizzing over.

"Nana."

"Hai. You coming to *younger* sister's wedding?" Her grand mom, Joy, had the sweetest voice, but her words often hid a scorpion's sting. Nonetheless, Hai loved and respected her. Her sister's wedding was this coming Saturday. She'd been to the bridal shower and every family get together. Each time, she got the same interrogation. Funny thing, her grand mom was not forgetful.

"Of course, Nana."

"You bringing date?"

"I don't know."

"I pay for table setting for you and date. Nine courses. Plum wine. Lots of plum wine. You bring date."

"Yes, Nana."

"Why you not married and your sister is soon? Sooner than you."

"Haven't found the right man, Nana."

"You no fool me. You not looking. Go find one and bring him to me. Saturday." Nana hung up.

"You're not getting any younger," Janine said.

"Thanks for the reminder."

"No problem. Can I have your fortune cookie?"

Hai watched what she ate, exercised and taught kids ice-skating pro bono on Tuesday and Thursday nights. She had always given her fortune cookie to Janine, who really needn't have one to go with that yummy, super-sized slice of chocolate cake Janine had a fork in. Maybe Hai would change her luck. With all the beating down she had received at lunch today, she could use a reversal of fortune. Not that she believed. Just this one time, she'd pretend. She'd believe.

"No, Janine, I've been stressed by everybody in here—you, Furgensen, and my very own grand mom. I'll eat the cookie." Why were the gods conspiring against her? Hai ripped open the plastic wrapper, cracked the cookie, pulled out the fortune and read it. "This is your fortune, Janine." She flicked the darn thing and watched it twirl down like a maple leaf seed onto Janine's plate.

The fortune read, *Lucky you. You will experience Double Happiness. Very soon.*

Chapter 3

What's the difference between a stand-up comedian and a psychologist? One, using observation and deep insight into the human psyche, would help you see incongruities in your life. On the other hand, the psychologist, Stella, a piece of work, made Troy laugh and a touch crazy.

Yes, she was gorgeous. Yes, she was off limits, and would always be, because Troy loved his brother. Stella had the habit of challenging Troy about the way people think, which was great for his business, but today he had to play the sad-sack role of a recovering alcoholic, and allow her to kick his ass in any perverse dominatrix way she chose.

Troy Chariote always enjoyed pretending to be his brother although his brother dragged into this one. Raphael had lost his ardor for swapping, but Troy would push it, if necessary. What could be more fun, as long as Troy wouldn't be forced to play stunt cock with Raphael's estranged fiancée? Not that Troy wouldn't ravish her if she were unattached and irrevocably out of Raphael's life.

Today, Troy would get a chance to play the role of the great artist. *How hard can it be?* He was always trying on personas on stage and Raphael's persona fit him like a second skin.

Exiting the jail and leaving his brother's behind, behind, Troy shook Deputy Max's beefsteak hand and stepped outside the building. He braced when an unusually cold, strong wind for a late April afternoon tried to blow off his mustache.

"Free at last. Free at last." Meandering about the parking lot, trying to keep his cap on, he pushed the car alarm button, and spied his brother's Prius. "I'm here, you dummy." The sun chose that moment to give up its fight with the thick graying clouds. He sprinted through the treeless lot, goblets of rain drenching him. He yanked open the door and swan dived into the car.

After leaving the lot, he tossed the fake mustache—like an unwanted snake—into the glove box. They planned one more exchange, unless Raphael was freed early by the, yes, competent and lovely, Ms. Hai Lo.

Troy drove down Route 70 heading west through Medford. Endless pine forests flanked the road showing hints of one-story strip malls and turn-offs to home communities. All of South Jersey lay flat and close to sea level. Next up, Cherry Hill, sported no real hills, just pimples populated with beautiful homes on generous lots. Cherry Hill, close to all, but far enough away from urban clutter, was one of the most desired bedroom communities surrounding the Philadelphia area.

He pulled up to the gate of Raphael's estate, buzzed himself through and tucked into a parking spot before the well-kept Victorian. He sprinted to the cottage studio, which was Stella's idea of jail for his lovesick brother.

The cottage displayed wink-at-you red-framed windows, right out of Disneyland, with white-slatted siding, rose beds and a flagstone walk-up. The cottage and all plopped on a slight grassy rise with a panoramic view of mixed trees and distant neighbors.

The door was already unlocked. He hurried in, stripped one soggy piece of clothing after another, dropping them on the floor where they belonged. He never enjoyed a shower more, rating it up there on the top ten list of life's experiences right along with a hotdog and frank at Lincoln Financial Field.

"You decent?" He heard his fiancée Stella, correction Raphael's fiancée, who must have just snuck in.

Ironic, he was naked just like the day he had caught Stella when she fell from the rafters over the boys shower. She really didn't care whether he and Raphael were naked then, why should she today? *Free-spirited Stella must still be giving Raphael the cold shoulder or she'd*

13

strip in a second and get wet. Back then, he and Raphael had slapped her JV ass and told her to run like hell so she wouldn't be expelled. Today, he'd resist the temptation to pat her lovely behind. However, this deliberately mistaken identity situation could get dicey.

It reached his consciousness that he had already made the mistake of littering his clothes. Raphael, even if his clothes were on fire, would strip each article of clothing off, and then fold and then put them in their proper places. Neatly.

"Rarely decent, Stella Adora." His bro sometimes used this endearment. "Give me a moment." While drying, he searched all over for clothes, oops. He hesitated to leave the bathroom, and look stupid or to the lustful Stella, rip-off-his-towel naked. You'd never know when Stella would end her starvation diet.

What if the identical twins weren't identical down to the tiniest detail? A very tiny detail in his brother's case.

"Stella. Could you grab me some fresh clothes?"

"What do you like?" He heard her mutter. "What a mess."

"I don't care." He realized his meticulous brother always cared. "I mean, I'd like to see what you pick out."

"That's a change," she said, with hesitation. He couldn't win.

"I'm just so stressed over Troy, I'm not myself." To put it mildly. He hoped this would fool a brilliantly observant woman. "I could have just as easily worn my pants backwards. He's got me so worried."

"Me too. You know I love him." *How sweet.* "How is he doing?"

"Well, he complained about his lawyer, asked me to track down some leads."

"With the amount of business you do, I think you can swing it." Dig time.

"Now, now, let's not start." That sounded like something his brother would say.

The door cracked open. A lovely, long, freckled arm neatly placed his clothes on the granite counter top. His brother had great taste in arms.

"Mrs. Shantel will be here in ten minutes. I left a sandwich on the table. See you." Stella's footsteps receded and the front door clicked closed.

Gone.

How in hell was he going to paint a portrait with his brother's client probably wanting to peek at the canvas? He had never painted in his life, except for the side of a house, but he had to have his twin's talent buried somewhere inside his brain. Besides, they talked all the time. Art and artists had rubbed off on him and his comedic sense influenced Raphael. He'd need it too, sitting in that stinky jail with a talking toilet. Troy ran around picking up his things and threw them in a lump into the closet. Then he got dressed as fast as a firefighter. Zipped over to the coffee maker, prepared a pot and breathed in his sandwich. All gone. Magic trick.

The bell buzzed and in swayed Mrs. Shantel in a long, yellow, vinyl raincoat and matching hat. She said hi and disappeared behind a room separator of three black wood and rice paper screens picturing two Geishas, trees, birds and balcony. Raphael always exhibited impeccable taste. She tossed her raincoat, hat, fluffed her hair and walked out naked. Had to be Raphael's idea of a joke. *Not bad* and certainly not looking like a boring side of a building, he'd have to paint. She twirled laughing him. *Lord, help me. She's built like a brick shit-house.*

"Have the brush?" she asked.

"Yes, yes, of course, ah, here it is." He perused an army of brushes, long, short, fat, thin, and one hairbrush.

"You sound weird. Your voice just cracked like a teenager's."

"Not me. I was just clearing my throat. Let me hold, ah, help you." Preening, his bro definitely did preening. "The rain has flattened your beautiful red hair just a touch. Here and there." He fluttered about her like a hairstylist, that is, his metro-sexual, or gay, brother.

"Voila." Troy tried not to notice her too-close curves, blue eyes, natural red hair. Tried not to pinch her deserving ass. Something was getting harder than he imagined. Life as a man was damn hard.

"I'll go over to the easel, and we'll just start."

She patted his behind as he escaped her.

Resist. Resist for Raphael and Stella's sake.

"*Coffee* should be ready in a moment." He lifted the cover of the painting. Mrs. Shantel had posed as a reclining Venus on the red couch, which he now noticed since she was undulating, well stretching on. The

15

couch was highlighted with close-cropped orange buttons punctuating the French curved headrest. Straight from a bordello, in his opinion, but maybe this is what she liked as fantasy for her husband.

Troy peeked at her as she absentmindedly twined her pubic hairs. Gulp. He could feel those hairs tugging at his libido. Entreating him like Medusa.

Damn you, Raphael.

He had to be careful, getting colors and thicknesses right, getting his mind out of her hair. The plastic-covered colors embedded in a wooden palette were neatly laid out and labeled. The mixing area of the palette also had a couple tags. This labeling had fastidious Raphael written all over it. The one, labeled crimson, spoke to him.

Got to start with the easiest thing in the world to paint, pussy.

He dabbed the red cup with the thinnest brush he could find, to do as little harm as possible.

His hand shook. *This is impossible. Damn impossible.* He'd study art techniques after she left, but knew it would take much more than a couple self-taught lessons; comics practice routines a hundred times.

A little later, after carefully placing a few red curls on her portrait twat, he asked, "When do you want to come back? I mean, my schedule is up in the air over some family matters."

"Well, I see no reason why we can't continue regular, do you?"

Regularly, he corrected without saying anything to her. His job as a comic entailed crafting words to suit an audience. Sometimes, he'd deliberately use poor English depending on his character, but his audience always knew where he *stand-ed.*

"I'll call you or text if anything comes up."

Comes up like my 'who who' a word my Mom used to say say.

"You're forgetting next Thursday. My husband's coming back for his birthday."

"I'm a dunce. We do need to get your birthday suit on canvas, to suit your husband's birthday."

"Well put." She was likely buttering him up for something and he felt he was about to find out what.

"You know, I could work in my spare time and put some finishing touches the next time we meet," he said.

"Or I could stay over. Stella wouldn't mind would she?"

Red hairs.

No, Stella would mind. If he screwed this woman, he'd have to attend either his or his brother's funeral depending on who Stella got her hands on.

The sheriff's jail started looking better all the time.

Chapter 4

Pressed for time, Stella ran into her mom and dad's home in Medford Lakes, New Jersey. She pulled the door closed; javelin-tossed her wet umbrella into the atrium basket, and started running again.

"Excuse me, Mom. I'll be right down." She bounded up the steps, remembering her parents laughing about their little flash. Was she really ever in one place, like an electron zipping about at near light speed?

"Dad's at work. Can you stay for…?"

Streak.

Out of earshot from her mom's last words—probably—*dinner later.* Stella raced down the hallway to her bedroom. She stiff-armed the bedroom door wide open, banging the wall. Oops. Dug through some photo albums. Found the one labeled Chariote Express, a favorite. Perhaps she could use some of the identical twins' pictures she had taken over the years to help finish off her Psychology Ph. D. thesis, based on identical twins. Naturally.

How juvenile of me, I'm not showing and telling enough for my committee of literally and figuratively farty professors. The album displayed a progression of the boys almost every month through high school, and less so in college, because she was two years younger, and not allowed to travel too much.

Her obsession with these twins smacked her professional self in the face. How could a psychologist be so—well—obsessive? Psychologist, cure thyself. She wouldn't. She knew what she needed to stay healthy, and besides, her colleagues trusted her as an identical twin

18

expert. Just the week before, she'd taken a call from some tweedy Harvard professor. He asked permission to quote her in a clinical study he was about to publish. *Oh, wow.*

Thinking. *Stella, you must stay forever strange and therefore productive.*

Her mom hung out in the kitchen, this time cooking up the always delicious, *rotini* pasta with red sauce, and minced clams fresh from Cape May. The Italian spices danced with Stella's nose.

Late for lunch, too early for dinner. She eyed homemade breadsticks just out of the oven on their pan. Her mom curled the sticks with provolone like a barber pole.

"What's the matter, honey?" mom asked, with that concerned look sometimes to be found on her dad's face.

What was it about moms? They always knew. Stella would like to 'know' something someday, but she had ruined her chance to have kids, *forever*, kicking Raphael out. No man, no babies. Well, no babies unless the last name of her lover and husband was Chariote. Period.

"I broke up with Raphael." She refused to cry, sticking her nose high enough to touch the recessed ceiling.

"Oh dear, he's such a sweet boy." Mom came over from the colander at the sink, and lifted her daughter's now dropped chin. She seemed to notice something deep within her baby. Then her mom's entire demeanor changed from concern to relief.

What is this sixth sense?

"What?"

"What, Mom," her mom corrected, always the gentle disciplinarian.

"Sorry, Mom."

"Stella, if you don't know what the problem is, I can't help you." There she went again, cryptic, and not at all helpful. Hey, didn't she just tell Mom the problem?

"He's been drinking too much. I'm afraid he's going to die young."

"It's more than *that*. It's something else."

She didn't know any more "*that*" she could tell her mom.

"What other 'that's' are there, Mom?" Her mom was harboring secrets, as if somebody wanted her spumoni recipe.

"I can't say. It is for you to take a journey of discovery."

"Oh, so I'm going somewhere out there to discover some truth and I don't know what truth I'm looking for?" Stella put her hands on her hips, as she had done so many times to Mom and Dad as she grew up. Little Miss Contentious and the Flash of course, never a middle gear on Stella. Yepo, they were her middle names, Stella Contentious Flash Maria Riccardi.

"Hey, it's your yellow brick road, not mine. Go on Alice. Take the first step on your journey."

"Alice didn't dance up the yellow brick road, Mom. She fell down a rabbit hole."

"Whatever…I meant Dorothy from the Wizard of Oz… Oh, you should tell Father Brian about this, so you don't mess up his wedding and couples retreat calendar."

"Can you offer any other advice, Mom? Please. Hey your sauce is spitting."

Oh that smell. She grabbed a still too hot breadstick, fanned it and downed it as fast as she could, with ooh ooh oohs and waving hands. Mom seemed amused. It wasn't the first time she watched the fire-eater devour her cooking. Her mom had expressed a theory that all the heavy breathing and noises emanating from Stella's ample chest signaled to the food 'go here.'

Mom seemed to collect her thoughts while lowering the heat on the sauce. "Of course, it's important to save Raphael's liver, but I think you should look to the root causes of his drinking. Come on, baby. You're the hotshot psychologist. Use that summa cum laude brain of yours. Help your man." Mom wiped her hands on her apron and then crossed herself. Her words sounded just right. Stella felt better already, but still Mom's cryptic behavior would have to be explained—at some point.

"Father Brian does late afternoon confessions. I'll use the confession as an excuse to tell him. I think, I'll run now. Don't know about dinner."

"I've made extra. Just show up, sweetie."

"Love."

"Love." They pecked, then her mom cupped Stella's chin again. "Gone on. Zip on out-a-here."

"Bye." She left in a flash.

She ran back in, leaving errant raindrops on the kitchen floor, grabbed her album and waved. Mom knew about this keepsake, and many others. She tucked the precious album beneath her raincoat, and in one of her leftover childhood fantasies, off she beep-beeped like Road Runner.

Mom had always known about her self-described *useful obsession* and probably realized Stella and Raphael would bounce back, because her daughter built her life and happiness around these boys.

Anyway, my dear Stella, what would you do without your manic fixes?

Nothing. Nada. No way.

* * *

Father Brian had transferred to Saint Thomas Moore in Cherry Hill from Medford some years ago. Since Stella lived in Raphael's Cherry Hill home, she had asked this priest to perform the marriage ceremony. Raphael, not Catholic, enjoyed Father Brian's progressive attitude, and leapt at the chance to make her happy; have a church-sanctioned wedding and Catholic babies.

Raphael had argued for one concession. He preferred his gated, private two-acre yard for the wedding instead of the church. Father Brian acquiesced after visiting his home. The bucolic backyard had a generous mix of trees, manicured flowerbeds, and a mostly level, impeccably kept lawn.

The middle of the week, late afternoon and intermittent downpours left the church without worshippers. Stella could deduce this from two unclean cars in the parking lot. Her powers amazed her, must have been all that training in the sciences. Saint Thomas always felt more like a sprawling mansion than a church.

Confession, now called reconciliation, was also available by appointment, but Father Brian would always chat with Stella. Whether they sat down at the kitchen table, or in the official old-lady box, the confessional, he'd make time for her. Plenty of fluorescent light replaced the hiding sun but it had no power brighten her depression. Besides, this type of lighting flattered no one.

She closed the door—light streaming in through small slits—knelt and crossed herself. The priest was already in the booth.

"Bless me father for I have sinned."

"What's troubling you my child? We need not be so formal." From his voice, he too must have sensed that something was bothering her.

"I kicked Raphael out of his own home, forgive me…and broke our engagement." Stella had confessed to Father on numerous occasions that she'd shacked up with him. She had lost her virginity to him in college without regret, so there, Father.

She wondered if sexual obsession with identical twins fell under the seven deadly or venial sins. She had forgotten her catechism. Perhaps she was crazy, in a highly productive, functional manner. If life with these passions were crazy, she wanted no cure.

"He's been drinking and I think it's because…there's something basically wrong with our relationship. I just can't pin it down."

"You two are more like an old married couple. The passion gone?" Father seemed determined to meander his way to another lecture on premarital sex. She girded herself. She'd be bold, and she could and had held her own in a debate with him. She had enough philosophy and theology courses—two every semester—to become a priest, if only the Vatican would change its policy. She enjoyed psychology better, much better. Celibate? No thanks.

"Nope, passion still there. That part is wonderful, was wonderful." Although she didn't know how long she could hold out. She cleared her throat and took a chance, once again, at frankness. "He's a kind and gentle lover, Father."

How's that for in your face, bold?

"I'm afraid we'll have to push the wedding forward, if there is one, to August. You'll have to catch up on the classes and the next engagement encounter is on the weekend starting Saturday, the twenty-third of July, in the morning. That one is better anyway. The Franciscan Monks will be doing an in-depth personality and conflict session for all the couples."

"I thought the parish was sponsoring it."

"You'll miss that one. The brothers take the same approach, tough love, you know. It's been known to break-up or bind completely and certainly bring dark issues to light."

Dark issues, what dark issues? Yeah perfect, a weekend of letting a bunch of strangers in on your innermost secrets... Raphael would be game, like his art, which has clarity. Well maybe I'll discover dark issues that will cure my twins' obsession, save Raphael from drinking, and win the Nobel Prize while I'm at it.

"A Saturday and Sunday?"

"A full eight hours each day. Saturday evening will be open to the couples. It has the feel of a ski lodge: fireplace roaring, hot cocoa, cheese, crackers, a little wine and good conversation. Don't worry, I'll show up for those who'd be pleased with a challenge on any subject and to make you two feel at home. The whole weekend is not for those who have little interest in the truth. It's not for those who fear cleansing their souls. Not for those afraid of their neighbor."

"Not me Father, not Raphael."

"You twisted your words, child. You mean of course, you and Raphael are game."

"Yes, Father."

"Remember how you were raised. Always apply the golden rule. Everybody there will love you as you love yourself."

"Problem is..."

"Don't blame yourself child. Fix it, no matter where it leads, find the truth, and then act on it. I am certain you will be there and whole, my child."

"We'll be there, Father."

"You'll have plenty of time to get your relationship back to normal by then or identify what's troubling you and you know where to find me. Now Stella, hear me for just a moment."

"Yes, Father."

Here it comes.

"Before you come to the retreat, and if you want any chance of surviving what we dish out, I want you to dig deep into your psyche and ask Raphael to do the same. Prepare for the encounter."

"We will." *Guantanamo Bay here we come.*

"Another thing before you leave." Father Brian's use of 'another thing' showed his love for detective shows, especially her mom and dad's favorite in the 'oh just one more thing' genre, Lieutenant Colombo.

"Yes, Father."

"Do you think Raphael would paint a mural for the church, maybe of Our Lady?" Father had fawned over Raphael's masterpieces when he toured his home and studio. His portraits captured a person's soul, according to Father, and Stella agreed.

"I'll ask him."

"We could pay."

"Nonsense, Father. Raphael has a big heart as you know but little time. I know him. He'll find the time, maybe not right away, and even if we breakup completely. He's a man of his word. If he says he will, he will. I'll let you know."

"God bless you, child." This Lieutenant Colombo always had an ulterior motive to his questions.

"Are you trying to convert him, Father?" *Got him.*

"It's my job. Now say five Hail Marys' and blabber the words. I absolve you of your frequent and only sin, in the name of the Father, the Son and the Holy Spirit. Go and sin no more."

A bit much to ask. The thought of Raphael in that towel, dripping wet had been almost too much to bear.

She blessed herself. "Amen."

"Amen, my child. Go in peace."

"Thank you, Father."

She practically had her doctorate in psychology and she left not fully understanding how Father Brian seemed to find the right path. Incisive, compassionate and a good old soul. Then there was the odd case of her prescient mom.

What to do about Raphael? She was sharp. She'd find her way. Both Mom and her priest wanted her to dig deeper. Both alluded to hidden problems. She'd *veni, vide, vici.* First, she'd see, then conquer, and then come, by hopping on her sweet Chariote. Not a problem.

Chapter 5

Max rapped his knuckles on the square iron plate in the middle of the jail bars. A sparrow friend abandoned breadcrumbs and flew off her jail window perch.

"So are you ready for another one?" Max asked.

Raphael still playing Troy had to pretend he knew what the hell Max was talking about. "Sorry, I dozed off. Hit me."

"Okay, a deputy, a minister and a rabbi walk into a bar..." Max waited.

He guessed Max was fishing, so he bit the hook, "What happened to the priest?"

"The deputy shot him." An embarrassing pause deadened the air. "Get it?"

"Got it. Tell me again, um, what are you going to do with your material?" He did not quite understand the joke, but Max's enthusiasm had to count for something. He wished he listened to more of his brother's lectures on stand-up comedy.

"Maybe in a month or two, I'll head over to The Freak for amateur night."

"I will definitely put a good word in for you. But how are you going to get somebody to ask you what happened to the priest?" He put on his I-know-the-answer and this-is-a-quiz face, but in truth, although he really got into comedy, and knew quite a lot, at least of what made him laugh, yes and even why, he hadn't a clue what Max was trying to do. Was he thick or Max?

"I'm not going to wait for the audience to answer. I'll be dressed as I am now. I'll pause, and then say I shot the priest."

"I guess it could work."

In a million years, he resisted saying. "You do look, well scary." He had a kind of Lon or Dick Chaney face. Ha, ha, he too could make jokes, even if unsaid.

"Do you spot anything else that could improve my presentation?"

What harm could dabbling in comedy do? Men could have worse hobbies. "Maybe if you pulled out a roman collar from your pocket, had a crazy glint in your eye, like you do now, and then sniff your gun and say, 'I shot the priest.'"

Max took off his cap and scratched his head, looking stupefied. Raphael had to have said something wrong, besides ribbing his buddy. Max's head could have subbed for a landing strip and therein a saving idea was born.

"Your camel-bristle hair looks like an upside down floor polisher. Maybe you should take off your cap, get out your cuffs and ask for some cute female to assist on stage."

"Assist at what?"

"You don't tell her until she's cuffed."

"Tell her what?"

"She's to assist with your miserable love life. Then ask her out on a date."

"Wow, Troy, you are a genius."

"Runs in the family." He felt vindicated and extremely lucky, but he loved his brother, and so he'd make his own luck.

Max squinted and said, "You aren't looking too good. I'm going to get you one of our sendoff meals." If it would cure blotches, he was all for whatever the food might be.

"You guys don't serve alcohol, do you?"

"I can't even drink a beer at the jail. I'd like to accommodate, but I'd get fired."

"No, I'm better off eating right, which might help these blotches. You're not serious about a sendoff meal?"

"These deluxe accommodations were temporary. When we stole you from the Cherry Hill Police, we made no promises."

"Are they still overcrowded?"

"Yep."

"Thank you, for lobbying your boss."

"Well, I'm sorry. You might have to go to the State Prison, maybe Rahway. Anyway, we're getting overcrowded. It would just be temporary." Max picked his nose.

Disturbed by the news, he asked for Troy's cell phone to do some texting and call his brother's attorney. Max relaxed the jail rules a little for his friend, another benefit. Max had to watch when he used the phone. Something he'd likely not get in the penitentiary.

Troy's attorney had to help keep Raphael in this jail. Besides, he had become attached to the toilet and now an inquisitive sparrow. Catching her on the phone, she promised to work on stopping the transfer and meet him 10 a.m. tomorrow. She sounded, diligent, sweet and concerned. His brother was full of misinformation soup.

Chapter 6

Night approached. Stella poked her head in the art studio. Troy snapped closed a drawer of Raphael's—no *his*—baseball cards. He should have known his brother had stolen and hoarded them. He'd get him for this.

"Hey Raphael honey, you're going to be late for the AA meeting. Want me to drive you?"

"No I'm fine. On another subject, I'm having Pierre come over to finish Mrs. Shantel's portrait. So let him in the gate."

"You really shouldn't, babe."

"Don't worry. Mrs. Shantel won't know, it's almost finished, and besides, she's getting a little too flirty. And my hands are shaking just a bit." He looked contrite and about to cry, held up his hand, and mysteriously, it shook. She ran over and hugged him.

"Oh baby. I'm proud of you. You are looking good. You're going to be fine. Say, you're going to be fine."

"You're going to be fine," he repeated. Troy knew Stella quite well indeed. She forever practiced both pop and real psychology. He believed this fell into the pop side of her bag of tricks. But was he too comedic?

"Smart ass." She broke the hug, and gave him a pose resembling a tiger sniffing something smelly. Just so she didn't sniff his true identity. He had showered, washed away all things jail-ish. She had to be

28

reacting to his joke alone. Best not get too close to her claws, for fear she'd rip away hid clothes or reveal the twins little hoax.

* * *

Troy entered a white colonial two story insurance building off Route 70 in Cherry Hill posing as his drunk but orderly brother. Going through the second floor swinging glass doors, he ambled down a wide hall with numerous employee-award plaques lining both sides. At the end of the hall beckoned a training room, dimmed for the occasion, people sat patiently with hands folded. The meeting started immediately.

"My name is Raphael Chariote and I am an alcoholic." He went on to entertain fourteen sympathetic listeners, regaling them with stories about his sad sack brother. How he stole altar wine right out of the sacristy of Saint Thomas Moore. How the dean of Villanova unknowingly ordered cases of Bourbon for every fraternity and sorority on an officially dry campus. On and on, he performed, trying not to elicit too many snickers. He had them eating out of his hands.

* * *

Later that night he entered Raphael's studio and picked up a note—attached to the cover of Mrs. Shantel's nude portrait—signed by Pierre, his brother's apprentice.

The note read, "You must have been fixated on her pussy. I toned down the curls. You joke, *oui?"* He stared at the now completed portrait and the more realistic triangular tangle of pretty red hairs. Apparently, he forgot shading highlights. *If there's one thing I could paint.* He was a pussy failure.

Damn it, he amazed himself about how little he knew of the art of being an artist. He vowed again to practice painting and sketching and branch out to let's say, flowers. Some flowers looked like vaginas, tsk, tsk.

Raphael had more than sufficient supplies, in the many white cabinets lining two walls, everything neatly placed, of course.

Tired, he slipped through the 'neat' one sheet and cover turned-down on the made bed. He made another vow to do the bed the same way his meticulous brother made it and keep the place in order. A cold sweat broke out.

"My name is Troy Chariote and I am a slob."

I'm such a slob. They named me a toxic waste site.

I'm such a slob. The CIA hired me to join al Qaeda… Not funny, drop in circular file.

I'm such a slob…

* * *

The rain pattered the roof; a dark grayish early morning filled the room and a misty fog hugged the window. Some woman had wrapped her arms around his curly chest snuggling from behind. Her large breasts with erect nipples assaulted his back, and thighs to thighs, made him feel comfortable, hardened, and then alarmed. He broke away from the nether world to fully awake. Did Mrs. Shantel sneak into the cottage? He turned his head slowly. Gorgeous Stella, with freckles everywhere, wore a contented smile—and nothing else.

God help me.

Or should I help myself?

Chapter 7

Morning had broken.

"Of all the jails in the world she had to walk into mine," Raphael said, under his breath, of the exotic beauty, Hai.

Troy's attorney was a minute early, but should have arrived years before. Perfect, if you liked a runway model Chinese woman with long, lustrous, raven hair and oh-my-God legs. She dressed impeccably in a white-on-white corduroy business suit with a twelve-inch black cummerbund, accenting her lithe waist, perfectly turned calves and ankles, suspended on modest three inch black and white heels.

Perfect for his brother, but sadly, not poor Raphael, the taken man. *Fidelity practice needed here*. Troy had ranted about a girl fitting said description for years and never landed one, no matter how he spiced his bait. Perhaps, he presented himself more sour than sweet. Raphael made another little joke, a case of brother on brother influence, no doubt. Okay, he'd have to work on joking. Troy had the audacity to describe this angel as ugly, with a rear to boot. Oh my yes, he'd pay.

"I heard that," she said. The door creaked closed.

"I didn't say anything," he said, focusing on the diminishing patter of light rain, the gray upon gray shadows, a dank and smelly world and the contrast of her female aura inviting color and brightness. He felt her taking him in as if she could read his thoughts. Maybe attorneys were big on laser-focused attention or she had *really* sharp ears? Yet he hadn't said a thing, except under his breath when she was halfway down the hall.

"Six cents for your thoughts." She demurred.

Sixth sense? Had the price gone up or was she playing with words to impress his professional jokester brother?

"Oh, I'm loving your business attire, and I wanted to thank you for your help this morning." He peeked at the embarrassing graffiti and wished Max had already supplied the requested paint. A latex smell would have been refreshing in comparison with this stuffed vacuum cleaner stink. The hint of chrysanthemum from Troy's attorney sent him flying through Longwood Gardens and then his long backyard of many flowerbeds and trees.

"Is that all you fancy?" She asked, hands on hips.

What the fuck. He'd take her. How could he feel this way? Was Stella's breaking the engagement like an on-off switch?

"Well, it goes without saying, my attorney is a knockout." Asian girls weren't first on his list. In fact, they weren't on his list. Besides, the list had narrowed to one, at least as of three days ago, before he was abruptly kicked out. Descendant from Florence Italy, big hazel eyed Stella Riccardi was a living doll and the love of his life.

"I thought you hated me," she said with defeated tone and cat sly look. His protective instincts compelled sympathy.

"No-o-o. Not at all. Whatever gave you that impression?" He worried about his brother. Perhaps, she had elicited a flight reaction in him. That is, she scared the hell out of Troy, who didn't believe he could support a wife, anyway. This was refined bullshit. As a comedian and part-owner of the Freak, Troy did more than fine. Raphael toyed with the idea that now was the time to find a wife for Troy.

She also demonstrated competence as an attorney. She had worked out an arrangement with the sheriff to keep him in his brother's cell as long as he'd allow miscreants to share the cell for short pieces of daylight.

"I'm trained to read juries and people in general. And I have acute hearing." She had an *a cute* everything, if he acknowledged the truth. "I bet you didn't notice my, what I was wearing last week?"

Oh God, the proverbial no win trap.

32

She could have shown up on that moment's notice for his brother's first meeting in a tennis outfit. *Best not to imagine her wearing anything.* Nonetheless, he pictured her bouncing back and forth swatting balls in skimpy white shorts and tank top, with black trim, of course. She'd showcase her well-rounded rear, perky breasts, lustrous raven hair. *Stop. Stop it.* Somewhere along the line he'd relish the chance to dress this Barbie doll, with a little more color, here and there, now and again, if only to mix it up.

He had to think up something cogent. "I'm sorry. I was so distressed last week, worrying about whether the young man would come out of his coma, worrying about jail." At this moment, he conjured up a little gift for his brother. He'd toss a curve ball at Troy. A not so straight, but narrowed path to a double wedding. This would be his best ruse yet—his crowning achievement—in the affairs of identical twins. He'd seduce her for Troy. So very honorable.

She smiled and teased. "I'm glad you find me acceptable. I was about to hand you over to Gertrude."

"No. No. Not Gertrude, Ms. Lo." She had to have made that up.

She must not know how beautiful she is.

"Call me, Hai." She did seem taken by him posing as his brother. The sleep had done his face some good, well good enough he hoped.

I had damn well better dig into my brother's jocular style a tad deeper.

They went on to discuss what Troy claimed and Raphael believed was an accident at Ponzio's diner. A witness, the comatose man's girlfriend, argued that Troy started a fight, pushed her boyfriend, Frank Greco, which forced Frank to crash head first into a concrete abutment. Manslaughter up to murder was possible, if he died.

Hai handed him the police report to review.

It read: *"I stopped at Ponzio's to meet a friend inside. Frank Greco got in my face after I parked my car nearly touching front grills with his car. However, they didn't touch, they were around four inches apart. He probably wanted to drive out using my now acquired spot. I wouldn't have parked had Frank's car moved an inch. It didn't. I don't believe, no he hadn't even turned on the ignition. I assumed, after noticing him in the car, he'd eventually be backing out of his space after*

33

he put on his seat belt or they had just then parked to go into Ponzio's. He hadn't done anything yet. I didn't know whether he was coming or going. I got out of my car, walked by his car on his passenger side when he got out and met me crossing to the last line of cars before the diner. I struggled forward with Frank close up, verbally harassing me, and then shoving me until we reached the handicapped parking spot in front of the entrance to the restaurant. I turned to face him and tried to get the measure of the man. I wondered how I could help him. I didn't see anybody else nearby. His girlfriend sat in the car applying makeup and faced away from me mostly, although I guess she could see using the side mirror. She seemed intent on getting her make-up right and wasn't looking at us. Frank seemed either drunk or just plain belligerent. He shoved me harder this time, with two hands to my chest. I asked him what he thought I did wrong and what was the problem. He did not listen and said nothing. The second time he tried shoving, I dodged him, as I had so many times when avoiding tackles during my football days. With nothing but air to push, Frank lost his balance and knocked himself out on a concrete car tire stop. I didn't see the abutment or I would have tried to stop his fall. I hope he'll be alright and will pray for him."

"God, that is tough," Raphael said. "I mean, I guess I wasn't very lucid in what I had told them. I meandered."

"No, this statement was accurate and emotional. I don't know anybody who cares for other human beings who wouldn't say and feel like you did. Besides, you had to be shaken up." Both Troy and Raphael were hardboiled due to the complicated, adrenalin driven game of football. They didn't shake up easily.

She went on to say she was trying to get Frank Greco's girlfriend to recant her charges. So far, no success.

"You or your investigator might see Raphael out there trying to get to know the Greco family, and Frank's girlfriend."

"He *needs* to stop." Her eyes narrowed. She obviously didn't like this news. "He's not a professional, and might make things worse. Plus, Frank's uncle is the reputed Don of the Philadelphia Mafia, maybe the whole United States. Romeo Greco is literally Frank Greco's godfather. Kabish?" *She's funny, too.*

"Sorry. I'll stress this to him."

Something Troy underplayed with him, probably to keep him from worrying. He played along with her continued protests, pretending the two brothers might actually know what they are doing. Hai seemed to care but was un-swayed.

"You've been saying sorry for a week now. But your brother could become an anchor in the Delaware River or cat food at the Greco fish plant. If he meets up with the wrong people, *finito*." Studying her body and face language—she did care.

"Oh that's horrible. I'll get a hold of him right now. Could I use your phone?" Picturing some cat eating his kibbled brother was not a happy thought. They made the call on speaker, but Troy pretending to be Raphael, said he had everything under control and knew about the whole thing. He did a very good Raphael impersonation, right down to the empathetic apologies. They hung up, but Hai still objected. "Get your brother in line."

"I promise."

"You're not looking so good, Troy. I'm going to bring you some of my home cooking tonight. If I'm held up, I'll call the jail." Maybe caring wasn't the right idea, she seemed interested in more than an attorney-client relationship.

If she cooked as good as she looked, his brother could skip becoming cat food and go straight to heaven.

"Just one paranoid thought for you to pass by Max and the sheriff. I don't want any mobsters sharing my cell and they should do complete pat-downs on all my visitors."

"I've already alerted them to the situation," she said. "They are way ahead of us."

"What's the chance Frank Greco's girlfriend will change her statement?"

She flicked a wave of hair off one eye. "Better hope Frank lives." Concerned.

The toilet said, "psst."

"I think your toilet's calling you or it just sprung a leak. See you later." She had a nice smile. "Oh my, you've got visitors." She pointed at two sparrows on the windowsill and her smile turned to that of a little girl's wonderment.

The sleek Ms. Hai Lo, did that sway down the hall, which no doubt made men recant their ways and yearn for freedom. Bump, bump-y-bump, de-bump.

A little later, the toilet spoke up. "Hey man."

"What's going down, Toilet?" Something Troy would say, no doubt.

"How'd you get sparrows?"

"I removed the screen. Hid it under my bed, just during the day. Mosquitoes, you know."

"Good info. Let me know when you remove the bars."

"The sparrows aren't the reason you called, right?"

"I like sparrows, man... Listen to me. The Grecos are all business. They are not goin' to waste some guy like you or your brother only for revenge." There were always exceptions and he hoped Troy wouldn't test the Grecos' patience. Troy's wit—if he displayed it in front of the mobsters—could sometimes be acerbic.

"How do you know this about the Grecos?"

"I'm a button man, man."

"Are you their tailor?"

Toilet laughed, then Raphael heard a flush from somewhere down the hall.

Chapter 8

Troy had torn away from Raphael's studio and the naked Stella faster than he could tie his shoelaces. He grabbed a coffee at the Seven-Eleven, and then waited for the library to open—more research on the Greco family. By studying the newspapers and internet, he was able to memorize the facial features of everybody connected to the Greco family, especially his demented, lying through her teeth accuser.

At West Jersey Hospital, he hovered at the nurses' station outside Frank's room. Every woman reminded him of Stella. He'd need his head examined, and that would lead him to a psychologist, Stella. Damn funny how that worked.

I must not covet my brother's fiancée.

I must not covet my brother's fiancée.

He stopped the mantra, long enough to rationalize—or legalize—his thoughts. True, she had cuddled from behind, not in front, or she would have been a corked goner. He wouldn't have been able to live with himself. Then again, he might have mustered the self-control necessary. After all, no matter how much he admired Stella, her strong personality, her caring heart, how sweet she smelled, how outrageous she looked. He wouldn't have her. He couldn't have her.

Aren't all men dogs? He noticed a male doctor walking by, stethoscope and chart. He would have liked to pose this scientific question.

'We all know if a man shouts in a forest, and a woman isn't present, he said less than nothing.'

What if a man is in a forest, and comes across a beautiful, naked woman, no idea of history, disease, or what, and she says take me? Who among us, doctor, would refuse, could refuse?

"Physiologically impossible for the male of the species,' he'd respond while tapping his stethoscope and pursing his lips.

I must not covet my brother's fiancée. And so, I won't.

Frank's girlfriend walked in dressed in a black micro-mini skirt and black blouse.

Give me a break. What an idiot she is.

Today's young should know black signified mourning, and Frank was not dead yet. If Frank's family saw her like this, she might get the boot, or at least he might be able to use her carelessness to undercut her credibility. She sat right next to Troy and had no idea who he was, so much for eyewitnesses. He played along, catching her eye. He turned so she could see his entire face.

"Pass me a magazine, would you," she said, fluttering false eyelashes on baby-blue eyes. Cute, but where was the please?

"I'd be *pleased* to, your first name?" He stressed 'pleased' as if he were pulling salt-water taffy.

"It's Jersey Malone, as in the state we live in. Get it?"

Jersey, as in the cow. He should find a way to take a picture with his phone, if for nothing more than a pinup shot, because in court the judge would rule her immaterial or not wearing enough material.

"Yes, I get it. Well Jersey, I'm John Doe. I just wish we could have met under better circumstances." Women had always fallen for the direct with him, God's gift. The sky opened and God said go forth Troy and make love to them all, all except Stella. Troy had a hard time with societal rules. He believed in a higher power, in the same way Einstein did, an impersonal God, although he fancied God's individual attention to him when called for.

"Hey, maybe we could go out for a coffee after I visit my friend. Who are you here to see?" Jersey asked. So much for dying boyfriends. This girl gave 'strange' a bad name. He couldn't quite pin her unique strangeness down. There was something to her in the way she talked and emoted. There was more to her than met the eye.

Unschooled, little doubt. Not trained in etiquette, no doubt.

Yet the girl had a certain, *je ne sais quoi*, something intangible. Perhaps it was the hankie she wore for a skirt that clouded his assessment. He felt a little sneeze coming on but no desire to blow his nose on her hankie.

"Yeah, that coffee is a definite maybe. I'm on call for brain transplant surgery." Humor would sooth his savage, woman-crazy beast.

"Oh, a doctor, and a handsome one at that."

He held back saying, 'remind me to wear a bag over my head.' "Let me have your phone number. I'll call," he said.

Oddly, she wrote her number from right to left, but legible, on the front cover of *Harper's Bazaar*. Then ripped the cover off and squashed it into his chest. Perhaps, she was, he'd forgotten the term, idiot savage, no savant. No strange savage lover sounded better. Once again, Stella would come in handy.

He noticed some grease-balls walk through the electric sliders in obvious military formation flanking the rear and front of Romeo Greco, Uncle to Frank Greco. Frank Greco's own father wouldn't show up on account that he had died, gunned down outside, To Die For Pizza, South Street, Philadelphia, four years ago.

"Excuse me, Jersey, nature calls," Troy said.

"What does it sound like?"

Usually, he could read people in an instant, due to his stand-up training. She seemed serious and a joke it wasn't. She seemed to carry her own fog machine around with her. Stella would know. Someday he'd ask her for help, better yet as soon as he dared.

Troy entered the bathroom and was about to pin the lock when Romeo Greco barged in and pinned it for him.

"You look just like Troy. You must be the illustrious and famous artist, Raphael Chariote." Troy sported curly black hair, thicker and blacker than Romeo's which had a touch of gray. Troy however was no Italian. He mixed every European country, including a dash of Italy with a touch of Cajun for spice, hence the rugged good looks, and modesty too.

"Yes, sir. I came here on behalf of my brother hoping to find, and then talk with you and of course check in on your nephew." Romeo had the intense eye-to-eye look of a man who always got what he wanted. Troy wasn't about to disappoint.

"Nice of you to show concern for my familia."

"Yes, sir."

"Well, I called this meeting," Romeo said.

"Yes sir."

"I want to take you for a ride, after I visit Frank."

"Well I…" Hai and Raphael had called to warn him about the Grecos, and tried to stop him, but he already knew what had to do, and wouldn't be stopped. He should have told Hai of his plan to swap with his brother. Not. He just didn't want to upset her or give her a chance to stop him or involve her in the slightly illegal act of being sprung from jail. She'd ruin his one chance. If he read this mob boss right, there would be no retribution. Perhaps, there'd be a price.

"I can see the fear in your eyes. Don't piss yourself. Clear your schedule, we're going to Philadelphia. Call Stella and tell her you might not be back until tomorrow." Well, the man did his homework or someone did it for him.

Troy tried to lighten up the situation and start to win him over. "As long as some good Italian cooking makes its way into the equation."

"It's a deal." Romeo grabbed his shoulder. "Nothing but the best Italian. See you later. I have to check in on Frank first."

"I already have." A little fib. Yes, Troy had peeked in the room from the corridor and saw Frank, still in coma.

Romeo left the bathroom. Troy took a moment feeling guilty of something, not sure what, and slipped out. He noticed the oh so strange Jersey staring at him. He mouthed the words "he's gay" and gave her the dirty grimace look. She seemed in shock. Her face looked like she had just been whacked with a giant powder puff, like in the famous Milton Berle schtick of yesteryear.

"Did you say he's gay?" she shouted. Normally, no one would notice loud conversation in front of doctors, patients, nurses, monitor watchers and who-nots. Romeo was walking right by her when she tossed out that little gem.

He spun around like a gunslinger but without any obvious bulge in his suit and said, "You're funny, just like your brother." He twisted back. "You, young lady, have a lot to learn if you expect to join my family."

"Sorry, Mister Greco," she said, with a sulky and childlike innocence.

"No problem. Next time, do not wear black. It's disrespectful." He patted her bleached-hair. "You're cute." He ascertained Romeo was bossy because he was the boss, smart because he graduated from Wharton, University of Pennsylvania, and like most men, giving pussy its own rightful stature in the world of men.

Embarrassed in black, she blabbered. "Oh didn't notice my clothes, this morning. I just...just ran out the door." She noticed, but there was so little black, perhaps a black washcloth would have been more modest. Wad natural hair color black or was the dark patch underneath her skirt, panties?

Troy walked by her.

"Mr. Greco says you got a brother? Is he a doctor too?" she asked.

Okay, lest belaboring the point about the density of the dense. He wondered if he were alone on an island, stuck with Jersey, if he'd make love to her. Well, yep, guilty, somehow he'd find a way to like her, as spacey as she was.

Males Anonymous. Hello, my name is Troy Chariote. I am a man, and I can't do much about it nor do I want to.

Later, Romeo and Troy slipped into the back of a stretch Hummer decked out limo-style inside, with Romeo next to him and the two goons up front. Another goon drove his brother's Prius. At first, the bodyguards said nothing. They didn't like Troy. They appeared to eat roofing nails for breakfast.

On Route 70 now, he must have looked longingly at Big John's Steaks Pizza & Deli, because Romeo had them make a quick gravel-throwing pullover.

"Let's get a Philly cheese steak hoagie for lunch," Romeo said. "I don't want to wait."

"My sentiments exactly. Their condiment bar with fresh bell peppers, kosher dills, fantastic, the best." Troy sprung open his hand over his lips for emphasis.

"Yeah, and we can talk. Tony, Marco, Joe, give us a little privacy. I mean take a different booth. Alright?"

"Yeah, boss," Tony said.

Oddly enough all Romeo wanted to talk about was art. Italian painters and sculptors. Troy tried to talk Phillies, Sixers, Flyers or Eagles until interrupted.

"I bet you're wondering why I want to spend the whole day with you."

"Yes, Mister Greco."

"Call me Romeo."

"Romeo."

"All I want to say now, is people have a big misimpression of my family. You might call us the mob, low-lives, grease-balls."

"I'll stick to Romeo and friends," he said, with a smirk and then smiled as genuine as could be manufactured.

Romeo explained how his family and friends were transitioning to traditional businesses, helping homeland security, rebuilding communities, etc. He was setting him up for something, and the best Troy could do, if he wanted to be a free man, was play along. He decided to delay his plea until Romeo's motives were clearer.

Back in the Hummer from lunch, Romeo gave Troy some quiet time with his internet cell phone. Romeo dug into a novel, on his iPad, about a quadriplegic New York City detective by the author Jeffery Deaver, rather than, 'See Spot Shot.' Troy no longer doubted the mob boss's intelligence. The man was certainly smart enough to know that killing a Chariote was always a bad idea.

Romeo closed the window separating the front and back, probably so he didn't have to listen to his men discuss what Broadway play they liked most while he was concentrating on the fictional detective. These bodyguards only looked like thugs. Troy resisted building some routine about them and their boss for the Comic Freak. Ever since he met Romeo, he shook slightly in short intervals as if a blast of arctic air periodically surprised him. He guessed he still and irrationally feared for his life. Right now, he couldn't punch in another text message or Google another mob link, besides, the possibility of being caught researching his foe was palpable. So he tried to focus on how he would talk with Romeo, when given an opportunity.

It wasn't long before they topped the Ben Franklin Bridge, a classic span. They looped left at the bottom of the bridge and toured by the Liberty Bell and Independence Hall. The car made an unexpected turn toward the river. *Bend over and kiss my ass goodbye*, but he was beginning to deny because of Romeo's renaissance demeanor that this was the end or that he'd have to kiss his end.

Naive?

"I have to stop at the cat food processing plant for a moment. You don't mind, do you?" Now Raphael and Hai's texting and commentary flashed by in his mind, like the glint of an automated fish canner.

"Cat food, fish. Sounds interesting." He couldn't hide his inner comedian. Fear and comedy had been inseparable since early Greek theatre and probably earlier in the caves.

"Well, it's not always just fish we use. Pusses have needs, too," Romeo said laughing at his silly joke. "We want our cat food to be the most nutritious on the market."

Troy wondered about the nutritional value of human parts. He couldn't come up with a reason why Romeo would want to kill him. But did the mob ever really have a rational reason for offing somebody?

"Yep, I've been thinking about felinity all day long," Troy said.

"Don't we all?"

Chapter 9

Raphael worried incessantly about his brother's predicament with the Greco family. He leaned over from the grimy jail bed and absentmindedly gazed at the curves of the toilet.

"Hey Troy man, I ain't getting any sparrows. Are you hogging them?" Toilet asked. It amazed him that this toilet could transmit perfect sound from another jail cell.

"No. Did you break the bread in little pieces? Sprinkle them on the ledge and back off?"

"I did, man." He seemed honestly stressed. Odd for a killer.

He told Toilet to have patience, wondering if his demeanor scared the delicate creatures. Toilet assured him he had a gentle heart. He would never knock-off a bird, unless he was paid to do so. Since all birds were innocent, he'd ask big money. Raphael remembered a not too innocent crow tantalizing the twins' childhood dog. This back and forth kept his mind off his withering lust for alcohol. Which, he decided was a minor distraction. He didn't shake. He didn't crave. He wanted, but didn't need a drink. Troy's visits to AA would do him little good, but Raphael felt something cleansing would come out of his stay in jail. He'd leave this crap hole somehow with a clean healthy body. The boys hiding in the latrine in 'Schindler's List' had it infinitely worse, but they purchased freedom. Of what did it matter, his silly little problem?

Anyway, supper was arriving soon, a little early. Out his too-small-to-escape window, the sun dried up the morning's rain off the swaying willows. The light for his gray and black inner world, the cell, blurred from one yellowed light bulb, dangling low enough to bat around, crusty with a cord to match. He hoped dust wouldn't flake down on their dinner, hoped she'd show up, his angel, Hai.

Bring me light.

Hai said 4:30 p.m. for supper because she had some evening appointments. She must have a boyfriend, or boyfriends. Raphael's plans to get Troy married, led him to worry some more. He couldn't very well deliver Hai gift-wrapped to a deceased brother. Troy was one tough cookie taking on a mob boss. But his bro knew what he was doing, or he wouldn't have gotten into Greco's car. Right? Had Raphael depleted his worry quota for the today?

The jail erupted in a few somewhat polite hellos, whistles, and complaints about room service, shortened no doubt by one look from the mountain called deputy Max. Hai sauntered down the corridor carrying a picnic basket, dressed in immaculate low-rider blue jeans, *oh God,* a belly button, a cowgirl checked blue-yellow blouse with two perfectly placed pockets, and red sneakers. She had to be five-foot-eight, maybe nine to his—he meant his brother's—six-three. *Perfect.* He decided upon further inspection, she was built more like a figure skater than a model because of very well developed legs and a round trampoline rump. This gave him an icebreaker in the personal arena, besides, he was more than curious.

"Thanks so much for this." He motioned his arms in a theatrical sweep of her basket and her body.

Her eyes narrowed for a moment. She laid out some hot and sour soup, egg rolls, tea and a shrimp with snow pea main dish.

"So you savor Chinese food?"

"I love Chinese everything." He assumed she understood his flirt, because of her coy, crooked grin and lowered eyes. Her body language, a shrug and eye flits, suggested, she decided to not take offense to his ogling or flirting and just enjoy the ride. "Did you actually cook all this yourself?"

"Well, just the shrimp dish. The soup and egg rolls, I picked up. I didn't have the time." She handed him chopsticks and a dragon embossed ivory soupspoon.

They had dinner for two on a table for one. They practically knocked each other out sitting intertwined like thick and thin branches, hands, arms, legs. He'd also say nose to nose, but she really didn't have much of one. Gazing into her black eyes, the cornea trimmed with burnt sienna, vexed and hypnotized him. That was just a starting point. God gave her sharp facial angles, high, round cheeks, extreme upwardly cut eyes. He taught the divine proportion in art and life. Hai could be his poster girl for the Golden ratio. He suspected, if he measured her body all over, every detail, it would yield the same result. An image of her naked and he with a ruler seared his brain.

All in the interest of art, of course. Maybe someday…

"Earth to Troy."

"Oh ah, I was thinking how busy you are. Why did you go to this trouble?" He sipped the soup. Excellent, breathed in the peppery aroma.

"You looked so healthy last week, but yesterday…"

"Blotchy."

"More like the walking dead, I was afraid I'd lose a client, before we had our day in court."

"Thanks, I guess. I hope you don't think me too forward. Were you an ice or roller skater? Your legs look athletic and your rear is very round."

"That's genetics on my sorry bottom, but my mom and dad had me ice-skating since the age of four. You're very astute and a little bit fresh."

He was surprised she didn't know how to put down a come-on. Being hit on must happen to her all the time. Perhaps, she didn't want to turn him off. He wasn't sorry at all for his remarks; only sorry he couldn't caress her rear.

All of her.

Meanwhile stick to the plan. Hardly free, he was just kicked out of his own home, a minor problem. Down but not truly out, as in out of Stella's life, who would take runner up in Miss Universe to this girl. Not that that mattered, when overwhelmed by extreme beauty and in both girls, caring hearts. On and on he could go about what made a near perfect woman.

"You're very beautiful." He could hear the faint chords of "Rhapsody in Blue." See the bold strokes of Michelangelo.

"Are you flirting, Troy?"

"What's for dessert?"

"Not me. I am not easy."

"I am sorry. I thought you were interested by what you said last time."

"I had just struggled through a hard meeting with a judge before I came to visit you and needed a little ego soothing. You seemed willing. That's all that was."

"That's too bad. I've always wanted to date a successful, intelligent, good-hearted woman with *slinky* eyes." He almost offered to do a portrait. She'd make a great study in black and white, shadow and light, and her exotic inscrutability.

She avoided his flirtatious assault while they ate, by going over presentation plans for next week's motion to dismiss. She had some tricks up her sleeve she assured him, but wasn't ready to elaborate. Meanwhile her breath filled his lungs. Getting close to her made his stomach twist as if peering into a volcano. Were there smoldering volcanoes in China? Google later. She blew him away more like Krakatau.

"My dear Hai, maybe when all this is over, well, I really want to date you. My parents have always told me to settle down, my brother too, and I have never felt the least urge to bring someone to meet them, until now."

What a load of bullshit. There was, oh by the way, Stella. What attracted him would attract Troy even more, because his brother was free to date.

Not much longer.

She reached across and poked his chest. "You...have a reputation."

Oh shit, Raphael had more repair work to do.

Damn it Troy. She poked the same spot. "You...are not the settling down type." Poked again. "And furthermore, you are far too handsome to be trusted. Besides, I can't get involved with clients. I use a three-strike rule, and you're at least four balls over the plate. You should be thrown out of the game."

"I only count two balls."

Maybe there remained a slight chance he would swat one over the fence and win one for the brother.

She wasn't shy with her personal space. Their eyelashes nearly tangled during the intense exchange of looks and words. He felt his sore chest, unbuttoned two loops, and peeked down at a small and probably temporary mark. She made a definite impression.

"Innocent until proven guilty, counselor."

He thrust his jaw forward just a tad and kissed her lips. She recoiled as if biting a lemon. Not quite the reaction he hoped for. His ego went down the toilet. *No offense, Toilet.* Then she slapped him.

Whack.

Apparently, she had well developed arms to match her poking finger.

"Don't do that *again,* Troy. Or the next lawyer you'll see *will* be Gertrude." She stood, gathered her things, leaving about half her food uneaten and called for Max.

"I'll call you," she said with a testy voice.

"Hai?"

"Goodbye-ee," she said, mimicking her singsong name.

"Not funny."

"You're the comedian, make it work." With that, Max rescued her, giving Raphael the too bad shrug with one raised eyebrow. The men locked eyes. Raphael eyed her sway, knew Max was doing the same and smiled that mischievous smile only men exchange, when desperate to spread their seed.

She glanced back, flicked her thick lustrous hair and softened her tone. "Listen sweetie, if you promise to be a good boy, I might bring supper again tomorrow. We have business to discuss, just business."

"Don't need your pity." He shouted after her, down the hall.

He could hear Max ask her what-the-hell was going on. She said something about saving the spoons and then her voice dropped below his hearing range. Guessing her facility with language and attorney-client privilege, Max would know nothing more than to heckle him. Tomorrow would be another gray day, until the fashion plate delivered sunshine and sustenance.

Leaning over the toilet and on an impulse, he considered flushing the delicious soup and everything else down. Whom would that hurt? Instead, he asked Toilet for advice.

"Yo, yo. You there?" He waited a couple minutes. "Yo-o-o."

"Yeah I'm here, I didn't want to move. I got a blue jay, here. Thanks, man."

"What? How'd you do that?"

"Don't know. Maybe this tree here is run by the blue jay gang."

"I don't think birds are like that," Raphael said, tickled. "I need advice."

"Hai likes you."

"She slapped me hard after I kissed her."

"You said she was an athlete, right, man?"

"Yes."

"Then, she could have avoided your lips. Eyes wide open, right?"

"Yes, I think so. No, I know so." Yes, she showed all the symptoms of someone smitten or intrigued.

"Open."

"Yes."

"Well there it is, man. She's a lovin' you."

"It's not that simple."

"Look, I'm a bad guy. I know when somebody's stealing stuff. You tried to steal a kiss from her. But, it was the mama, who stole the kiss from the man. She is lickin' her lips right now and drivin' with her head up."

If Toilet was right, and she didn't have an accident, all he had to do was plan his next moves, and make damn sure they were smoother than today's fiasco. He had a distinct advantage over Hai at this point. She was busy, and until supper tomorrow, he had nothing better to do than role-play, consult his toilet, feed the birds and maybe paint over the obscene graffiti.

Before he got down to the business of planning his seduction, he broke off pieces of egg roll skin and put them on the ledge. He clicked and whistled, but no blue jays showed. He went up on his toes, only to

49

spot sparrows twittering on the willow branches. He'd try again, not that sparrows weren't delicate, sleek and beautifully colored in browns and grays.

Chapter 10

In Philadelphia, Romeo brought Troy to his grandmother, who was staring out the picture window of their row home, located a block off Rittenhouse Square on Manning Street. They owned the block according to Romeo.

They needed to, for protection, he assumed.

"Na Na, I'd like you to meet Raphael Chariote, the famous artist. Raphael, you can call her Rosa."

"A pleasure to meet you, Rosa." He bowed and took her hand.

"You're a very good looking boy. You taken?" She pinched his ass.

"Na Na. No no. Shame on you."

"You've got strong fingers." He rubbed his butt and laughed. "And you're cute, but I'm engaged." She had a handsome if wrinkled face, tons of teased out black and white curls and a petite figure accented by a sunflower festooned apron.

"Too bad. Can't blame a girl for trying. Need your booboo kissed?" She wouldn't have to stoop over.

"Na Na, I love you so much, but sometimes you're too much. We are going into the library, and will see you for dinner. Would you have the maid bring us ah, grape juice?" He had to be considering Raphael's alcoholism.

The considerate mobster.

"I'll send Hilda in. Dinner at eight. Be prompt." She walked off tapping her cane, humming "La Donna E Mobile." What a kick, so full of life. He wished he'd stay that alive that long.

Romeo led him into the library. "I have a number of ideas I want to share with you and then we'll discuss your brother, okay?" he asked.

Was it really a question?

They had settled into a beautiful walnut library with inlaid floor to ceiling bookshelves surrounding three sides. The fourth side had two doors and Romeo's diplomas and family pictures, hung with care. Comfortable sofa chairs, map table, chess table, globe and sliding ladder added charm. He spotted business books, *National Geographics*, various novels and non-fiction in hardback.

Troy settled in next to his chair, separated by an end table with a bust of Gioacchino Greco.

"An ancestor of yours, I take it?" he asked.

"We think so. He was the unofficial world chess champion back in the 1620s. You play?"

"I've always wanted to." He didn't want to admit to knowing the game. The twins had played chess along with every other game while growing up. He had a gift for quarterbacking and chess, but never took lessons or read a manual on the game. Raphael sucked at chess, Guinness record sucking.

Hilda rolled a cart carrying a carafe of grape juice and a jumbo shrimp cocktail. She was dressed in a professional blue and white uniform, covering her knees. The pretty, maybe twenty-one-ish girl caught Romeo's eye. They gave each other a non-verbal hello, suggesting familiarity, something like *meet me later in the broom closet*. Troy wasn't going to go there with his wicked tongue, considering the relative formality of Romeo, and his need not to become cat food.

The cat food factory had seemed like an invitation to eat, drink and wear fish scales. The men, who worked there reeked; coated head to crusted rubber boots in scales and guts. Romeo boasted they were paid two dollars more than minimum wage with benefits. The workers took turns squirting the fish guts on the concrete outside the high roller doors into the Delaware River, to which Romeo went on about sometimes-stupid regulations, claiming fish guts were good food for the living waters. Troy felt there was likely a flaw in his logic. He dropped the thought.

"We don't have much time before dinner, and I never keep my na na waiting. Here's my ideas."

"Shoot."

Romeo smiled rather than commenting about the lame joke, which he had probably heard his whole life.

"I have some ways you and your brother can help me, and I think I can help you. In no particular order, my mom, Graciola, is an artist. I think she's has talent. That's why I tried to talk art today. I realize you, Raphael, are way ahead of anybody who isn't in the art business, so I decided I'd show her work to you. You can decide. The second idea is for me to meet your brother face to face. And I'd like you to set it up."

"You know we're identical twins. We are so close sometimes I get confused as to who is who." Therein lay the joy of fooling the whole world.

"I see you have a touch of your brother's wit, but I believe in the direct approach. It shows earnestness." Fish guts went swimming through Troy's psyche, but his worry ebbed long with the tide of living Delaware River waters.

"Well, if you insist, but how about a hint, to whet my brother's appetite."

"Let him know, if he likes my proposal, I might be able to clear his name."

Troy straddled, holding back elation with paranoia.

What was this guy's angle?

"You mean you'll persuade Jersey to tell the truth. No offense." Romeo seemed displeased with the girl, so why not push.

"No, I couldn't. She marches to a different beat, a very different beat. Oh, she's odd, no, something more interesting than odd. But Jersey is another set of problems, which I'm probably stuck with and I don't really want to discuss." Fair enough, if Romeo had another way to drop the charges.

"If there's anything I can do to help my brother," Troy quickly added, "I'll certainly consider your request." His gut told him, he had better not make a promise to a Mafia boss. Refer to cat food.

"She's a bad influence on my nephew, God bless him. Sometimes he acts as if he time warped to the 1920s or '30s. It's a stupid way to do business. If I can find a way to prod them apart or change the way she acts, I might have a chance at saving Frank's life." He understood Romeo's suggestion; belligerence begets the same. Romeo wanted to reason with the two of them, and then kill'em.

"Well, for what it's worth, she flirted with me, today," he said.

"Well let's table that, for now." Romeo's man-of-the-world attitude struck Troy as if Romeo had heard similar remarks in the past about the young lady named Jersey. *She's a flirt.*

Troy changed the subject. "You can visit Troy anytime you want, but I will clear it for you, tonight." He wondered what problems he might create if he confided in Romeo—a likely opportunist—his true identity. No, he could not risk it.

"Maybe in a couple days, I'll visit him. Let's talk about Troy after dinner. First I want to show you my mom's work."

Chapter 11

Shortly before 8:00 p.m., Stella trekked over from the main house to Raphael's studio. Aghast over the mess he had left behind, she decided to tidy up. Raphael, the neatnic, had run out distraught over something. She hung his pants in the closet and then jerked clear a suitcase to save some shoes it was crushing. They weren't Raphael's.

Girls knew shoes. That's the way God created them.

Troy's shoes in Raphael's closet.

She then remembered tripping over them and then dodging socks, belt, pants, boxers—they both wore boxers—and shirt on her way to the bathroom where he was showering. In high school, she peeped a couple times, but having seen it all numerous times, she didn't think Troy baby would ever shower in front of her voluntarily.

'Are you decent?' she had asked.

'Rarely,' he said in a jocular style.

Daaah.

It rained yesterday, so she'd thought little of the mess or his joke. Being an observant psychologist and a lover of mystery novels, she deduced the man she hugged while she lay naked in Raphael's bed was, drum roll, *oh my God, Troy.* The twins had done it again. They switched and if she had to breathe her last, she'd do something to stop their legendary nonsense. It would be their last time, but it would have been nice to see Troy naked as a man not a boy, or maybe not, being identical you know, can sure twist a fantasy.

Fuming, she dialed Hai Lo, Troy's attorney.

Answer. Please answer.

"Hi, Hai here."

Interesting Hai sounding like Hi ee. Troy had to have enjoyed this or was it, Raphael?

"Hi, this is Stella, Raphael's fiancée." She resisted saying ex-fiancée. Holding her Yogic breath, she continued in an unemotional tone. "Do you have any time tomorrow? I want to talk with you mostly about a personal issue regarding the boys, and a little about the case."

"I was going to stop by the Echelon Mall at lunch time to look at shoes."

Shoes, shoes, the magic word. A shopper no less, I like this girl already.

"How's noon at the food court for a quick bite, then I'll join you on your shoe hunt?"

"How's 11:50?"

"Done." This could be the beginning of a beautiful relationship. She toyed with the idea of wearing blue jeans, maybe a dress. Raphael would buy her a dress and shoes, tomorrow, in absentia, since he was in jail.

This is so ridiculous, moronic, goofy.

"I'm five-five, twenty-five, one-hundred and fifteen, northern Italian, freckles, and sandy-blonde shoulder length hair, top heavy." She tried so hard to keep her college weight. That scale had to say one-hundred and fifteen pounds in the morning or she wouldn't eat, much.

"I'm Chinese." Hai giggled. They'd have a great time.

"See you there." They hung up.

What on earth are the boys up to?

He had to have seen her in her birthday suit, no present, when he slipped out of bed, because she had tightly wrapped herself to him. He had politely covered her, so Troy, before running to the bathroom. Raphael would have stopped to kiss both her erect nipples and tucked her in, or he'd start by licking around them, then her lips, oh, then, *oh, now's not the time.*

How embarrassing can it get? Oh, they will pay. Pay. Pay. Pay. She cleaned up the studio some more.

Double Happiness by RW Richard

How much will one brand new dress and a pair of shoes cost you, my dearest on-again, off-again Raphael?

Chapter 12

Romeo preceded Troy up two flights to an artist's penthouse studio with full skylights and wrap around balcony with some interior and exterior greenery. His mom, Graciola, had a somewhat complete setup, suitable for sculpting and other media. He worried if he could pull off masquerading as an artist. He had accompanied his brother to a fantastic Slater Bradley exhibit in Manhattan, and he knew the difference between a Picasso and a Matisse. The twins shared each other's worlds with interest and earnest suggestions, as best friends and brothers would. Once upon a time, he was a maestro with crayons. Bravo.

Graciola's works were under linen shrouds.

"I know you won't be shocked, my mom is an outside-the-box thinker," Romeo said. "She thinks everything you are about to see, is serious art."

Oh no, he'd need his A-game.

"Impact, in today's art scene, is where it's at," Troy said, painting resolve on his face.

"Okay, don't say anything, until I unveil them all."

He worried. The probability was perhaps one hundred-to-one against Graciola being sufficiently professional. Like any other field of the arts, including comedy and or writing comedy, it took a lot of dedication, some luck, being open, accepting criticism, and a hell-of-a-lot of God-given talent.

How did you get to Carnegie Hall?

58

Troy couldn't stop laughing at the sight before him, in spite of the risk of becoming cat food. He knew immediately, Graciola's work would be a hit, but not in the way, the Greco family wished, perhaps. "Romeo, this is amazing. I hope I won't shock you."

"Go for it." He twisted a smile, obviously tickled.

"You know how I told you my brother and I are very close."

"Yep."

He came up close to the pieces as if the artist. "And, your mom is correct, these are serious thought provoking pieces, but—and this is a big but—if she could create maybe three more original pieces to go with these, we could guarantee her debut at the Comic Freak. Please don't misunderstand me, depending on press coverage, the audience reaction to the art…she'd need to present her descriptions in a completely serious professorial manner, and remain unfazed by the audience's reaction. We might be able to book talk shows, and then galleries. She'd back into the place she really wants to be in, an art gallery, with a little luck. You see, a strong audience reaction is the first step to making a lasting, thought-provoking impression."

"I think I see what you're getting at," Romeo said.

He couldn't stop staring. She had painted Mona Lisa in precise and beautiful detail, honoring Da Vinci's exquisite composition. Except, she had Lisa in full smile, showing off chipped, missing and crooked teeth. Mona Lisa was now the ugliest woman he had ever seen. The painting titled, *Her Secret Revealed,* an understatement, showing comedic training or talent.

Next, a scaled-down but perfectly rendered Michelangelo's David, except David's now too large penis stood straight out. He remembered art history. The hands on David were sculpted, too large, to denote power. Now they were normal size. She titled this, *How'd you feel if women and some men stared at your privates for four hundred years.* He suggested for the purpose of the show and any TV spots; she put a hand towel over the offending protrusion, with maybe a hotel moniker or bird design, but a hat rack came to mind. "Maybe, if we display in a gallery, she could go back to her original."

Next, he enjoyed a statue of a pudgy, balding, gap-toothed man in a rumpled business suit, mismatched socks, and elevator shoes, lugging a briefcase with one strap broken and papers hanging out. The inscription at the base read, 'Statue of Limitations,' rather than statute. Below the first line read, 'Nevermind,' referring to the deceased twentieth-century comedian, Gilda Radnor, playing Emily Litella. Oh God, he missed her smile, her quirky brilliance.

"Well Romeo…" Troy's eyes watered. He sat down for a moment. "I have got to meet the artist."

"She'll be home soon from yoga. I'll introduce you at dinner. Do you think…?"

"I know"—Troy interrupted, with passion—"success depends on how she presents herself. She has to practice being deadpan and professorial, maybe a little absentminded. My brother and I will work with her on this project. She'll be great, but she'll have to produce three more pieces. I'd like her to call the two of us with ideas."

"Deal. We better head down to dinner or we'll suffer my na na's wrath."

Dinner started without the artist, Graciola. The family held hands for a prayer. Rosa claimed credit for the meatballs, which were the size of grapefruits. Romeo sided Troy saying into his ear, "they get bigger every time she makes them" his eyes rolling. They were spicy, juicy, and the best meatball to go with spaghetti he had ever had. She garnished the dish with *grigliati,* strips of bell peppers soaked in olive oil with oregano. Everybody drank grape, carrot juice or plain water. The dinner sides were *esquerrole* soup, Italian bread and eggplant with endive salad. Sitting at the table was another Don, Uncle John, in from Chicago, Romeo's two children, Bobby and Emelia. Troy had learned Romeo's wife was deceased, natural causes. Also at the table, his grand mom, Rosa, or affectionately, Na Na, then Hilda, and a place set for Graciola.

"Sorry I'm late." Graciola ran into the room, dressed in tight faded jeans, attractive lithe body, a tie-dyed shirt with psychedelic spirals, a bandana and an Indian necklace with a sunbird as centerpiece. She looked a lot younger than her maybe sixty years. Troy stood while Romeo introduced her.

"I'm already a fan of your work," Troy as Raphael said.

He explained his plans for her, between sips of piping hot esquerrole soup. She nodded from time to time, but jumped all over the idea of explaining her pieces while people chuckled, as if nothing was happening. She understood the wisdom of his approach immediately.

Sharp cookie.

"I'd love to. I'm thinking of a piece already."

Her voice trembled with slight stutter. The delivery reminded him of an absentminded professor, in love with what she was teaching.

Perfect. The audience would love her. He pictured the crowd leaving the Comic Freak talking about the unusual exhibit, the artist, and then later to more friends.

With actual excitement, he prodded her to let all in on her new idea.

"I picture a sketch of the White House, except it's repainted in black and white stripes."

He said this was okay, but he felt polka dots showing equal amounts of black and white would be funnier. *On a roll.* He also felt the laugh for this idea would die too quickly. Comic success would come from her halting in-depth presentation of each piece.

"The laughter might die out too quickly on this one, unless you presented a quick slideshow at the finish with maybe four other sketches. This will still leave you with two more major deep and unique compositions. You don't mind the work?"

"I'd love to. It is a piece of my heart," Graciola said. She did remind him right then of the late, great Janis Joplin, in looks: straggly hair, freckled face, lusty voice and just maybe, talent.

"Aren't you the brother of Troy Chariote?" Uncle John interrupted.

He explained why he was here and finally made his plea. "Since my brother will be proven and is innocent, and we care about your family, I'm here to offer our prayers on his behalf."

"I'm afraid, young man…your brother may have to pay a price," Uncle John said. Oh no, not two hundred cans of cat food.

"John, we are not going to do business this way anymore," said Romeo.

"You know, Raphael, may I call you Raphael? In Sicily, in the old days, whether a man was innocent or guilty, something needed to be exchanged. An eye for an eye, if you know what I mean. If you slip on your ass in a K-Mart, you might sue, but who was guilty? In Sicily, the courts are all corrupt, no justice there, we have learned over hundreds of years to balance. It is our way. Here in America, so many Americans can't get a fair shake with the government, and don't tell me republicans, democrats, they're all full of themselves, and crap. An impolite debating society. Listen to me—we might be primitive or simple—but we fill a need. Some of us, Romeo, do not follow the traditions anymore." John glared at Romeo. "Some of us—are asking for too much—too soon."

The two men started arguing loudly in Italian. Everybody including the kids dove into the discussion, also in Italian, to the point knives might fly. After a while, Rosa stood up, glanced at their guest and then everybody else. She banged the table, and then they all shut up.

"*Scusa*," she said to Troy, while blessing herself with the sign of the cross.

Uncle John said as if nothing had happened, "So Raphael, Rosa's spumoni is better than her meatballs."

Romeo's mood had soured. After dinner, he did however assure Troy that John was just blowing hot air and they were in the process of exchanging for his brother's sake, even if fathead didn't see it that way. Therefore, the old way and the new way weren't much different.

He and his men saw him to his brother's Prius. Romeo promised he'd call or text soon to pin down the meeting day and time with Troy in jail. Troy got in the car and began to shake again. Apprehensive, he wasn't used to losing, and at this moment the possibility all could go wrong was too real. He waved and leaned into the back seat to hide his trembling. Tomorrow, well, there would be a tomorrow. Perhaps, he'd need to switch back with Raphael.

When he reached home, he found Raphael's studio tidied up. He had rushed out that morning. What else could he have done, with Stella naked in his brother's bed? He spotted a note and read it:

Dearest Raphael,
*   I'm visiting my mom and dad. I'd like to go out to dinner with you tomorrow night. See you then. I'll be wearing a new*

dress and shoes, which I just know you want to give me as a present.

    Love,
    Stella

    Raphael can afford it, and Stella is worth it. Tomorrow night I'll patch things up with her, just as my brother requested. What am I to do with her for a week and a half? I have to come up with a new improved plan to include extra alone time with her.

    Raphael's instruction rattled about Troy's brain. 'Don't touch her.'

Chapter 13

Deputy Max interrupted Raphael's morning's routine. Raphael was in the process of removing the jail cell's screen for the day to let his little friends perch on the window ledge. He called out for the winged beauties when Max appeared at the bars.

"You talking to yourself, Troy?" Max asked.

"No merely practicing a comedy routine."

"Try me."

"I'm not ready yet. You know me, a perfectionist. Later, okay?"

"Deal. I wanted to ask you what you did to your attorney." Max said while sticking his nose and big face between the bars as if he was pushing a football tackle rack. He grinned like the winner of a pie-eating contest. His crew cut ran parallel to the bars and had the makings of a good pencil or charcoal sketch. Cop on the outside looking in.

"I didn't do anything to her. I only complimented her about the way she dressed," Raphael said.

"Well, Troy, whatever you didn't do to her, did upset her. I caught a glimpse of her driving her expensive Mercedes over the tire stop twice, both front and back wheels. I could feel the car's pain." He groaned. "I didn't know whether to run out and give her a ticket. I guess I figured she learned her lesson right away."

"Was she alright?"

"Yeah, she just sat there stunned for maybe a few moments, then got out, peeked under the car, and took off. Whatever you're doing to her, please be careful. She's a real sweetheart who cares about you, and she's a powerful woman."

True, true.

"You know Max, you've been bugging me to settle down, even though your last date was with Dairy Queen. Seriously, I think, this time could be it. Don't know for sure."

Of course, if I couldn't find a way to hook Troy at least into dating Hai, I'd have to eat crow or more likely a perfectly spiced moo goo gai pan.

"Well, if the state doesn't throw away your key," Max said, sadly. He continued to press the bars.

"That's another thing, Max. Ms. Hai Lo is doing a great job. I'll be out of here in a little more than a week and then you can give this cell to some other poor schmuck."

"I hope so. Invite me to your wedding."

He assumed Max was jokingly referring to Hai and played it flat. "We'll get together before then."

"Be there, when I try amateur night at the Comic Freak or for a beer, anytime."

"I wouldn't miss it for escargot at Le Bec-Fin," he said, figuring Max would need at least one person clapping and whistling with wild abandon. Raphael surprised himself by thinking breakfast instead of alcohol. He also wondered about the sound of one hand clapping, or if the audience likely half-assed, half-handed response to Max would hurt his dear friend.

No, not that tower of strength.

Chapter 14

Stella settled in outside the Dunkin Donuts at the Echelon Mall food court. A tad early, at 11:35 a.m., she waited for her meeting with Hai Lo. She sipped a coffee and cracked open her mystery novel, *The Outreach Committee*, by C. L. Woodhams, and rapidly left her troubles behind, oblivious to the smells of deep-fried chicken, French fries...

The plot centered on women banding together to kill their evil husbands. She'd have to Raphael first. She read on, maybe a loophole would present itself. Perhaps Raphael could accidently impale himself on his paintbrushes. She considered why she had said yes to his marriage proposal. Aside from his beautifully sculpted body and face, fine introspective thoughtfulness, big cock, well maybe she needed more. Not more cock, more something. Maybe she needed to move on, maybe not. He loved her—or did he?

* * *

Hai peered around the food court for a young Italian looking lady. She wondered about why Stella called this meeting, but was excited to at least bond with her. They might become sister-in-laws if she read Troy right and luck was on her side.

For the first time in her life, she could relax around and trust men, at least one man. Oh, they were fine creatures until they wanted to steal her panties.

Her career had moved ahead with power and grace, chalking up one acquittal after another. With job stabilized and the firm encouraging families, she was ready to take another step forward on life's exciting journey and find a man. Maybe.

Troy might be that man. She loved the way he looked at her. He was gorgeous, not that handsome men hadn't chased her in her unready-for-love past. Troy was more than a hunk, there at the right time. She admired his refined perceptions of beauty, including noticing her clothes, and his celebration of the harmony of all life. She loved the way he cared for the sparrows. He had a kind heart and for some crazy reason ravished all of her, with his eyes.

She tried so hard to dress professionally and couldn't help that genes gave her an overly round derriere. A drunk-on-wine friend, some friend, once accused her of stealing and hiding balloons in her jeans while at a kid's birthday party.

She adjusted her black slacks where the pleat stopped and spotted a thin top-heavy woman in a unique, sleeveless pink blouse with blurred lavender starfish of various sizes. A Subway sandwich boy planted his face inches from the woman.

"Hi, Hai." Stella, seeming relieved, waved her over. The young man retreated to his workstation three stores down along the line of eateries. Stella's polished oak table had no Subway stuff, just a jelly doughnut, which had holes picked out of the top, as if a bird had pecked away at something too big to eat. Stella devoured a gooey morsel and licked her fingers.

"Nice to meet you, Stella." Stella had a welcoming smile, framed by bowed lips accented with a touch of powdered sugar. Her wide, hazel eyes lit up an exotic roundish face. Hai stepped between the Subway shop and Stella's chair, pointed through her body at the young man, now behind his counter. She tilted her head, pulled the bow of her lips and raised eyebrows to ask the unspoken question.

"Can you believe it? He asked for my phone number." The young man, probably a college student, stood tall and very thin, not good-looking, but not bad either.

"Your Raphael could snap him like a twig."

"Raphael and Troy," Stella said absentmindedly, her smile wavering. Something troubled her. Funny, men troubles seemed the order of the day.

"Hungry?" Stella asked.

Hai knew from experience in interviewing to allow the person with the problem, a little time to collect thoughts. She glanced around, spotted a Pic Up Stix, but decided to have whatever Stella wanted. "I'll go on your recommendations. It will give us more time."

"I like their pizza," she pointed, "goes great with beer."

"No alcohol for me, it makes me dizzy, and then I break out in hives," Hai said. She rolled her eyes to make the point. The last glass of wine she had downed was at her oldest sister's wedding. She had had more bumps on her body than a horny toad.

They ordered two slices of vegetarian pizza and ice water.

Back at the table, Stella flipped over the jelly doughnut on a bed of napkins. "If you are not squeamish, you can peck at this side of the doughnut. In this way, if you like, we can pledge our sorority."

Hai had researched Stella's background the night before. She did belong to an off campus sorority at Villanova, graduated with honors, had moved on to Princeton for a masters in psychology and was nearly through her doctoral thesis. Pledging sisterhood, with the jelly doughnut as the instrument, was a zany and memorable touch.

Hai laughed. "Well, okay, if I don't taste just a little, the doughnut will keep shouting at me, and I won't be able to hear you." Hai pictured a sculptor forming a dab of clay about the size of a finger-pinch worth of doughnut, and applying the dab to the rear end of a statue, which looked suspiciously like hers. Oh well, someday science would make signs to direct doughnuts and the like elsewhere in the body.

"You are game, girl. I like you," Stella said.

"The same." They locked pinkies and tugged. *What a great start.*

"How do you like working with Troy?" Stella asked.

"Once you get to know him, he can be so charming. He seemed to open up a completely new side to me this week. How's your Raphael?"

"Raphael is a thoughtful retrospective artist, an appreciator of all of God's beauty. Troy is brash, funnier than hell, but with a pure heart. He's a tenacious student of human behavior."

This description surprised Hai, having observed the opposite in Troy. Perhaps the jail weighed on his mind, made him reflective.

68

"Interesting," she said.

"I thought I'd catch you perplexed. There's a problem. I'm almost certain Raphael and Troy have switched places." Stella showed no tells, she seemed earnest and truthful.

Hai held her tongue. How could this be? The bachelor Troy kissed her a short but dreamy one. She could tell by his incredible hazel-blue eyes he wanted her, wanted all of her, heart, body, and soul. Hai nodded and silently repeated a mantra.

I have two ears and one mouth, therefore, I listen twice as much as I speak.

Stella tipped her head to the side. "Well, the reason I think so, I found Troy's shoes in the closet and I'm certain he, that is, Troy, wore them home from Raphael's visit to jail the afternoon it rained."

Hai decided they'd have to graduate from doughnut sharing and tackle a bigger problem. What were friends for? She had to tell Stella, no matter how much the truth might sting. Before Stella married, she had to be told.

"Sorry for the delay, you gave me a lot to think about. I don't think they switched. Your fiancée would never have kissed me." Stella's on-again-off-again happy face disappeared like a Venus flytrap and her petals turned scarlet. Some awkward moments passed. Stella finger tapped the novel she had on the table.

"Do you enjoy the story?" Hai asked and touched the book, trying to give some breathing room. The book touch was more a caress of the beautiful woman's spirit.

"Oh, it's great fun. I'm sorry, here's the thing. If you could check the shoes of the man claiming to be Troy…"

Hai interrupted. "He's wearing brown leather slip-ons with tassels." Hai had checked the man claiming to be Troy from toe to head and every bump and muscle in between. Women, at least sharp attorneys, take stock and inventory.

"Troy always wears the same black leather Oxfords from Sears, six loops. Has for years," Stella said. "And Raphael loves slip-on brown or tan loafers, because he works at home. Troy generally dresses in black for his stage persona. In fact, all I've ever seen him wear is black sneakers or black oxfords, since high school."

"Oh Stella I'm so sorry. There must be a rational explanation or maybe we're wrong." Hai was sorry, now she'd have to start her search for a man in earnest, and Stella might have to lose Raphael.

Hai contracted the hunt-down-a-man bug. She would find time, her career was in high gear and she only had to put in ten hours a day, six days a week. There'd be time, besides her paralegal, Janine, was getting more efficient and knowledgeable by the moment, and therefore would take on some of the load. She'd check out e-harmony dot com and other sites, as soon as she went home and sat down with her laptop.

Finding her mate in jail was too easy to be true and the worst place to look. She had a lot to learn about men. Damn it. Troy or Raphael only wanted what any other man had ever wanted from her. S-E-X.

Want to screw me, mister, take a number, get in line and be prepared to wait for the rest of your life. Surely, someone out there would be attracted to a pretty, Chinese lady with a successful career and a good heart. In China, she felt she'd be one of many, very many, pretty girls. Here now she aspired to be someone's rare pearl.

Stella tapped Hai's wrist. "Those two have been doing this swapping crap for years. In high school, the Cha Cha DiGregorio types used to nickname them the double your pleasure twins. Nobody could ever prove the ever-ready bunnies were taking turns dipping their wicks. And the Cha Chas of the world—not me, I was a virgin—they weren't about to give up none-stop crazy passion with the two, star players on the football team by blowing the whistle. They'd rather, ahem, you know." Stella popped her facial cheek with tongue to get her point across. Hai liked direct, forceful personalities as girlfriends, but she believed she'd require some tickling, lavishing, and courtesy (TLC), from her future boyfriend.

Stella laughed and Hai caught the bug. "Oh Hai, they were hot, but for good girls, they were not."

"Troy or should I say Raphael is very attractive," Hai said. What a disappointment. She had wanted to make it work. The guy was perfect. *Why can't he be true, be mine?*

"We need a plan, but I don't know where to start," Stella said.

"Well, in law school they teach you to lay out your case. That is, we start with the obvious. We prove beyond a reasonable doubt that they have switched places."

"Since I know both of them better than you, let me think up a way," Stella said.

"In the meantime, let's give this doughnut a proper burial and go shoe hunting," Hai said.

"Strawbridge and Clothier is having a sale. They have the nicest pumps in spring colors."

"Okay. Let's kick it, girl."

The two girls marched off arm-in-arm giggling.

There would always be shoes.

Yes shoes, but without that other necessary accessory, a man, might as well be barefooted.

* * *

Stella hoped, at least, Raphael would learn some life lesson in jail. She prayed he switched places to please her by detoxing. She was no child, no girl with a frog down her shirt, no kissed twice bimbo.

She hoped some jailhouse thug wouldn't torture him. *Just please, Lord, don't let my pretty boy be ravished.* That was her job.

Why had he kissed Hai? Had Stella pushed Raphael too far? Or was there some other reason?

* * *

Unfortunately, Raphael had to pay an unhappy price in jail due to overcrowding. A little after lunch, Max escorted a drunk named Dirk to his cell. Max had already filled Raphael in to ease his anxiety. Max had said Dirk was a white-collar guy who had too much to drink at a luncheon, started trashing the restaurant and danced on some strangers' tables.

Nothing worse than an idiotic drunk. Max un-cuffed him, introduced them, and said it wouldn't be long before his family rescued the surprisingly stinky offender. Raphael would rather stick his head in the toilet than breathe this air.

"That is sooo disgusting, having a bare-assed toiletry in the middle of this," Dirk said, waving his hands likely in search of the word, cell.

71

"I got used to it," Raphael said. Maybe this guy was a little like him. No. No. No. He'd never get so drunk he'd dishevel and puke on his white Arrow dress shirt. *Beyond disgusting.*

"I'm not going to shit in front of all of you. What's your name—again? Huh?"

"It's Troy Chariote. Listen, I don't want to shit in front of you, *either,* sir. So why don't we make the best of it? Let's talk." He motioned for Dirk to take the chair.

"I'm not touching anythings in herere. You profiably have AIDS."

"No, I'm only accused of murder, well, probably manslaughter if he dies, well…" Raphael felt like murdering somebody, but then he'd have to *touch* him.

"Guard, gird," Dirk shouted.

"Hey, Dirk, it was an accident. I'm innocent."

"Yeah, that's what they all say. What did you say your name isn't?"

"Never mind my name." A sparrow tentatively hopped forward on the window ledge. It seemed to hesitate at the sight of Dirk.

"How do you feel about sparrows?"

His puke had migrated from his shirt to his red power tie. Nice tie, checked pattern, too bad. Dirk's stench might have been worse if Raphael's sense of smell hadn't been diminished by whatever mold, dead rat, toxic waste lingered in his cell.

"Oh God, guard, God, ah guard," he shouted again. "Those creatures carrys all kinds of diseases and stuff. You touch them and your hand will fall off."

Gently, Raphael had to persuade his little friend to leave, and pronto, because he guessed Deputy Max might show up soon and the little visitor would be busted.

"Here Dirk, I found this tiny screen. I'll keep the bird out. See, I'm putting it in place." He blew on the bird to encourage it to leave, but it just ruffled its feathers. So Raphael walked his fingers toward the little one. The bird got the message and left.

"What's going on in here?" Max asked with an, I'm-busy-stop-bothering-me look and a deep authoritative bass.

"Whatshisaname has some kind of bird visiting."

"Look Max, Dirk here, also claimed to see tiny alien spaceships fly in here."

"I-I-I did?" Dirk asked.

"Hey Dirk, it is okay by me, alcohol will do that to you, sometimes." Raphael said.

"Yeah. Yeah. Aliens are real. They don't have any of those germs. I was ah cleaned up once—by them beans. They gave me ah um a super emena, full tank."

Yep, tanked, indeed.

"I think you should listen to Dirk's ideas. He's a manager at one of those financial firms." Max caught Raphael's eye and then crinkled his lips into a put-up-with-him frown. Dirk was facing Raphael and missed the signal. Emboldened Max whirled his finger around the side of his head, and then jogged down the hallway.

Maybe I should find out what Dirk drank and drop that from my shopping list.

Troy, get me out of here, before I go nuts.

Dirk soon departed and Raphael's mind became overwhelmed with nostalgia to a simpler time before he had started drinking. They'd played through a classic scene from *A Streetcar Named Desire.*

Hey, Stella-a-a. Hey, Stella-a-a. In the scene he knelt and wrapped his arms around her upper thighs, burrowed his head sideways onto her belly, and said, *Don't ever leave me, baby.*

Why would he leave her now? They had laughed and cried. They had made love. They loved each other. He'd stay focused on his brother's needs. His attraction to Hai was a potent mixture of her overwhelming exotic beauty and his doubting his feelings for Stella or Stella doubting him. Yes, he'd plead guilty to enjoying his seduction of Hai for his bro's sake. *So what.* Troy put him in this trash can aka jail. He needed something beautiful, no offense sparrow, to lighten up his artist's soul.

No doubt, Raphael would patch things up with Stella after he got out of here. After all, Troy was on the job, representing him. There was no better ambassador. No one in this world he would trust more.

Chapter 15

Shopping for shoes did little to diminish the deep pain and a dark secret Stella harbored. Raphael had crushed her heart by drinking, but so had Troy in a different way—a long time before—without Troy knowing it. She could not force herself to tell Hai now—the long complicated history of why she chose Raphael—so they ogled shoes. She couldn't stand the idea of breaking a very sensitive Raphael's heart. So let the skeletons stay in the closet.

She had to get a grip. Troy had always been emotionally unavailable to Stella except for outrageous and deep conversations about human frailties. Raphael wanted to settle down. She wanted children. Therefore, Raphael and she would have to find a way back to each other.

Stella and Hai admired the round glass-topped shoe displays in Strawbridge and Clothier across from the escalator on the second floor.

"I love these flats, feels like silk on canvas. The shoes will go with what I'm thinking about wearing tonight when I meet Raphael, if he is Raphael. I am so sorry," Hai said again. From the expression on her face, she must have realized her insensitivity and truly regretted it.

"No, that's alright, I don't want him anymore," Stella said, damn sure she didn't want him unless he fought off his demons and offered a rational explanation for kissing Hai. Fucking men. She'd grow a friendship with Hai, at least.

"Isn't that a bit hasty? What if we find reasonable explanations for all this?" Hai asked.

"I've been thinking about breaking up with Raphael for a long while, but I do want to know what's going on. And, my new sister, I really appreciate your honesty."

"What are friends for?"

"Exactly."

Hai picked up another pair. "I'll get his fingerprints, but how do you want to play our time with them?"

"I think we should play along as if we were in the dark, see what they're up to and meet after you get the print results," Stella said. In an afterthought, she added, "Hai, can you allow Raphael to do whatever he wants to you?"

"Only so far. Is there any way we can ID them, before I get the print results back?"

"Well, there's the embarrassing way."

"What do you mean?"

"Before I kicked Raphael out of his house, I had bit him near the top of his rump."

"Oh no, I couldn't do that."

"You don't have to bite him." Stella raised her arm to signify a joke. Hai smiled as if she suffered from whimsical thoughts of men's asses a tad beyond her reach. "The blemish was near the top, maybe if he bends over you'll see the top of the bruise."

"The last time I saw a man's crack; he was fixing the drain in my home. That splotchy, hairy eyeful traumatized me. I'm afraid, forever. No more asses." Hai said, tongue in cheek, of course. "Any other ideas, Stella?"

"Raphael is introspective, forever observing the world around him. Stealing moments of beauty trying to capture the essence of life. Although they are identical twins, Troy is his opposite. He wants to change his environment and then observe it."

"Insightful."

"Well, I've had Chariote-itis since I was a little girl." Again, Stella avoided saying she still carried a crush on Troy. Her hots for that man were strictly juvenile. Give the world a break, Stella. The twins came with the same equipment, and both with good hearts. Live with it.

Hai smirked, as if she were reading Stella's mind. "They say the talents in twins should match. That is, Troy and Raphael could duplicate each other if they chose," Hai said.

"Tell me about it. Since high school, the psychology of identical twins fascinated me. Because of them, I read everything on the subject. Imagine a high school girl reading treatises, studies and doctoral dissertations. I conducted double blind experiments right up to and including my thesis. You could say I'm obsessed."

Hai giggled and then cocked her head and smiled kindly. "No, you found an area of research, a specialty, and you dug in. Passion builds careers."

"I'm so glad you understand, Hai. When they were in grammar school, Troy decided to chase girls instead of taking art lessons. Oh, he's no slouch, and knows a lot about art, because they share each other's dreams. But he's unpracticed."

"So let me make a try at this," Hai said. "Troy chases girls, looks for the comedy in everything, and because he's a professional comedian, he won't settle down. Or to look at more negatively, everything is a joke, including women."

"I'm afraid you're right, counselor. I'm afraid you are right."

"Do they have any other physical marks that might give them away?" Hai's eyes blew up to twice their size; apparently, she liked talking about men's bodies. All talk, perhaps. Stella couldn't resist a deep dive into Hai's psyche.

"Raphael's penis is really big and circumcised." Hai exhibited no facial reaction.

"I can't go there." Now a bit of red showed in her new friend's cheeks.

Stella continued on, ignoring Hai's embarrassment. "I've never seen Troy's unless they switched on me, the bastards." Stella lied and smiled. She massaged Hai's shoulder to get a sense of her reaction and let Hai know she was teasing and bonding. She also didn't want to mention her secret hiding place in the boy's shower and locker room. If the two penises were in a line up, not even their mother would be able to tell them apart.

Hai didn't miss a beat although her face turned Chinese red. She deadpanned. "They were likely circumcised one after the other at birth. Is there anything else physical or otherwise that I can actually inspect?"

No blushing here.

"Yes, as a matter of fact there is. I think I talked a little about this before. Raphael is a neatnic, and Troy a slob." Stella picked up sandalwood tan-leather high-heels with a bird of paradise pattern on the straps. The on-sale rack carried all the name brands at reasonable, marked-down prices. These would do, indeed.

"They're stunning," Hai said feeling the fabric.

"Like our boys."

"Yeah." Hai swallowed. Stella wasn't sure whom or what merited the gulp. Had Hai suffered under the same Chariote spell? Who hadn't? Was it time to cut loose, Raphael, to give Hai a chance? All she knew now, an old crush bit her behind, a crush dormant all these years. Troy was within her grasp, if she did the unthinkable. What was the point to making love if there was no prospect of marriage? Troy wasn't the settling down type. Raphael loved her. However, by forcing Troy to make love to her, she could wash that man and fantasy right out of her hair. *Bagging both Chariotes could merely be a subconscious bucket list thing.*

Did Raphael really love her? Was Troy the better lover?

Maybe she'd have to visit Father Brian for confession, because she was confused as Hell, and extremely horny.

Tonight, tonight. Stella gonna get her kicks tonight.

Chapter 16

Raphael started pacing his cell. Toilet, his philosopher in a bowl, was taking a late afternoon power nap. He mused. He had to be careful when Hai arrived with dinner, not to overplay his hand with one special lady. He had to do better than last time. No one had ever slapped him before. Well, there was the day the twins visited the Wildwood by the Sea boardwalk and made a contest out of asking cute girls if they'd like to make love under the boardwalk. He swore Hai tossed mixed signals. Today, he'd pay better attention to her body language, eyes and words, and land a very big fish for Troy. A mermaid, with a nasty flipper.

Max accompanied Hai to the cell. Turning to leave he winked approval. Raphael gawked at her, shame, shame. This time she had outdone herself with her look and attire. First, she had a fancy new hairdo: two long corkscrew curls resting on her bosom trundled from two interwoven side-buns. Her forehead combed back tight to show off a thin tiara. She wore a long white silk gown topped with a traditional Chinese collar. White on white sewn peacocks adorned the gown. He pictured himself in a tuxedo and going to a wedding, his. She had to be dressed for one, maybe her own? She propped a see-through umbrella in the corner by the jail bars. Out the small window, a light mist tasseled with late afternoon breezes and shadows. The natural light flickered and breathed life onto her gown's peacocks.

Speechless, he jumped up, smiled broadly and blurted out a bit of mindless drivel. "You…are so cute." Why hadn't he said gorgeous or beautiful or anything else?

Cute, puppies are cute. What is wrong with me? He had to get a hold of himself, lusting after a woman he was trying to recruit for Troy all the while kind-of-engaged to Stella. He was a dog with many fleas. What became of all his resolutions?

"Thank you. I thought I'd try this outfit," she twirled, "out on you." She spread out the dinner and popped open the top of some wonton soup. The aroma made his stomach attempt to escape his body and attack the food.

He wanted to joke, to put on his brother's comic mask, saying something like the dress wouldn't fit him but undressing her would be worth the try. She kept talking.

"I'm going to a wedding in Chinatown Manhattan, this weekend. So you like it?"

"I love it. I love the girl."

"Troy, don't tease me. I think you need to clarify."

He felt uncertain. *Tread lightly.* Normally this was the part where he'd get close, put his arms around her back, pull her to him, kiss.

"I mean, I could fall in love with you, if you gave me half a chance." He glanced at the window, the freedom beyond, and worried about Troy. His brother would want him to go only so far. Raphael would tell him soon of her, before things got out of hand, and then he could let go of the exotic, exciting, and talented woman who so tantalized him. If he pressed any further, he'd risk confusing his own feelings.

"I thought you weren't the settling down type."

"My brother, Raphael would love a double wedding and has always pushed me. Maybe it's time."

"Yeah, you won't know unless you try."

"Yep."

"I need to get you out of jail. You could be going crazy in here, without any women around. You might be lonely. Starved. Horny. Not yourself." Yeah, literally not himself. He had gone crazy years ago. She had a coy demeanor. Hands on hips, eyes dropped level to his.

Mesmerizing. He flashed a moment, on Olivia Newton-John, 'You're the one that I want. You better shape up, because I need a man.' Does she ever. He'd supply the remedy. The Chariote brothers had always supplied the remedy. He had the ball. Straight up the middle this time for a touchdown.

Wait a moment.

"No, I'm not going crazy. Well maybe." He bit his tongue, losing his mind to her charms. He could have said to her, 'I've had far too much experience with women. I can wait.' Or 'hey, I'm an artist'—big mistake, an artist equals hedonist. Or 'I only need beauty to survive, and I find it in the finest of details.' He was happy for this moment, maybe happy for the first time in a while.

"I read in the *Courier Post* that Raphael is your identical twin."

Oops, what's next? "Yes, and he's my best friend."

"I have three sisters. My baby sister is the one getting married this weekend. It must be wonderful, to be an identical twin. You two must have a lot of fun?"

"Great for your sister. Is your family pressuring you to marry your boyfriend?"

"I have no boyfriend Mr. prying man, and they know me better, well except for my grand mom. I can't scare her, can't satisfy her. Witness, please answer the question."

"Ha. Well, identical twins are tempted by all sorts of advantages." Oops again, too much information. "I mean, I feel as though I can almost read his mind, and we help each other all the time."

"Weren't there studies about identical twins reading each other's minds?"

"Yeah, it's probably true at some level. You should meet Stella. She's the expert. She's a practicing psychologist, almost has her Ph.D."

"I look forward to seeing her. I hope Raphael's trip to Philly was successful. Did he report anything good?"

"Well, Romeo Greco wants to visit me here in jail."

"You need to tell me these things as soon as they happen. This could be dangerous. I'd want to be here. What does he want?"

"Raphael thinks Romeo has something to swap that might benefit me and him."

"A Mafia trade always benefits the Don. Let's be careful. Anyway, his proposal could involve something illegal, but we should hear him out."

"Well, I'll hash it out with my brother, and call you later as soon as I know. What is this spongy stuff?"

"Rice cake."

He had eaten fast. His portion of broccoli beef, fried rice and eggrolls was down to a couple of bites. She was pecking at her dish like his sparrow. One of the benefits of taking a woman out to eat: You eat one-and-a-half meals.

"Yum." The rice cake had a gelatinous quality with tiny grains lined up like soldiers row after row.

"If only I could get you out sooner, I'd invite you as my date to the wedding. My mom and dad would meet you. I could do my duty."

"Is that all this is, duty?" He pointed at his chest, with a comic, sad face straight from a Greek mask.

"It depends on the man."

"So I have a chance with you?"

"Maybe. It depends on who you are...*as a person.*"

What kind of attitudinal statement is this? Did she sense he had switched with his bro? If only his brother would grow up. See women as more than a fun time. Feel their passion, their lust for life, their nurturing ways and the pure joy when their eyes melted you.

Earth Goddesses all.

He choked on his thoughts. She stood, laughed and patted his back. It seemed to be a funny situation so he laughed with her but didn't know why, aside from the laugh being a contagious piece of human nature.

"My dad is very protective of his available daughter. You think you have problems with the Mafia." Maybe this was her joke, had to be. The Mafia slays people; fathers slay marriages. He felt somehow that he'd meet her dad, maybe even this weekend.

"Someday your dad will have to let his little bird fly." He said, touching her hand. "Whether it's to get married or stay independent."

"He loves me." She didn't withdraw her hand. "And he's very pro marriage but even more pro allowing me to do what I believe is right for me even if I never marry."

Here again, he should have wrapped his arms around her and kissed. You can't hurry love, Mama said.

Am I losing my touch, out of practice?

He wavered. "What are you looking for in a man?"

"I wasn't looking until you kissed me, yesterday. Don't get me wrong. I've been very busy with my career. You awakened my primal urges. The idea of a special somebody for me. I had shelved these thoughts. Just the same, you stole that kiss."

'Twas the maiden who stole from the man.'

He ignored her accusation and felt he should take her now. But getting to understand her remained more important. "Okay, but if you are going to be successful at finding a mate, you need to use the scientific method. Just my opinion."

"I don't think it's the same for a woman. Since you brought it up, why me? And what about you applying the scientific method?"

Putting on his Troy: "I too wasn't looking, until I met you and had plenty of time in this dump to think about it. I can tell you for now, you are oh so beautiful, smart, and funny and have a great heart. You appreciate my sparrows, my way of looking at the world. You're nurturing, warm, and I think the sexiest woman I've ever met. Um, what about you?"

"Well, in no particular order. There's looks, Troy, something you have in abundance. Chemistry, right?"

"Chemistry, sprinkle in a little biology and *voila*, we have at least a romance."

"Then there's a man's heart. It must beat true. He must be looking for a best friend, in your case, another best friend. Do you think any woman could replace your brother?"

"No, but she wouldn't have to. Love is infinite. You can't slice it or dice it."

"I really do have to get you out of here." She winked and stabbed her eggroll with chopsticks.

"Go on."

"Well I adore your gentleness, your adulation of nature. I know I said that already. Your brother's an artist and yet you seem to be the sensitive one, and for that matter, not at all that much like a comedian."

There it was again, but this time in his face. Had she really caught on to their little scheme? *Couldn't be.* She hardly knew him or her brother enough to jump to that or any conclusion. Still, she had been asking or implying a few too many twin questions.

Just small talk. Right?

"Sitting in jail with your future up in the air dampens the mood for jokes. Twins share all their God-given talents. Developed skills are different, but we always kept each other informed and educated. Raphael is pretty good at making jokes and I'm pretty good at art."

"Show me."

Whatever did she mean by that? Her face displayed that inscrutable coyness once again, this time harbored in her eyes held shut a bit too long. He remembered his baseball coach's rule—don't take the third strike in baseball or life. If you allowed it, you would have lost your opportunity to get on base, that is, accomplish something. He didn't want his brother to fail before he started.

He worried about all this rationalizing over analyzing, so he stood up, paced a moment, uncertain, walked behind her, cupped her elbows and tugged her a tad upward. She sprung up and pirouetted into his arms. Eager. Her wanton stare, questioned what he was doing. She had little or no experience. He pulled her close, and bent down, just a little.

"I'll show you," he said, but really asked.

"Show me." Her eyes welled. She trusted him. Their lips barely touched and then separated slowly like a sticky-note. He raced his hands all over her back, resisting the only-a-little-farther to what he really wanted to squeeze. He then touched her cheek, kissing his way to her ear. She trembled. He had her now. He meant his brother had her now. He could kick himself for his temporary confusion. He returned to her mouth, attracted by her trembles.

Troy would love these pillow lips, her creamy smooth face, her mix of confusion, fear and joy. She had absolutely no experience: show me, take me, but take me gently, be good, but be bad, very bad. I'm ready for love. Hai presented a clean canvas on which to paint a masterpiece of wanton desire and abiding love. Absolutely perfect.

"I love this. Some more. I want more." She seemed to mean it. He looked around and out into the hallway, then at the disgusting bed. Surely, she hadn't meant, make love to her here, now. He kissed her again. They became one in the kiss, two bodies floating off to some dream world, now as one.

The more he gave the more he got. He became lost, swirled in a fog of two souls, of Troy's, of his. He reached out for his brother's blurry ghost. He absorbed Troy and savored it. He blushed, she noticed.

"Will you teach me how to kiss right?" she asked. Somehow, he felt she could do the teaching.

"Don't change a thing. Let Mother Nature guide you. I'm not saying we couldn't or shouldn't learn…*things.*"

"Things?" she panted, arms wrapped tight, hands cupping his shoulders. She shivered and held tighter.

"Delicious things."

"Touch me."

With his pointing finger, he raised her jaw. "I'm not as fast as people think." He had better not touch her. It had been great to share girls and then women, but Raphael was playing to lock up his brother's heart so that Troy would never want to switch again. Anything beyond kissing and hugging was taboo. Besides, she was too little experienced and he was too much willing to teach her.

"Psst." Toilet was calling. "Pssst."

Their lips separated. "Wanna get that?" she whispered cracking a dreamy smile.

"Is she still there?" Toilet asked.

"Hello." She bent over a bit too close.

"You'll soil your beautiful gown."

"She's wearing a gown? A gown?"

"Toilet, I'd like you to meet Ms. Hai Lo, my attorney."

They exchanged hellos and shared a little bio, button man— lawyer, lawyer—button man. Hai then observed that pipes transmit sound, and she had heard of this phenomenon before in other jails.

"You shouldn't call him Toilet. What's your name?"

"I'm likin' toyo-let ma-ma. You likin' the man?"

"And the man likes her, Mr. Toilet."

"Oh, this I know. You have it bad, man."

"Well, we'd like to…"

"Get back to your kissing. Indulge yourselves. I'm seeing my blue jays now. Goodnight to you, young lovers. Goodnight." They said goodnight back. The sun parked at a deep angle ready to wink away. He could never get Toilet to talk at night. The man had discipline. Raphael respected his privacy, alone time and sleep.

"He has blue jays?" She asked.

"Yeah, he thinks a tree controlled by a blue jay gang right outside his window."

"That's adorable. I always wondered what men did in jail."

Hai had to leave. He asked her to discreetly check the other cells for a Caribbean man or ask the about to come on board night shift. He placed the screen back on his window to avoid the now awakening New Jersey state bird, the mosquito.

Hai left anxious and promised to see him tomorrow.

He couldn't wait.

Shame on me, but hey, I'm an artist and I appreciate beauty. He not only needed AA, GA, girls anonymous, loomed.

The sparrows moved to number two on his jail list of pleasant activities, Toilet third. He wondered what she'd wear tomorrow. Stella somehow dropped out of his thoughts, and he felt rotten about it. Troy and he needed to meet or at least talk, before Hai came back. Raphael would tell him what he did for him by seducing her, before it was too late for his heart *and hers.*

Troy, you dastardly philanderer, recognize greatness. Recognize your soul mate. Settle down. I'll be your best man…or was I just the very best man?

No, his brother was also the best of men, just in a different way.

At some future double wedding, they'd be each other's best man, always had been in every sense of the word. If anything ever happened to Troy, Raphael would feel as if his heart ripped away from his chest, and he knew Troy felt the same way.

Chapter 17

Change of plans, went the note from Stella.

Dearest Raphael,
I decided to cook. After all, I am Italian. See you in the main house at 7:00 p.m. Come casual. You'll be getting a fashion show, thanks to your pocketbook.
Love,
Stella.

He knew his brother enjoyed cooking, and he had little experience. He could wing it if she enlisted him. Being in the main house with Stella worried him. He worried he'd be dessert. She had always been a pest in high school, two years his junior, alternate junior varsity cheerleader wannabe varsity, with a straight up-and-down figure. She was cute, had potential. *A crazy gorgeous face.* He'd lost track of her in college, and missed most of her transformation, until that fateful day Raphael had brought her home.

She displayed her feathers like a swan. Her big round wide eyes could hypnotize Dracula.

With trepidation, he knocked on his brother's main door at exactly seven. It was drizzling out. No answer. He gently pushed open the door, and shouted hello. Stella, in the kitchen, was singing "Stop In The Name Of Love". He tossed his raincoat, and then remembered whom he was impersonating. He picked the coat up from the floor, neatly ironed it with his hand and parked the raincoat in the closet, front of coat facing the door. He bent over with his hankie and absorbed some telltale water drops from the oak wood floor. His brother was such a, a metro-sexual, limped-wristed artiste, pansy.

She stuck her head out the swinging door to the kitchen. "Come on baby, I think I burnt the carrots, but everything else is fine." The smells from the kitchen weren't horrible.

"Hey, no harm, a little carbon in the diet is good for the soul." He couldn't die from burnt carrots, could he?

She banged the table with the main dish, his knees jerked up knocking the underside of the table. The dish, some sort of seasoned lamb chops with a side of mint jelly, beckoned him. *Eat me. Eat me.* He would with relish. The aroma masked the carrot disaster.

"Sorry about the bang. I put out the dress on the dining room table, and a pair of shoes, what do you think?"

She wore tight jeans accenting her curves. A pink cotton shirt sported blurry starfish crawling all over it, two of which helped caress her breasts. Nipples erect. Worked for him. He traveled over to the dining room table and made a fuss over a pretty dress, an above the knee number in white with tropical colors matching shoes with bird-of-paradise straps. He supposed that if he were a girl, he'd like it. He forgot his brother was half-girl in attitude.

"You'll model these later?" He said effusively with a breathless air and this wasn't just acting like metro-sexual-Raphael. He remembered one of Stella's chats. If one of the identical twins was gay, the other one was too, even if separated at birth. It dawned on him exactly how macho his brother really was.

"You've been so *incredibly* good about drinking. Of course, I'll model for you."

A little later she added, "I'm finishing up my thesis modifications and my faculty advisor, you know Dr. Jacobs, well he's asked me to flesh out a couple of the case histories with a heavier lean on the psych angle. Would you mind if I asked you and your brother a couple more in depth questions?"

"Not at all, and the same goes for Troy, I'm sure."

"Well I'll catch up with him later. Now my tall, dark, and handsome guinea pig, let's start with who's dominant?"

"Neither, and that's by design. We made a pact, at our mom's suggestion when we were six and we stuck to it."

"Good. Sorry if I asked that one already in the past."

"No problem."

"Who's stronger?"

"Well, Troy and I aren't ego driven with each other. I probably developed more upper body strength because I played halfback to his quarterback. Maybe his throwing arm is stronger." It dawned on him; she may not really be interested in who was stronger, but really more in how he felt about his brother. *Those devious psychologists.* "The next time I catch up with him I'll challenge him to a left-handed arm wrestle." He'd act like himself, well like his brother, to keep Stella in the dark.

"Don't hurt the weakling." She smiled, reached over and squeezed his bicep.

"Never."

"Would you commit a crime to help your brother?"

He pretended to think for a while, since he already had committed a victimless crime swapping with his brother. "Neither Troy nor I would ever do anything morally or ethically wrong." Did she know how to read faces, as they did on that old TV show, *Lie To Me*? Little doubt, she was the real deal, but he'd try to deceive her.

Stella had taught him many psych tricks. He cleared his mind of all complications, to present a grimace free expression. You can fool some of the psychologists some of the time...

Meanwhile she paused. Then she perked up. "Oh, I'm sure. No, I meant something illegal."

Had he been found out? No, ethically speaking, he and bro screwing all the senior cheerleaders hadn't counted. Had it? Perhaps that would be his cover if she read his face.

"If it would harm no one, we'd consider it."

"Can you give me an example?"

Again, he took a little time responding and finished a bite of crisped lamp swirled in mint jelly. The dish was perfect just like the chef. He rearranged his silverware perpendicular to his plate and moved her wine glass an inch to her left so that his glass was exactly diametrically opposed just like he had observed his bro do a few too many times. Stella starred fascinated and then seemed to move on with only the slightest hint of disapproval.

"I'm sorry, Stella, I can't think of a situation." Actually, the comedian in him could think of quite a few silly examples.

"How about swapping girls? Remember how you two switched in high school and summers during college until I took you off the market?"

"We outgrew swapping the moment I brought you home to meet Mom and Dad and see him."

"What do you mean, the moment?"

Oh shit, he screwed that one. "I mean, the moment we fell in love, of course, honey."

"And when was that?"

"You should know, you were there."

"Humor me."

Luckily, Raphael and he shared every detail when it came to women. "Okay, okay, technically, it's never the same moment. I loved you for months before I told you and you had waited too."

"Let's revisit the night."

"Late afternoon, technically. We reenacted *Lady and the Tramp*. When I recover, you'll be spanked for this." He paused. She just took a bite of her roll. "When we had no more noodle, we parted lips and both said I love you at the same time. It will forever be one of my sweetest memories of my life."

"Me too. Just one more question and then you can relax."

"Stell, around you, I'm always relaxed."

"You never swapped me, with your brother to—you know, have sex?"

Forget relaxed. "Never, honey. I swear to God."

"How's your belief in the Creator doing?"

"She exists. Listen to me a moment. Troy could see we were in love. My brother and I matured. Swapping wasn't and is not okay anymore. A woman must be respected."

Did he look and sound real to Stella? He folded his napkin in a perfect triangle. She crumpled hers and tossed it half way between them. This was a challenge. He smirked, turned his head away from the supposedly offending napkin and studied the drapes.

"And a girl isn't?"

"The girls we played with, well honey, we were immature and so were they." At least she got off the Stella swap idea.

"You were jerks."

"Okay, jerks. But weren't we all jerks in high school?"

"Not me, but this isn't about me. Just one more question, promise."

"Okay."

"Do you think your brother will ever marry?"

"If he found a girl like you, he would in a heartbeat." God, he put his foot in doggie do-do this time.

"Did he ever say that to you?"

"Yes, he had. I mean, not about you specifically. I meant to say, the idea of you, a fine woman with a great personality." He held up his hand to stop her next question. "I know my brother. He meant it."

"He probably just likes my rack."

He sputtered his wine. "No doubt about that."

"Okay. Off the record. No more interrogation. Do you think Troy would go for his attorney?"

"Have you met her?

"I've checked her out online. She's quite a catch."

"He'd never go for her. Yes beautiful, but not his type."

Something was turning her pensive. "I thought he lusted after Asian girls."

"The last time he discussed preferences with me, was freshman year in college. I think, Thanksgiving, at home. He declared this in front of the whole family. Check with Mom and Dad. Since then, he's become more rounded."

"Notorious."

"Nowadays, I firmly believe he sees you as an example of his ideal woman, driven, lovely, funny, insightful, discerner of but human nature." He decided to try to change the subject to family matters, before he went too far. Stella allowed this.

After dinner and a short fashion show, she said, "Let's play strip scrabble."

"I'm still withdrawing from alcohol, I promised myself after I'm clean maybe ten more days, I won't get these headaches and then I'll prepare to lose to you."

"My poor baby." She started to rub his shoulders, then ran her hands up and down his back. This reminded him of an Electric Slide dance.

"Take your shirt off."

"No... In order to keep my promise to you, my AA friends and myself, I swore off all forms of gratification. You kicked me out, remember?"

"I'm trying to help you with your headache. That's all silly. It's medicinal." Damn, she was persistent.

What gives?

He took his shirt off, and wobbled his pecks for fun. Her eyes lit up. She grabbed some olive oil and went to work. He felt like a tossed salad and wondered if he'd go well with croutons. Her treatment was a bit harsh—a sort of Japanese karate massage—but it worked. Either that or she wouldn't need a punching bag for Christmas.

Soon she fagged out.

"Remember last week you promised to teach me how to draw the human figure?"

"Oh sure." Raphael failed to mention this, probably not expecting art lessons to come up so soon.

"Fine, take off all your clothes."

"But..."

"No buts, just your butt, now."

"Honey. This comes under my pledge to AA and to myself."

"But you're a professional artist. And hadn't you boys danced for Chip-n-Dale for extra cash in college?"

"Well, that was only for one summer, and part of the next."

"Come on, baby cakes. I gathered from your studio a sketchpad, a bunch of B graphite pencils. Right? A blender, a sharpener and an erasure. What more do I need?"

"Well." He couldn't say charcoal over graphite to stall her, because he didn't know.

"Well Raphael. Do you love me?" Now, that was a tough question in reality. His heart ached, probably due to the tremendous temptation, hovering near him.

"Of course I do."

"Off, off, now, come on." He had to.

Raphael, I promise you, nothing will come of this. He stripped, hoping he wouldn't become ram hard. *Think pigs rolling in slop, John Brown moltin' in his grave.* He felted calmed, in control, dick dangling. There were no body differences between him and Raphael, all joking aside. Raphael sported no tattoos, no scars, nada. He was safe as long as the sight of one thing didn't lead to another. She asked him to pose like Michelangelo's David. That was his undoing. Her suggestion brought him back to the night before when Romeo Greco had shown his mom Graciola's rendering of David on which she sculpted an erect penis. Like a philosopher, he ruminated on David's plight, posing for hundreds of years, and big-eyed Stella staring at him, her eyes truly bulging…

"I notice you're happy to see me."

He broke out into a sweat. "Of course I am. You're my sweetheart." He put his hands over the offending object but the horse done run clean out of the correl.

She squirmed, obviously wet and ready to trot. His control, yeah where was his control. She knocked over her chair, ran, laughed and clicked the lock on his brother's master bedroom. Phew…and down it went.

"Good night," she said breathlessly. He wondered what she'd do in there without him and smiled. She definitely had the hots, and somehow found the courage to stick to her promise of no-sex for a minimum of what remains of two weeks and until some progress with AA was noted. She could use AA batteries to get off, but poor him. He was tempted to pound his meat, something he had forgotten how to do. Besides, he'd feel guilty.

"See you tomorrow." He was relieved, but he needed a cold shower. He walked out the door naked, into a downpour under a full moon. Luckily, the neighbors weren't close enough to sing, 'there's an ugly moon out tonight, wo, ho, ho, ho.' He had to consider, that his admissions in front of Stella could come back to bite his ass. He had to consider, if he really did covet his brother's fiancée. Their styles matched, her body was just right, but who would want a comedian who might travel, anyway. She was feisty, no pushover, and he had always liked that. However, he loved his brother like life itself. Nothing or nobody would ever break that trust.

Easy now to say. Stella, Stella, what do you want from me? What do you want from me?

He'd get the clothes tomorrow. He double locked the studio door more to keep him from turning into a werewolf than to keep Stella from jumping into his brother's bed naked again. Although from her insistent good night, he doubted anything would happen. He wondered if the 2:00 a.m. hornies would overwhelm her, perhaps fueled by dreams of his posing as Michelangelo's masterpiece. David was ugly in comparison to the Chariotes. Modesty, modesty. Stella was a direct girl. She'd probably pull out a vibrator.

I'm so handsome New Jersey started a lottery for a date with me.

I'm so handsome George Clooney visits me to learn how to get a woman...

Clunk.

* * *

Bacon and eggs, pancakes, maple syrup, and the remainder in a care package for Raphael, a peck on the cheek from an oddly red-faced Stella, and off Troy drove to swap with Raphael again.

The first thing he noticed about Raphael was his complexion. A miracle had taken place.

He whispered. "My dearest Raphael, please don't ever drink again, if you love me."

Naturally, Raphael cried. He knew how to get him. They hugged. Troy pushed the Phillies baseball cap tight upon his brother's little head, wiped Raphael's nose with his sleeve, and stuck the mustache on him.

This time neither of them stumbled while changing clothes. Troy wore an identical pair of his brother's shoes so they wouldn't get caught.

"Mr. Greco will be here at 1:00 p.m. with Hai to make a deal." Raphael understood why they had to switch back. Troy resisted saying good news, Raphael, a horny Stella awaits you. Forget AA, Take her. Raphael tugged Troy by his sleeve over to the corner near the newly painted wall.

"We have to speak softly or in whisper, I don't want Toilet to hear." He pointed for emphasis, but really, Troy knew what a toilet looked like. The next thing he told Troy blew him away.

"I warmed up Hai for you. She's perfect, just what you've always wanted, and it's your time, to get serious, join me at the altar, settle down." He wasn't going to burst Raphael's bubble with argument. He watched him wax ecstatic.

"She has the sweetest lips. She's smart, successful, thoughtful, appreciates my sparrows." He pointed up at the window with its missing screen. "The screen is under the bed; put it back on before dusk. She's the sexiest and most loving woman I have ever met, on an equal with Stella. I think Mom and Dad will idolize her."

Sweet lips. Well, in a pinch, I could do kissing.

"It sounds good. I'll look into it. Thanks." Okay he was short, but Raphael had to know it was a lot to absorb and that he would consider his brother's idea, a little.

The tall athletic Hai had a sensuous face, with high cheekbones, slightly parted lips showing perfect teeth, which to be honest was a bit distracting. She outclassed the beauty of any number of Asian actresses in his opinion, but he had no feelings beyond the normal lust for her and every other good-looking woman. Anyway, she was more his brother's type, artsy, fartsy. He wouldn't suggest that to Raphael, who was having enough problems with Stella.

If Troy ever got hitched, this bore repeating, it would be to someone similar to Stella. A girl that gave as good as she got, a type A personality with a sense of humor, and loyal to the death, like a dog. Wolf. Wolf. Okay she wasn't as perfect as Hai, but just as pretty, not as tall, maybe a little extra baby fat in the right two places, but one look into those gaga eyes... *I will someday find a girl like her. I will.* The

94

perfect places to shop for such a girl were South Philly's Italian neighborhoods or maybe the same in Brooklyn. They grew them feisty there with just the right seasonings. Catholic girls with patent leather shoes, he remembered watching the Camden Catholic bus unload its horde of beauties. He always wanted a tough but loving critic to practice his jokes on.

Some day.

Transfer complete they hugged again.

Before Raphael, playing himself left, he whispered. "I call the toilet voice, Toilet. He's been my common-man philosopher. He likes his name. He wants to hear about the sparrows. Please feed them. He has blue jays. Not that I don't like sparrows. Love you, my Jedi clone."

It was like Raphael to get sappy. The sappy brothers. Maybe he could talk him into playing straight man in a routine. Who said comedy pairs were dead anyway, Penn and Teller were fine. While he would once again rot in jail, he decided to work on a routine for a once-in-a-while surprise at the Comic Freak, perhaps on the crazy love lives of twins. That'll slay the audience.

Raphael left.

Troy fed the troupe of gathering sparrows, and then sat down for a long stink. He stared at the toilet, wondering if the toxic cloud he was manufacturing would herd itself over to the toilet and obediently wait for a flush. All that Italian cooking from the night before, he guessed. The sparrows, not canaries in a cave, paid no mind to his toxic fumes.

"Hey sparrows, I'm not my brother, do you care?" he whispered naturally. He wondered what stupid jokes Max would hit him with today. Although he displayed a compelling comedic mask—the brawny, not brainy cop—a little pathos in the romance department would help. Max lacked timing and material. Fatal for a comic.

"You two guys really love each other," Toilet said through the haze.

Chapter 18

Hai met Stella at Garden State Bagels off King's Highway in Cherry Hill, for a quick lunch. The noon sun blared, so Hai took off her suit jacket, folded it over and left it on a hanger at the back door of the Mercedes.

She looked down at her breasts. They were still there under the silk. *Nice to know.* Stella's big knockers put her off. Hai loved her perky ones. They fit her frame, didn't droop, but still, you always wonder what little detail would turn a man away, now that she was officially looking. The romance sites on the internet she perused the night before made her want to sanitize her hands.

Big boy wants loving chick, be submissive. Okay, maybe that was the wrong site. Corporate attorney, successful Philadelphia practice, owns large estate. Twenty-nine, considered handsome. Yes, the male prospect was a bit better than that. She had researched, using Google and Lawnet, identified the firm, and opened a picture of an elderly man with white hair, what was left of it. The best sites were mostly honest as far as she could tell, but nobody turned her on. She had been Charioted, perhaps.

"Hey, Stella."

Stella sat on the clean carpet of the cargo area of her old Sport Explorer. Two bagels, a Philly Cream Cheese, and coffees rested on a plastic tray.

"Are you sure this is enough?" Stella pointed at the bagels.

"It's an everything-bagel, right?"

"That it is."

"Then I have everything, including your company."

"Did you get the fingerprint results?" She asked.

Hai opened the lab envelope. "Just picked this up from my investigator. Yep. They switched, that is, Raphael is in jail, and you have Troy. What a mess." How Stella was feeling after all this? "A dollar for your thoughts." She loved inflation when friendship was at stake.

"You said, I have him, Troy, my God, he could have had me."

"Ooh ooh, this is juicy. Tell girl." She hesitated. This was getting curiouser and curiouser. Hai waved her pinky; they linked.

"Spill it, soul sister." The two had started a sorority of two and forever two, the day before, so she knew Stella would have to tell the whole truth.

"Well, at first I pretended to interview him for my thesis, but he didn't break under my subtle interrogation. Then, desperate and a little curious, I decided to inspect his body. He claimed to have a headache after I suggested strip scrabble. So I made him take his shirt off for a massage, but again no tells. So after beating the crap out of his back, God that felt good, I asked him to pose nude for an art lesson I had vaguely talked to Raphael weeks before about."

"You were playing with fire."

"No, not really, after I saw more than I wanted to see, I ran away to the bedroom, locked the door and asked him to go away."

"What do you mean, you saw more?" Hai raised her eyebrows. She wanted every big detail.

"His thing didn't take long to get as hard as a week old baguette."

Well, she had asked for it. "Maybe he likes you?" Hai asked.

"No, he's just a dog, like all men. How'd it go with you?"

"Are you sure you're over Raphael?"

"Hai, my feelings are already hurt." She grabbed Hai's hand. "I cried all last night over this ridiculous pair of adolescent miscreants. Breaking up is hard to do."

Hai remembered her Nana's old records and sweet songs.

"I'm sorry." Hai said, meaning it.

"I don't blame you, Hai. The boys are nearly irresistible. I want to know everything that happened to you. Knowledge is power and with power, we might change these bad boys, if not for us, then for some other young pretties. So do tell."

"We kissed. We lingered. I was so wet. I only wish he were real." Heaven, had she mentioned heaven on earth? No, of course not.

"So you enjoyed your assignment?" Irrepressible Stella seemed saddened. Hai was glad she stopped her description of the most romantic, sensual event in her life. Raphael's attentive loving... By his kisses alone, he had told her all she needed to know about his heart. He would love Stella forever, if they were meant to be.

"All I can say, if we plan this right, maybe we can both get what we want." Hai said.

"What do you mean?"

"Remember motive?"

"Yep."

"I believe they switched so that Troy could confront Mr. Greco and Raphael could get a little time to detox for you, sweetie. You noticed any blotches?"

"No, well the night before they switched I think Raphael went on a binge. But why did my fiancée kiss you?"

"This is the best part. First, they love each other right?"

"Let me finish your thought." Stella's mind was quick.

"Okay Stella, but before you do, are you absolutely certain we have a sisterhood?"

"Absolutely, come hell or Satan's twins." Hai smiled as if she held a baby, and indeed four people had been born today and needed nurturing.

"Raphael was warming you up for Troy, the confirmed bachelor. Troy, for his part, played it as cool as he could with me, like running out of bed two days ago from my *delectable naked* body without ravishing me. Darn." Stella held her hands and arms open around her chest area to show off the points she was making. Whereas, Hai hid her balloons over her rear, Stella kept hers right up front where she could keep an eye on them.

"Exactly." Hai said. She wished she knew how it felt to be naked in a man's arms, ravished. Perhaps she'd learn soon, if two girls could outsmart two too smart for their own good twins.

"Makes complete sense, so what do you think we should do about them?" Stella asked.

"Complicated." Hai shook her head. They hugged. Stella knew Hai was short of time. They would table the discussion until after the meeting she was about to have with the Mafia boss, Romeo Greco and Raphael. Then they'd devise the perfect trap, the kind of trap that could include wedding bells for at least one couple. The kind of trap that might change Hai's life.

What was she thinking all these years, denying earthly pleasures? No wonder guys wanted to get into her pants; she could no longer blame them. She now wanted to get into theirs. Well, one guy's pants.

Hai worried about her growing feelings for Raphael. It seemed with a little luck all the girls had to do was decide who would end up with whom. And then, off with his pants. Well, she'd marry first or maybe not, as long as her parents wouldn't find out.

Who would make a play for the hard to catch Troy? Maybe Troy would be as nice as his brother. Hai left Stella with barely enough time to get to her meeting. Her heart pattered with hopes she could land a beautifully sensitive man, an artist who appreciated inner and outer beauty. Who lit her vista like a shooting star? Just the same, comedians were artists, too.

Someday she'd be ravished by Raphael or Troy. She was sure ravishing included two naked bodies. If only Stella would find a way to bring Troy to his knees, with a ring, of course. Then, they'd all live happily ever after, sisters and brothers, wow.

Fairytale, just a fairytale.

Her head spun with the complexities. She had to go on two assumptions: Raphael when reunited would reconcile with Stella, and quite probably, Stella still loved him. Hai was the latecomer to this crazy web, and would graciously give way. It was the right thing to do. Besides, Raphael was fooling with her. Or was he? Could his lips lie? His sweet passionate caresses lie? She knew body language. What if Raphael was merely, severely attracted to her? She made him pant.

Maybe it was just physical. In any case, it was wrong to take another woman's man.

Maybe, when all this was over Troy would chase her. The two brothers had to know what the other was doing or why would they have done it? Maybe Troy would be just as nice and a great kisser. Maybe the identical twins' hearts beat identically. Her passenger side tires flung gravel. She swerved back onto the lane, and focused on the road.

It should be illegal to drive when falling in love and doubly illegal to be love's fool.

Chapter 19

Hai entered Troy's cell at 12:55 p.m., leaving Romeo Greco with Max for a couple minutes. Although she seemed beleaguered by some unknown problem, she planted a very sweet kiss on who she thought was Troy. Today was their lucky day. Troy loved her kiss. But without knowing it, she liked Raphael not him. He played along, naturally, very naturally.

He asked about who Toilet might be. She reported that no Caribbean men were in this jail, but he and his brother had had conversations with Toilet. Maybe a prisoner had manufactured an accent to hide his identity. She also said she had called Raphael, actually Troy at the time, to admonish him about horse-trading with the Mafia, and then called for Max to escort Romeo Greco to the cell. Max would stay as a witness.

Romeo shook Troy's hand and nodded to Hai. He took her hand. "You're lovely."

"Thank you, Mr. Greco."

"I'd find some excuse to get in jail if I could hire an attorney like you."

She nodded, with a touch of crimson on her cheeks.

She's a blusher. Raphael and Troy had shared as much as they could about Hai in the time they had, but this was a sweet touch.

"I've never been in jail or prison, can you believe that?" Everybody was a comedian, but knowing Romeo's educational background, philosophy and a team of good lawyers, maybe it was the truth.

"I wanted to say how sorry I am about your nephew." Troy said this, more for Hai's consumption, than Romeo's. His nephew, Frank, was still in a coma at the local branch of the West Jersey Hospital system. The chance of Frank recovering was fifty-fifty, according to his doctor.

"I'm going to make this short and maybe sour. My nephew went missing. We don't know what happened yet, but the surveillance tapes will give us some clues."

Max jumped into the conversation. "Hopefully, he woke up, and just walked out. It's happens."

Troy pictured a young handsome Italian running through the parking lot in a hospital gown, two cheeks to the wind, hailing a cab.

"Not at all likely." Romeo's demeanor changed. "My nephew is a vengeful old-school bastard, who got it in his head that he's Al Capone reincarnated. If he remembers anything about you, the drunk, and he was drunk that night, might beat you up or worse. He doesn't fight fair. Watch for brass knuckles or worse." Romeo shook and lowered his head as if remembering something violent. Drunk or other, Frank wouldn't have a chance in a fair fight.

Troy glanced at Max, who was shaking while he ran his hand over his landing-strip hair.

"The hospital comes under Voorhees's police jurisdiction. They have a good staff. I'm certain, they'll get to the bottom of it," Max said. He flipped his phone. "I'll ask them to call the hospital to offer assistance and or receive updates."

"Originally, I was coming here to trade and give you a little good news."

"Please, Mr. Greco, bear in mind your company. We're here to help." Hai didn't have to say 'keep it legal' Romeo with little doubt understood her meaning. He flashed recognition, as if he had thought of or lived through the situation before.

"I have nothing to offer that isn't strictly legit." He waved his hands. Troy supposed by his hand waving, he'd start speaking Italian, but he didn't.

"You, Max or any of you may not know that I own the company, SirVale, Inc. We sell and maintain surveillance equipment at Ponzio's diner and a number of other businesses. The police reviewed a corrupted disk that should have proved Troy's innocence. They unwittingly handed the disk over to SirVale to try to reconstruct it. Hold your thoughts, counselor. I want you to consider something."

"I certainly will." Troy jumped in, interrupting Hai before she objected. She closed her gaping mouth and starred at Troy.

"I'm thinking of buying the majority share of the Comic Freak business and the building completely, but I don't want the star of the show and I hear a twenty-five percent owner of the business to lampoon my family, without passing it by me first." He stopped speaking and allowed a pause. Troy jumped right in.

"Well lampooning the Mafia is not my usual shtick. Since you might be buying the place, well, let's say, you did buy the place. In my opinion, you as owner, set the parameters for the comics, not too much profanity, no cripple jokes, whatever. It's your right, because you have to market your business to retain your asset." He meant it. He felt Romeo could be trusted to make informed decisions.

"That's just it. I'm an American, I believe in the principles of our country and I'm sure you all do too. I want to encourage free speech and besides I think it will sell more tickets and booze. The comics know exactly how hard to push their audiences. I don't want to scare them off. Listen, we can talk about this issue later and thank you very much for you and Raphael giving my mother a chance." He pulled out from the top of his opened briefcase, a sealed package.

"I hand to you attorney Ms. Lo and before witness, Deputy Brunkowski, evidence in the form of a disk that upon review will acquit your client. In short, my geeks retrieved the data. I am also posting bail. I must strongly recommend that you Hai find somewhere safe to hide Troy for maybe a week at most. And, ah, don't hide in Atlantic City. That's Frank's hangout and playground. I'll call and text you when my friends or the police find Frank. I hope that my nephew will grow up soon. And if he doesn't I'll teach him a lesson, the old way."

"I'd like a little alone time with my client, the cell will be fine," Hai said. She couldn't wait to get Raphael alone and it wasn't the

103

procedural items created by Greco that she wanted to go over. She'd—watching Raphael fail to negotiate his brother's 25%—have to help him later. Max and Mr. Greco left for the front desk and some paperwork.

She grabbed Troy's belt buckle and pulled him to her, boldly for a novice, she surmised.

"Kiss me."

He obliged. The kisses were shorter, but just as sweet, his body more insistent, more urgent. He must have been thinking about their limited time and his freedom. Freedom, Hai was proud to be part of this moment. As a professional, there used to be no greater satisfaction.

She'd be able to kiss him whenever the mood struck her, if Stella let him go. Finally, her adolescent hormones caught up with her, because she realized, due to the way her body was going crazy, she'd always be in the mood, for him. What a nice fit. Merely speculation, counselor.

DOUBLE HAPPINESS
ACT 2

Chapter 20

Stella's cell phone chirped, competing with the birds on this glorious sunny day.

"Hey Stella, it's Hai. Raphael's been bailed out by Greco." Stella plopped into the living room loveseat and listened quietly to the whole story.

Hai finished with, "Romeo wants me to hide Troy for a week or until crazy Frank is found. If Frank suspects they switched, he could come for Troy."

"Unlikely." Stella needed time with Troy to see if her feelings were only an old crush. She felt selfish, because if it were only a crush she could consider reconciling with Raphael. All she'd need to do was call him to bed. On the other hand, Hai might have intrigued Raphael. She was pretty, not much in the boob department, great ass and a really nice and successful career woman.

Hai continued. "Well, also, we need an excuse for all of us to be together. If any of us have a chance at a lasting match, we should try now while we have them off their normal routine."

Maybe Hai was right. Put four of them in a hotel room and let nature take its course.

"Where would we go?"

"I have my baby sister's wedding in New York tomorrow and I think I can put you all up at my mom and dad's and get you all on the guest list. Either we can go up together or you can meet us later. You free this weekend?" Stella's thesis was practically finished. She had to build up one more identical twin case study. What could be better than to have both of them together to torture in equal parts? Perhaps a unique observation at the wedding might put a topper on her thesis.

"As long as I have my laptop, I'm good. But…"

"Make it quick. He's coming." Hai lowered her voice.

"Just delay one hour, then when you get here, I'll let you know what my concern is, if any." Stella didn't want to lose the opportunity of testing Troy's feelings toward her, before they switched back, and then she'd never know. Never know if she missed something or not. Why couldn't they have toyed with her as they used to with other girls in high school? This would have left her un-conflicted as an adult.

"Okay." They hung up; she'd get her time alone with Troy.

Stella slipped out of garden clothes, all her clothes, and put on a short denim skirt with daisy-may ruffles. Took off her bra, flung it over her shoulder, as Troy would do if he were a woman. He'd make an awful looking woman. She wiggled into a cotton-polyester T-shirt, which accentuated her positives.

D-day has arrived and I have a plan.

"Knock, knock. I hope you're not decent." She said at the studio door.

"Come on in, I'm cleaning up," he said. He respected his brother so much, he'd clean, he'd act the part. She'd see just how much he'd act.

"I wanted to say goodbye, but give you a going away present. Sit down for it." Direct worked with Raphael or she supposed, Troy. Nonetheless, she only ever knew one way to act, forthright, in your face, on your lap.

"Where are you going?" He sat on the bordello couch and looked concerned.

"I'm going away from you."

"But honey, I've decided to quit drinking for good."

Call the academy awards.

"Here's the thing…" She let him interrupt since his mouth looked constipated.

"I love you, Stella."

"That's the problem, although we're on the rocks about our engagement. I think I know why you drink and why I'm a pain in the ass. All along, I have had a kind of subconscious love for Troy. He wasn't and isn't available."

"Is this like, every time you make love to me, you see him?" They both laughed. That was a damn good subtle touch, a la the comedian. Just one more tell that she was seducing Troy…successfully. Maybe. Still, it took tremendous presence of mind, to put himself into his brother's persona and then think about the irony of her crush as his brother might see it. Mind boggling, right?

"No, you silly boy, I like his comic style. He and I talk psychology as students of human nature. Your interest is just passing. Besides, I liked the quarterback more than the halfback in high school."

"Oh come on, a school girl crush. And I've always listened to your psych stories." Yes, Raphael had been more a passive listener, but he had always managed to add something to the conversation. Troy, you devil, once again, well played.

"Don't argue. I can't explain myself. I like his personality better than yours. You're such a ah…metro-sexual."

"We both have the same heart. I could do stand-up and be a slob as easily as he could do art and clean-up his perpetual messes. It's practice and habit, that's all. I will change for you."

"I don't know."

"Come here, baby," he said.

He put on his sad face, but his eyes told her he was up to something. Maybe she'd get her chance finally. Just who was seducing whom?

This was the point where he'd have to fall into her trap. He'd console, she'd seduce. He would have to accept her wish, because to say no, meant the destruction of his brother's relationship with her.

She sat on his lap. "That's the other thing. I wanted to give you a present."

"I don't want it, if it means losing you. You're shaking, baby." He caressed her. She pushed his arms away and took off her T-shirt. She felt his hot breath on her newly freed breasts. Her light red areolas and nipples engorged at the thought of his adoring eyes.

107

"Now I feel better. Take me if you love me." This should force Troy to oblige, for his brother's sake, honor, duty, God, country, whatever floated his boat. She grabbed his ears and sunk his face into her bosom. Surely, the man Troy, couldn't refuse now, otherwise she'd smother him. A cruel orgasmic death.

His breathing heavy, he sucked her nipples, licked around, buried his head again. Yes. Oh, God yes. She twisted his thick black curls, pushed his head to her heart. So far, Troy was no different from Raphael. Maybe all men suckled the same way.

"I love you," he said.

Could it be this easy?

He licked and nipped her neck. She swooned, so very wet. Still the same Raphael moves, kiss-by-kiss.

Did the boys study sex together? Didn't matter, oh my God. She throbbed. She was so adored, so loved. Well, she was wet the moment she came up with this idea.

"Oh, my sweet one," he said. She didn't know how much longer she could hold out. He really wanted her. How many days, weeks, months, years had she fantasized about this boy? She couldn't get enough of his hard body, his manliness set her adrift.

"Please, your pants. Let me slide down on your beautiful shaft. I want a pony ride." She hiked her skirt revealing, oh my, somehow she forgot to wear her panties. She pounded and rubbed his lap with her bottom. Up and down. Come on out and play.

He nipped her ear lobe. He whispered with hot breath. Her ear vibrated.

"Te adora Stella." Often said by Raphael who also sometimes called her, Stella Dora, his tasty cookie. Oh well, she guessed the boys really did share intimacy secrets. Meanwhile her cookie was crumbling.

They were incorrigible, but that's why she loved them. Them, how did she get to this ridiculous and untenable position? Her rationality had long since abandoned her. Oh, she loved him and he definitely loved her. But who did she love?

He shimmied out of his pants while sitting. He sprang out hard, tip wetting. She bent over and kissed him there while he was still trying to remove his pants. He wouldn't need any encouragement or stimulation.

She loved going south and whenever she wanted it, all she'd have to do is ask, Raphael that is. She was too hot today for any more foreplay.

"Oh honey, you aah drive me crazy," he whispered through a sturdy breath.

He rubbed her back and then cupped her head. He surely wanted into her, now. Getting her fill of his shaft, she looked up. Kissed him once more there, knowing she drove him crazy.

He pulled her up eyes swimming. She straddled him, faced him, to watch his every ecstatic moment and his movements. She grabbed his shaft with both hands and, so wet, slid down slowly until their bodies meshed tight in perfect harmony.

For her, it was always a problem of reaching multiple climaxes too soon, but now with Troy, she felt way past due. She couldn't hold off. But she tried to help him catch up. She squeezed him as hard as she could with her hidden muscles. He raked her back, bit her shoulder, grabbed her bottom and thrust harder. Over and over, he rammed her. She wiggled and gyrated like a mad woman. Dirty. Hot. Hard. They gasped. Erupted together in climax. She shivered one wave after another, to his hard cock driving deep within her. She squished down and took all of him. Their bodies in ecstasy. He sighed as he held her tight, smelled her body and came in her deepest recesses.

"My God, Stella," he cried.

"I love you, too," she said, trying to figure out what it all meant, what had just happened. Forget the figuring, she wouldn't stop her multiples.

He'd never forget her now. What had she done? She squeezed for every drop. She pulled up off him, and bent down to taste his tip. One quick lick. He shuddered again.

"Honey," he said, eyes dancing.

After they made love, Stella began to feel peculiar. Nestled in his arms, pants still around his ankles, with not much time left before Raphael and Hai would arrive, her eyes now closed, she smelled him, loved the scent. The boys used the same soap. She went back over every intimate detail, feeling, touch, never wanting to forget her only opportunity to complete her teenage crush, her only time with Troy. She would memorize every precious moment.

Then it hit her; hit her hard. Troy had made love no differently than Raphael would have, not even one movement or one starry eyed expression.

Couldn't he at least have spun me around a couple times. Do anything differently?

No, he was the same old same wonderful, perfect lover. So true. She thanked him with a blush of kisses, as always.

What had she done? What was she thinking? It was wrong to touch Troy. She wasn't thinking. She was still obsessed. Well, at least, she got it out of her sexual system. She knew better, obsessions were obsessions for a reason. She'd need to see a therapist. Hell no, nobody would ever know her deceit. She could cure herself. *Mea culpa, mea culpa. Mea maxima culpa.*

Enough prayers.

She'd have to buy a book on lovemaking in one-thousand different ways. Maybe she fooled herself. The only difference between the twins was the mess Troy left behind both literally and figuratively. She languished on the couch for moments more of his tender caresses, his staggered breathing. Nice doing that to an athlete.

Receding from the fog, she reasoned in purer tones. Sure, she had parked her mind at the door, letting her wild woman free from self-imposed and sometimes stupid society shackles. God was merciful and surely didn't mean to stop people from loving each other, as long as nobody got hurt. Still, she realized in all the just past lovemaking coincidences, her redemption or rationalization would save her.

Troy had to be Raphael. Right? Her mind had blown a gasket. Somehow, the girls were wrong.

The place was immaculate. If this man was Troy, why did he enjoy so much, too much, their little tête-à-tête? In other words, if he were Troy, why did he dishonor his brother? Yes, she pushed him into a corner no man could refuse or resist, but could he have come up with some creative way out, or at least tried, or performed dutifully instead of conducting their rhapsody on a par with a great maestro?

110

The Chariote brothers vexed her for the umpteenth time. She was no closer to a solution than any other day of her obsessed life. As a Ph. D. candidate, she felt a fraud. Where to go from here?

She and Hai would have to grab the boys by their horns, pun intended. She'd go to Hai's family wedding with a warning for Hai. All *may not be* as easy as they had hoped. All may not be as they had thought.

"Raphael sweetheart, get ready, your brother has been sprung by Romeo Greco and he's been proven innocent, and we're going to celebrate by going to Manhattan this weekend with Hai and Troy. Go shower, you're sticky." His naked body, so beautiful, glistened, every muscle ripped. Stop it girl. He did look a little silly with trousers as socks.

"Wow, oh my God, thank God. Let me make some calls, shower, straighten up some more. I'll pack," Raphael or his pretender said, standing up and then falling over. He wasn't hurt. Now that pratfall was pure Troy. Stella's head was spinning like something from The Exorcist.

Maybe this straightening up of the house thing was an act. He was after all playing Raphael. He did it exactly, precisely, move for move like Raphael.

She didn't know why she felt guilty about one of life's special pleasures. At least she kept her lust in the family. She had made love to Raphael after all, but how? Fingerprints don't lie. Identical twins do not have identical fingerprints. Identical penises, yes. She had noticed that years before when in the rafters over the boys' shower. Now she jumped in the shower and washed him. Then she scrubbed her quick, well quickly. He always loved to watch this rubbing and bubbling of soap on her, Raphael, that is.

Was her distress and confusion, because she might have made love to Raphael, while harboring a crush on Troy? Or had she made love to Troy while half-engaged to Raphael, the man who still had a big piece of her heart?

He got on his knees and kissed her.

"Oh honey, we don't have time." She gasped. "I think you knocked all the juice out of me."

"Just one kiss, is all I need." He did, with a little tongue, a little too much tongue.

She felt a Motrin moment fast approaching.

"Eiye, yeiyei," she sighed, pulled his head up, and peered into the eyes of the man who had undone her, one way or the other, one man or the other. He rose, grabbed a towel and wrapped her, patted her behind, and kissed her nape sweetly.

She stared at the pink and white tiles, cross-eyed.

Chapter 21

Hai had exchanged pleasantries with Romeo before he left and then sat on a side chair at Deputy Max's desk. Troy grabbed the other side chair to fill out his release papers. Thank God.

He seriously doubted Frank would remember him. According to the court medical reports, he was pickled, that is, beyond drunk, which likely insulated his brain from permanent damage or death. If his girlfriend, Jersey, was any indication of his mentality, there wasn't much brain damage to be had, anyway.

Today I live. I will not worry about screw-loose Frank…much.

The sunny day streamed through skylights showing riffs of dust dancing down. The jail office was little better than his cell, except it didn't smell like polecat. He had just promised Raphael he'd clear up one mystery before he left.

"Did you have a Caribbean man in one of the cells, while I was here?" He asked Deputy Max.

"Nope."

"Maybe somebody from New Orleans?"

"Nope. Why?"

"Just one more question, anybody with any kind of accent like the ones I said?"

"No, why?"

"Well you know the pipes to the toilet carry sound. You can hear voices sometimes. I heard an islander voice."

"Ms. Lo." Max tapped her hand and scratched his flat top with his other hand. "I think you can take Troy from here to a psychiatrist's office." He gave Troy that crazy, I'll sit on you look, as he had during so many football games and practices, long ago.

"Come on, Max."

Max beamed.

"Okay, Okay, you better be kissin' on the lady, man. She be the prettiest seashell on the beach, like rum and lime in da' coconut. She's a ray from heaven's gate, man." Max coughed as he waved the air. He finally pulled one over on the *hell on Chariote* twins, after all the rotten things they had done to him. Like, setting him up with Cecelia, as a blind and mystery date for the prom; the smallest girl in school with the biggest, what three hundred and fifty pounds easy. They were the cutest couple though, but as usual, Troy won prom King. Max picked Cecelia up for a kiss like Andre the Giant used to pick up his opponents or cars.

Yes, Max over the past week, you've been fooled too, and I'm certainly not going to mention what Raphael and I did to you.

"I'm going to beat your ass, man." Troy said, tackling Max. But he didn't move an inch, of course. Yeah, Troy was two hundred and twenty pounds in his birthday suit and strong, but Max, well for all his flab, he had more muscles than Troy had body. So he rubbed Max's flattop, just as he had before every football game they played together, everybody on the team, the water boys and the coaches. They dared not get the cheerleaders in on it, or the girls would all move to Philadelphia and cheer lead for Central.

"Wish me luck." Troy said.

"Luck, schmuck. What, just a bit ago, you threatened a peace officer? Maybe I better put you back in your cell," Max said, in jest. They shook hands.

Then Max bear hugged Hai, who appeared to faint, eyes closed, big smile.

"Thanks Max, for watching out for him," she said, reaching up to rub his crew cut. She giggled.

"You two call me if you get into trouble. I will personally come to the rescue and get NYPD's best to your aid as fast as possible."

"Thanks again, Max."

They said their goodbyes and headed out the door for her Mercedes. Max called out from the opened door of the jail. "We don't get blue jays in these trees. They are run by robins and sparrows, man."

"You might have a future at the Comic Freak. We'll talk." He put an imaginary cell phone to his ear. Once in Hai's black leather Mercedes, he relaxed, reclined the seat and patted her hand. His sorry ass could have kissed her upholstery.

Off they went to Hai's place, then Raphael's, skipping Troy's place in case of ambush. Hai's plan to protect both twins was inspired by necessity, because Raphael could easily be mistaken for his brother. The four of them would head ninety miles north to Manhattan for R&R and a wedding. Hai seemed excited. But he spoiled the mood when he dropped an energy bar wrapper onto her pristine carpet.

"Alright Troy, how'd you two switch twice?"

"What, who?" Switched twice. He knew Hai was sharp, but this would put Sherlock Holmes to shame. She had to be talking about something else, but what else.

"You're Troy, you are really Troy, aren't you?"

"Of course. I've always been Troy ever since I could remember."

"Please pick up the wrapper and put it into the container."

"Sorry I didn't see that and I was going to get it after I picked a speck from my eye." He backpedalled with logic as fast as her car powered forward. She increased the speed.

"Stella and I decided to take your brother's prints while he was pretending to be you. Want to answer my question? Better yet, why did you kiss me?"

He couldn't figure out what gave them away. They had never been outsmarted in their lives. He hummed a few bars. Although he guessed she used conjecture, they did at least know of the first switch. So why fight it? He had everything to gain by being contrite in his own insufferable way.

"You know, this is the first time we've been caught. When I received an A+ in Physics on the finals. When Raphael and I switched with Maria …w-well, countless times, countless girls. Guess we're getting older, losing our touch."

"Is that all you can think about is yourself? Treating us like Barbie dolls. I have a problem. I do not like you." Her nose wrinkled and her lips pursed as if she bit into a lemon.

"What, I didn't do anything. Hey, you kissed me. Can I be blamed for kissing back? My God, Hai, you're a desirable woman." Her speedometer crossed sixty and she continued to press deeper on the pedal. He uprighted his seat. They tore down Kresson Road, passing Saint Thomas Moore Church. He noticed the thirty-five mile per hour sign next.

"Hey, there's a speed trap around here somewhere." From time to time, he had spotted the Cherry Hill Police out here nailing drivers.

"I thought you were Raphael." She slowed down. He let go of the handhold and took his foot off an imaginary brake.

"Why would you kiss an engaged man?"

Now I got her.

"He started it."

"And you went along." Troy understood Raphael was trying to set her up for him, but how would he explain that?

"I can see we're getting nowhere. At first I thought he was you."

"But you don't like me."

"Circular argument," she said, with her own gotcha smile and cocked eyes. Jeeze, he wished she'd keep her pretty peepers on the road. He had to tell her, no matter the fallout.

"Look, Raphael told me afterwards he was trying to get the girl of my dreams for me."

"Am I?" Good, so far. He feared she'd see Raphael as a manipulator, which they were to a degree, about three hundred and sixty degrees. In this case, her lovely end justified the means.

"Well, a girl like you floated in my head when I was in college. But I..."

"But?"

"Well, I'm not ready for marriage. Who'd want a comedian, anyway?"

"I'm sure somebody would like you, just not me."

"Plenty of girls like me. Why wouldn't you like me?"

"You're not my type."

"And my brother is?"

"You're a slob."

"And Raphael is a drunk. Well, maybe ex-drunk." He had to be honest with her, but he left out the obvious manipulation charge against his brother. Somehow, she didn't see it, now. He'd leave it to her steel-trap mind to solve that problem. Something told him—call it intuition—this woman would be part of their lives. At the very least, he owed her for the party she'd throw this weekend.

"Did you not say plenty of girls like you?"

"Yes."

"You stand accused of shallowness in the first degree."

"Punishable by spanking."

"How about castration?"

Ouch.

"Maybe we got off on the wrong foot. It isn't shallow if all you want to do is date, and have some fun. I'll know when the right girl comes along." The problem: Stella was taken. They turned off Kresson Road into the upscale Eagle Oak neighborhood and then pulled up the driveway to enter her garage. Her home, as were all the homes in this neighborhood appealed to Troy. Her home and grounds charmed him, from its shaped boxwoods and multi-colored spring flowers. Black walnut trees didn't quite hide a pinkish one-story flagstone with runs of tan vinyl-clad aluminum on the sides. She claimed to have the smallest home in the neighborhood.

"Come on in. I won't take long... Sorry, I don't have any Playboys for you to drool on."

"Thanks, Hai, Knitting World will do nicely."

"You can switch on the TV. Raid the fridge. As you like it."

As You Like It, whimsical Shakespeare. Shakespeare's play, Comedy of Errors fit better to this situation. He would someday have a pleasant conversation with her about her choice of words. Right now, she probably thought he was an illiterate dolt. Comedy of Errors was often the subject in High School English class as one student after another tried to top the latest fictional Chariote misadventure. The students at Cherry Hill High loved Shakespeare like no other school in the country, or so went the boast. SAT scores hadn't lied, with his class being the dump up in average.

"I might take a short snooze, your couch looks inviting." She had good taste in furniture. Her plump Lane sofa beckoned. He'd speak to her about the Bard some other time.

She showered. He listened to the sounds of water dribbling all over her lithe body. Next, she dressed and packed. Knitting World held his interest right up there with Composting Gazette.

"Since we're going to be together…" She paused while making her entrance in tight black jeans and a modest white cotton blouse. What a knockout.

"And you're letting us join your family for the weekend…" He filled the silence as if they had practiced for years.

"We should get along." She finished his thought. This woman was in, if she'd accept the gang of three, they'd become the four musketeers.

"I'd like nothing better," he said.

"Besides, Stella and Raphael have split, I think," she said. This split wasn't unfixable or absolute, but he played his part for the sake of four and a less stressful ride to Raphael's.

"Maybe this weekend will give us all time to sort out the mess Raphael and I created. At the least, we can all become great friends." He believed a man and woman could be friends without sex as much as a lion and lamb could take a nap together. He then remembered YouTube and so many unlikely videos of prey and hunter in harmony, no doubt buddies from a young age. *Let me amend that to adult human strangers of the opposite sex meeting in strange ways*, although napping with a human female was a good start.

Troy volunteered to drive Hai's car over to Raphael's home, both out of a sense of self-preservation and enjoyment for her Mercedes road-ability and handling. They would soon head north to Manhattan for a hoped-for unforgettable weekend, with much to celebrate, and just as much to worry about. Hai seemed pensive, busying herself with eyeliner on eyes needing no adornment.

"Five bucks for your thoughts." He prodded, and played the inflation game she started with his brother.

"You boys are exasperating."

"I'm sorry, sweetie. What would you want us to do to make it up to you?" He really wanted to turn the corner with Hai and change his life's direction.

"I think we messed up Raphael's and Stella's engagement."

"I was thinking the same thing, but they're adults."

"We should try to put them back together." Like Troy, she had similar ethics and heart, a good sign that at least they could work together.

"Humpty Dumpty sat on the wall," he sing-songed. "Well, when we get there, we'll feel them out and compare notes. Maybe have a four-way show down."

Chapter 22

While they waited in the kitchen for the boys to pack, Hai lifted the plastic protecting her peacock-embroidered, full-length gown she'd wear at her sister's wedding. Stella expressed some well-deserved oohs and aahs. However, Hai would appear stunning wearing overalls.

Hai smoothed the front and back, pulled down the sheath and hung it in the entry closet.

One of Stella's favorite musical mixes shuffled on the house stereo. The boys were taking too long, so the girls contented themselves with conversations about two maddening men as they swiveled their stools to the songs' rhythms.

Stella panicked at the prospect of losing Raphael. She needed to find a way to stop the boys from playing any more cruel tricks—intended or not—especially those performed on her new friend. Hai had no idea how crazy a Chariote ride could become and Stella wasn't going to let her find out.

Hai swiveled a full 360. Easy for ice-skaters, Stella supposed. "Your Raphael has an outrageous eye for beauty and function." The latest and best appliances adorned a sharply designed black and white kitchen.

"Where's Raphael's ferret?" Hai asked.

Raphael had a black and white ferret named Jerry who liked to rearrange salt and pepper shakers among other black and white items. Stella had never seen Jerry outside of the kitchen.

"Jerry hides somewhere in these drawers or the tunnels Raphael built during the afternoon. I'll hunt for him and introduce you when we get back. Yes, it seems out of character for a neatnik like Raphael, but his appreciation for the beauty of nature trumps neatness. By morning light, he photographs what Jerry left or videos him in the act or rearranging. His YouTubes are viral. He peppers his gallery and road shows with Jerry's antics." Stella helped keep the rest of Raphael's home in perfect order, which in the past equaled perfect harmony.

Three dull thuds and the familiar sound of raised male voices invaded Stella's consciousness. Given the least provocation, those boys cultivate the bad habit of wrestling. Generally, Troy started fights by destroying the harmony of an artist's soul by rearranging Raphael's things. Troy had never understood how these bunk-bed boys could grow up so differently. Of course, for identical twins, Stella had theorized they vied for their parents' love by differentiating themselves. Therefore, Troy—it could be said—used comedy to attract his parents' love.

"What are those two up to?" Hai appeared startled as she slipped off the stool ready to either run or rescue.

"You don't have brothers."

"But I thought boys grew out…"

Stella grabbed Hai's hand and stopped at the kitchen door to raise the volume on the house stereo. *All About That Bass* just started. The girls danced their way out of the kitchen.

"We shouldn't eavesdrop, Stel."

The song sang, *I ain't no size two,* and Stella bumped Hai's hips. Hai was obviously offering token resistance. Stella couldn't pass up the chance to pick up one more insight into identical twin psychology that just might finish off her thesis. Besides, the boys, if history were the judge, were up to something nasty, aside from roughhousing. Listening in, the girls would get the upper hand. This time. Future generations of happy children depended upon it.

They sloughed off their shoes at the hallway. Stella put her finger to her lips, "Shh."

Hai shook her head and whispered back. "We're stooping to their level." But Hai kept walking. Curiosity had done-in this sloe-eyed cat.

121

"Step where I step." Stella knew all the creaks in this old house's wood floors.

As they approached the double, closed doors to Raphael's bedroom, they could easily tune into the rowdy argument. Meanwhile the stereo switched to an Ariana Grande song that suited the situation. *I Got One Less Problem Without Ya.*

The girls froze in front of the doors.

"You're going to create another nice mess. Stella will kill both of us."

"Both girls will appreciate the relief. This is the only way."

"Every time you say that, something goes wrong."

"Bullshit. Remember Marjorie, Hilda, Jennifer, Rose and countless more."

"We're adults now, schmuck brother."

"I promise this will be the last time...my metro-sexual bro." Stella squeezed Hai's hand. They suppressed a laugh. Were the boys considering switching again? She wouldn't mind Troy taking her but she didn't quite like the idea or this very pretty Hai making love to Raphael. Her intuition told her they were up to something far more insidious than switching places. A headline flashed. *Stella Riccardi, renowned psychologist and identical-twin expert has just been arrested for the murder of her lifelong friends, the identical twins...*

"Get that fuckin' toothpaste out of my suitcase."

"What?"

"Toothpaste goes in *this* traveling case."

"The shirt's white."

"Put that toothbrush down."

"I forgot mine."

"I've got new ones. Dammit Troy."

Stella whispered to Hai, "He probably tossed the brush into the suitcase." Both girls covered their mouths again. Thud. From the sound of it, the boys seemed arm-locked. Thud. Thud.

"You ought to stick that toothbrush up your."

Slam.

"Here's some toilet paper. Chinese don't use it." Hai pursed her lips.

Bash, thud, bang.

* * *

Inside the bedroom, Raphael pointed down at the shadows at the bottom of the double doors.

"Listen Raphael, Stella likes me better than you and I think we should duel. Loser gets the skinny Chinese chick."

"Have you seen her rear end?"

"To be honest, I don't know which is more impressive, Stella's huge knockers or Hai's booty."

"How dare you insult my fiancée. Put up your dukes."

"This time we fight to the death."

Groan, clatter, bang. The boys readied pillows. Both of them had accurate throwing arms.

* * *

A seemingly perplexed Hai whispered, "They're going to kill each other?"

"No, let's do it for them."

Stella swung open the doors and shouted over the din. "You insufferable misogynistic pigs." In that moment, the girls got smacked squarely on their kissers by pillows.

"War?" Hai asked.

"War."

Pillows swinging, the girls attacked. Advantage boys. They wore no shirts. They had bigger muscles, but who the hell cared. Stella went for one of them who flipped over the bed. Hai tried to anticipate the same maneuver but was de-pillowed if not deflowered on the bed. She was summarily spanked with the pillow as she begged for mercy.

One of the boys flipped her over and pinned her. *No way this will stand. The culprit could be Raphael.* Stella jumped to Hai's defense and onto the attacker's back. The other boy piled on, turning the whole mess into a football scrum. The bed held. Stella raised her head from a half-hearted arm lock, her attention diverted by the tail of a toilet paper roll hanging from the suitcase.

After a bit more jostling and a couple stolen kisses, they collapsed against the side of the bed on the carpet. Relaxed now, they laughed it off.

"We don't have much time left if we want to beat the traffic," Hai said.

"Okay, here's our point," one of the boys said with the other signaling his agreement. "Choose one of us, without the prejudice of preconceived baggage."

* * *

"To what advantage?" Hai felt she knew where this was going. Stella had an old crush on Troy. Troy thought a woman like Stella would make a great wife. Hai felt affection for Raphael and his way of looking at the world, and he seemed taken by her. Stella and Raphael probably loved each other. One thing was certain Troy loved Raphael and Raphael loved Troy. Would there be any love left over for the girls?

The other twin spoke up. "Our point is—you think you know us—but you're wrapped up in preconceived notions. You said it yourself, Hai. You don't like Troy. You'll trust the gossip but not the man. Stella, for God's sake, it's time you get over or forever keep your cheerleader crush on the star quarterback. It's only for this weekend. After you make your choices, we promise to identify ourselves and to never deceive either of you again."

Stella blew her nose on one of Raphael's handkerchiefs, but the boys just stared at the ceiling mural of treetops mixed with rays of sun and clouds, Raphael created. Hai felt she knew which one was Troy, because Troy clipped his ear and nose hairs in a half-ass way. Raphael's were trimmed minutely. Their chest hairs looked like an unruly jumble. No difference there.

Stella let her hair down and confessed what she had done with whom she thought was Troy and—crying—asked for Raphael's forgiveness without knowing who to look at. Both men hugged her and tenderly removed her tears with their fingers. Hai felt left out but could not jerk a tear. Obviously, Stella was trying to figure out which one was Raphael. Well, probably.

After some jockeying over who would choose first, Stella insisted Hai go.

"I choose you." Hai leaned into and kissed the one she thought was Troy. Stella recovered from the shock. "Unless...if you want him, Stella?"

"I don't know what I want anymore. This whole thing, thank you boys, has been therapeutic." Stella plopped onto, likely Raphael's lap and gave him a steamy kiss.

Phue. Voice softened, Hai said, "Get dressed. I recommend jeans for the trip. We must leave," she checked the wall clock, "in seven minutes."

"I'll need a little more time to straighten up my room," Raphael said.

Stella put on the stern mother face and tapped her toes. "We'll straighten it together when we get back."

At the double doors, Jerry, the gorgeous black and white ferret, dropped a black fork, stood on his hinds and stared at four ridiculous humans.

Hai had hoped she could introduce a real boyfriend to her family. Raphael seemed as perfect as perfect could get: handsome, smart, an accomplished artist, with a big heart. She had never felt giddy before until he held and kissed her. High school, university and certainly grad school were all about achievement. Dating, a means to an end: be sociable, relax on a regular basis, network, become successful and make her mom and dad proud.

But the boys were right about preconceived prejudices. She hadn't been fair to Troy. If she had chosen Raphael, she wouldn't have been fair to Stella who loved Raphael. Troy was correct. Raphael and Stella deserved a second chance to make a life together work. Stella had called a halt to the engagement, but she had kept the ring. Case closed.

If Troy was serious about wanting to settle down, maybe Hai and Troy as a couple could also work. His career was on the rise. Romeo had guaranteed him first billing, a generous buy-out of his quarter share in the Comic Freak. Troy could settle down.

Troy needed to be set straight on one thing. *Chinese do use toilet paper.*

Chapter 23

Frank awoke in a hospital. His vulnerability here, wore thin. Jersey was filing her nails with her baby blues focused on him.

"Let's blow this joint." They ran out of the hospital, his gown waving, and hopped into her Jetta for a clean getaway. Jersey drove, Frank dressed with the clothes Jersey grabbed from his room.

"Yo Jersey, you are looking good." He reached over and flicked her golden locks.

"The same." She said in her typical high-pitched sour-apple voice, but the fruit was sweet.

"Why was I in the hospital?"

"You was knocked out by some lug."

"Who?"

"Troy Chariote."

"Did I get into a fight?"

"You was trying to get out of Ponzio's when he blocked your way. But baby, you was drinking, so you lost the fight."

Maybe he'd lose a fight someday, if it wasn't for dirty tactics or brass knuckles. He wasn't the world champ, okay. So what happened here?

"I don't lose fights. Where is this guy?"

"He's in jail for beating you up."

They pulled over. Frank asked Jersey to call the Medford jail. They found out they just missed Mister Chariote. Somebody had sprung him, and Frank knew better than to have Jersey try to bribe a cop for the dirt. After all, he had almost one year as an art major at the Ivy League Princeton University. He was smart.

So sometimes, I use the king's English and sometimes it uses me. Got a problem wid dat.

He had stayed almost a year at Princeton until the day he beat up his art professor over whether Jackson Pollack was an artist or not. Frank could go home and look at wall paint if he wanted texture. So he textured the professor's face with tawny red tones.

"How long have I been knocked out?" he asked Jersey. They drove off heading for Atlantic City.

"Maybe a week."

"You know what I need?"

"You won't beat me. It's not in the cards." she said. Rummy to be exact.

"As soon as we get to the hotel room, I will beat you."

"That'll be the day, Frank." Jersey formed a large zero with her hand and took it to Frank's nose. He had never beaten her, but he'd keep trying.

"How's you doin'? Staying true to me?" Frank loved his tough guy image and wasn't about to speak proper for nobody.

"Well, there was this doctor who came into me." Oh the image.

"What? It's *on to* me." With her, sometimes, some words needed correction.

"No, not you, came into me."

"Nevermind." The word 'hopeless' made sense here.

"Don't you want to hear?"

"Yes, baby."

"Yeah, he was waiting for a brain transplant and sweet talking me." Jersey had her qualities, really. *I swear.*

"What's his name?" Like nine pins—these guys—Jersey set'em up and he knocked'em down.

"Doctor John Doe."

Jersey's IQ rivaled iceberg lettuce. "Doe is the name of a dead man."

"Don't kill the doctor, honey. It's not fair."

"After I take care of this Troy guy, I'll make sure the doctor thinks he needs a new head, but I won't whack him, sweetie." She seemed mollified. "Hey, guess what, John Doe is a fake name he gave you."

"The nerve."

"Did he touch you?"

"Just our knees."

"A knee-knocking pervert." He fumed. This was getting interesting. Maybe this guy's knees would meet-up with an iron pipe and give him problems for the rest of his Doe-life.

"He is kinda ultra cute."

Dah.

He knew Jersey liked to flirt. He'd beat the doc up. He'd beaten them all up. They charged down the Atlantic City Expressway for a forty-minute ride through flat lands trimmed by the infamous Pine Barons and its magical inhabitant, the Jersey Devil. Of course, it was the right place to bury Jimmy Hoffa, a little here, a little there, in a little nowhere, so he had been told.

Before they went up to their comp ocean-view suite at the boardwalk in the old Claridge Hotel, they picked up some Philly soft pretzels and cheese steaks at the corner of Park Place and Boardwalk. This food always went good to warm him up, for what he planned for Jersey. He'd take care of the latest two Don Juans, tomorrow.

First, a little fun. While waiting for their sandwiches, he studied the glades of sun speckling the mostly gray ocean. A strong southerly wind drove the white caps sideways slicing them through the posts of the Ocean One Pier. He breathed in the drizzled air and took his lady's arm. Atlantic City, any time of the year, was Christmas.

After settling into the room, showering and dressing comfortably in white robes, he readied to beat the crap out of Jersey.

"You can *try* to beat me, Frank. But you can't do it." She smiled broadly with that teasy, eyes-a-flutter look.

A–dorable.

He marveled at Jersey's idiotic savant mind. She was generally unbeatable at most card games, for which the two of them made a bundle. They'd try various tables and casinos until they found marks

128

ready for the big fall. The house always got their cut, so they didn't care. Jersey was a regular force of nature. She was strictly legit, but she was not human.

Robes folded and on the chair, they sat on the bed naked and cross-legged facing each other. He did try to beat her at gin rummy, again and again, until cross-eyed.

Collapsed onto the bed, defeated per usual and exhausted from trying, he fell asleep dreaming of Jersey saying, 'hit me.' Dollars fell from the sky, which he then used to buy her diamonds.

Chapter 24

Late afternoon traffic near Manhattan could be brutal, so they decided to take their time, by stopping for dinner. Raphael took the wheel of Hai's Mercedes, while brother Troy jumped into the back with Hai. They decided on her car, because when parked in lower Manhattan near Chinatown, outside of her mom and dad's co-op the neighborhood kids would recognize Hai's car and not create some unwanted artwork, or steal a hood ornament. There also remained the small matter of hiding from Frank Greco.

The long flat New Jersey Turnpike could easily lull anybody to sleep. Raphael kept his eyes on the road, mostly. Hai nestled against Troy's chest under his protective, caressing arm. Raphael could feel Troy's infatuation with the exotic woman growing. Troy sniffed her lilac-scented hair for the umpteenth time. She fit his body as God meant it to be. That would mean it had been the same for Raphael's body, but he refused to allow jealousy an entrance into his psyche. Her blissful upturned lip, closed eyes showed contentment. What a beautiful structure to her folds over sleek eyes. God didn't make junk, but he must have favored the female of the species, especially this female.

"Yo, Raphael, ease off the gas," Troy said. He guessed Troy was right, his mind was drifting. They were not in a rush.

"Will do." He had learned over his entire twenty-seven years to cede the easy points of possible contention to his twin. Troy did the same.

Although Raphael contracted a severe case of the hots for Hai, he would never stand in the way of Troy's truest desires. Which, now, were written all over his brother's face. Troy would get his Asian doll. An old David Bowie song started playing in his head, *China Girl, da-da-da, da da*. Besides, although Raphael held reservations about Stella after her latest antics, he still loved her. She'd soon get over Troy, if there were any real getting over to do.

They pulled into the Molly Pitcher restaurants and tourist trap for gas and a meal. Hai cautioned them to eat light, because her family was obsessed with making sure their guests ate good Chinese food, some home-cooked. Then her family would stuff them again.

"We're going to have to decide how to introduce you two," Stella said, interrupting her love fest with a large bowl of lentil soup and her favorite, nose-twitching, garlic bread. Although not Italian, he loved garlic-enhanced dishes, and nearly all Italian dishes, especially a dish called Stella. Way back in high school he believed that all Italians had raven hair. God adorned the lovely Stella with sandy blonde hair, a roundish face, wide, round hazel eyes matching her facial lines, resulting in an exotic impression for an Italian beauty. Although her roundness projected naïveté, this driven and brilliant woman was anything but. Mona Lisa, move over. Although Mona Lisa wasn't all that pretty in a modern sense, just striking, as the greatest master, Da Vinci, probably intended.

"We'll make a choice of introductions for the weekend and try to stick with it," Troy said.

"You'll be my boyfriend," Hai squeezed Troy's arm, and Raphael's heart sank. How the hell was he going to get to know her better now? Perhaps all would be the better for it.

Was the game over? Knowing Troy, well no, the game was just beginning and these two girls could play too.

"Funny—I would have chosen you too," Troy said, obviously cruising for a knuckle sandwich to go with his eggrolls. Well, Raphael had set Troy up. *Time to stand as a man and take ownership.*

Raphael changed the subject. "I've decided if it's all right with you, Stella that we turn on our engagement plans again, at least for the weekend."

"Why?" Well, forthright Stella struck again.

"I think if we're engaged we'll be able to sleep in the same room, saving Hai's parents valuable space."

Stella broke out laughing. "Oh yes, of course." You couldn't miss the look she gave Hai, one of those eat your heart out things women do to each other. Raphael would make sure Stella had a great night, but didn't he always.

"How liberal are your parents?" Troy asked, obviously trying to get into Hai's magic kingdom. Fat chance, that girl had virgin written all over her plump, enticing lips.

"You'll have to wait until we're engaged," Hai said, smirking with just a touch of confusion. But she didn't say if, she said until. Okay. Okay. This was good. Finally, his brother would settle down just as Raphael had always wanted. *Own it.*

Troy sprung up from his cheap plastic chair and knelt down on the well-traveled, scuffed, macaroni littered terra-cotta tiles.

"Marry me, Miss Hai Lo." Some nearby patrons and a waitress started applauding.

Hai uttered something guttural in Chinese and looked as if she was going to bop him.

"Maybe, someday."

Troy rose. Raphael pulled him over and dusted off his knee with a napkin. Cleanliness was next to getting married in a woman's mind. Later, he'd lecture.

"Peking wasn't built in a day," Troy said. That pretty much was the way the trip went. They crept through the Holland tunnel, then down a faster Canal Street. Canal's complexion changed slowly from predominantly industrial grunge in dark and dirty tones, to lively multi-colored and multi-lit Chinatown with dark but still dirty tones as backdrop. Just before the Manhattan Bridge, they snaked around and under the bridge to drive onto Eldridge, her parent's street. At 7:55 p.m., they found a spot about a half-a-block, from Hai's parents' home. The neighborhood seemed alive in a hidden way, windows backlit, music muted, exotic cooking teasing his nose.

Most of the kids were probably inside by now, likely due to darkness. However, one nose turned-up *tween,* waved at Hai. Another walked up, basketball in hand, pants on the ground, almost, and said hi to all of them. Hai said something in Chinese and the boy walked by smiling.

Personally, he was conflicted about Hai, but it seemed they all had their roles to play, and not a bad play at that. Not a Shakespearian tragedy. Perhaps at this point, the Bard's Comedy Of Errors once again would fit the boys mess. In any case, meeting her family and attending her sister's wedding would bond the three of them to Hai even more. For this, they were all lucky.

Chapter 25

Hai introduced her new friends to George and Hui Lo, her parents. Everybody else had abandoned ship on missions of mercy, getting her baby sister's wedding ready to go without a hitch. Well, one hitch. The moment she'd tell her grand mom Joy, about Troy, well, Joy would implore Troy to marry her. Yep. She would not avoid telling, could not avoid telling her family because it would go a long way to reducing her parents worrying about her.

"Please Troy, Raphael and Stella come into our kitchen. The dining room is piled with things for tomorrow," her mom said.

"Very nice home, Mr. and Mrs. Lo," Stella said, and the boys chimed in. She made idolizing comments about the tiny terracotta soldiers, Ming dynasty vases, and other knickknacks.

"Please, we have lots of food from tonight's rehearsal dinner."

Hai opened both doors of the refrigerator and smiled broadly. "Troy is my new boyfriend." She didn't have to mention to her frustrated parents that he was her first boyfriend and maybe only as a trial boyfriend or a one weekend date. She felt the friendship of the four of them would guarantee she'd become closer to Troy.

"What do you do for a living, son?" George Lo asked.

"Papa, let him relax. He didn't bring his financial portfolio."

"No, no, Hai, I don't mind. I make people laugh."

A silence overwhelmed them.

"He's part owner in a Philadelphia comedy club and he is the main attraction. They say a stand-up comedian," Hai said.

"I know what a stand-up comedian is," Hui Lo said. "We love to watch Chris Rock." Maybe, too much information.

"He's a great comedian. My subject matter is often family-oriented, but sometimes sexy."

"You like families?" Hai wanted to object, but Troy responded immediately.

"My brother and I are identical twins. He's engaged to Stella. I can't let him get ahead of me too far."

"So you are saying by inference, or in a funny way, you would want a family, sooner than later?"

"I'm sorry, Troy. My father argues law on behalf of the Mayor of New York City. He prefers everything tied down."

"Well, Mr. Lo, I would like to tie down your daughter, but we're new to each other, so we'll see."

"Yes, I heard about your unusual release from jail on the national news." Oh no. Hai didn't need a conflagration. "Your benefactor couldn't avoid the publicity."

"I can assure you, sir, it was just business with him."

"That's right, Daddy, I was there. Mr. Greco has enough problems with the Mafia's image than to let his nephew go around beating up innocent people."

"I see."

She had simplified Greco's story, leaving out the sale of the Comic Freak. It would have muddied the waters and served no purpose at this time. Mom had laid out egg rolls, noodles, wonton soup, dumplings and fortune cookies along with tea. All chatted for a while but had to get to sleep early.

"I'd like you, Troy, to sleep in this sleeping bag and an extra blanket on the rug next to the couch. Hai, you can have the couch."

"That would be fine, Sir. Thank you for trusting me near your daughter."

"My daughter can take care of herself, but just in case you'd like me to show you how I use that sword over the mantle, let me know."

"Father."

"It is a *joke*." Troy looked a little pale. She stood an inch taller than her dad, but he packed a beefy frame, and could hold his own with bigger men. It hadn't hurt him to have earned a black belt and it held his pants up too.

Hai had set up her bedroom for Stella and Raphael. The lights were all off, except for a tiny footlight near the bathroom. Everybody and the dog slept.

"I think we should kiss." Troy said in a whisper.

"Silly boy. My dad is very good with his sword."

"Where'd he get a samurai sword?"

"My grandfather brought it home after World War II and taught his son how to use it, to defend against burglars."

"In perfect condition, a thing of beauty."

She leaned over and whispered in his ear. "Kisses. I need more of them to compare to Raphael's. I already love your body, handsome face, and you are so tall."

"Gladly."

"Shhh."

"If you just start kissing me, I wouldn't be able to talk," he said, "much." through closed and joined lips.

They pecked at first, and then she became hungry for more, hours of more. Deeper, wetter, sweeter. Troy seemed unable to get enough of his new exotic girlfriend. *Nice to be wanted.* Maybe the upturn of her upper lip attracted him. The hue and texture of her skin or her unusual facial curves. Would he tire of her someday when he discovered she was like every other woman on the planet? *A girl just wanting a boy to love her.*

His kisses brought on euphoria. Yet something was missing. She'd figure out the missing ingredient as time went by. She wouldn't mind doing the homework.

Chapter 26

Frank Greco woke up sweating. His cell phone was probably still at the hospital. Jersey lay naked and slumped in the downward dog position again in her bedroom. They hadn't eaten beans the night before.

It had to be fish, yep flounder, well maybe she's comfortable. He'd rouse her after a shower and then they'd rake in a little cash from a poker game, to pay his deductible to the asshole administrators/racketeers at the hospital. Technically, he had insurance through his uncle's fish factory.

While he showered, Jersey wondered in bleary-eyed. He made room for her.

You scrub my back. I'll scrub yours.

"You up for a quick out? Maybe a thou at the poker table?"

"Yeah, that's okay, or a little roulette," she yawned and stretched, "if there ain't nobody down there yet, what." She paused looking down at an imaginary watch on her water-speckled arm. "At 10:37 a.m." She probably remembered the bedroom clock and added time in her computer like head. He liked her mathematical precision and that she never poked him with questions about his decisions. Besides, he always got around to discussing his ideas with her and she always agreed.

They dressed, descended and trekked through the Claridge to the adjoining Bally's noticing a poker game now forming. With a little luck, they'd stuff their pockets and clear a g-note in a couple hours, make an excuse, and clear out.

A guy in a black leather jacket and black cargo pants pushed off the wall and turned to face Frank.

"Hey, Pisano," Tony said. They hugged.

"What are you doin' here?" Frank grabbed his chest. "Come to get rid of a pest?"

"Never. Your uncle wants us to show you something and he wants to talk to you on the phone after you see it." Frank reached for his missing cell phone.

"Is this important? Can't it wait? We were going to pick up a large."

"Hey, you know Romeo. He likes everything, yesterday. What can I say? Your grandma wants you to take the time." At least he knew he wasn't going to be iced, turned into cat food, unless his na na had ordered it, laughing out loud. Tony always had a way with words, a way of letting you relax. Frank didn't understand Romeo but he was the boss, *capo di tutti capi*, Don of Dons, and he'd do what he could to get along. Someday, with a little luck Frank would bring the family back to its former glory.

Down the hall, Joe, Tony's sidekick stuck his head out a conference room. "In here, bring Jersey." Getting Jersey involved in family business had never been done before.

The four sat down and watched a video of the night Frank got knocked out. They watched a drunk Frank get out of his car, accost some stranger, Troy Chariote. Frank started pushing Mr. Chariote, and then flat-out fall on his face on a concrete barrier, lights out.

"Well, what do you think?" asked Tony.

"He's still a punk."

"He didn't touch you. He didn't do anything to you," Joe said.

"He could have caught me. Where's his Christian charity." They all laughed.

"That's the doctor who felt me up," Jersey said.

"What?"

"Yeah, that's the doctor who was waiting for a brain transplant, and played knee knocking with me." It became obvious Troy Chariote was a pervert jerk who played Jersey for a whore. Brain transplants were impossible unless you were Frankenstein. He knew that. He chuckled.

138

"I'm sorry, Jersey. He is really not a doctor. He was sitting there in the hospital checking in on Frank, to see if he was okay. Then we showed up with Romeo. You remember?" Tony asked.

"You see this guy's a pervert." Frank said.

Tony and Joe had a short whispering talk.

"Let me call Romeo now. Maybe he can clear this up," Tony said.

Tony handed the phone to Frank, speaker on. No secrets today, Romeo had Frank's na na, Graciola, with him. The bodyguards could listen. Romeo trusted Tony and Joe with his life and considered their advice. Tony was ex-green beret, and Harvard educated. Joe was ex-secret service and a Catholic University grad. Not only were they smart, which was exactly the kind of people Romeo wanted to be surrounded by, they were street savvy and tough as nails. These praetorians were loyal to their boss.

"Okay Frank, me and your na na met Troy Chariote's brother Raphael. They're identical twins. First of all, these brothers are good guys, and second of all, Raphael probably didn't want Jersey to know who he was, because Jersey was ready to testify that his brother tried to kill you. Jersey, what is going on with you?"

"Nothing, Mr. Greco."

"You can't keep doing this to Frank. You're going to get him killed someday."

"I'm sorry, Mr. Greco."

"Baby, I know our Frank loves you. If you love him, you must start telling him the truth," Na Na said.

It seemed Frank beat up too many Joe Publics, but so what?

"Sorry, Na Na."

"Tell us what really happened," Na Na said.

"He didn't do anything to me. But our knees did touch," Jersey said, off point in la la land as usual.

"That man is engaged. It was probably an accident. Moreover, your legs are everywhere. Stop wearing those micro-mini skirts and give Frank's fist a rest," Na Na said. Hearing the modesty argument from a not so ex-flower child was a kick in the pants. Unfortunately, he pictured his younger na na running around naked, except for a bandana, at

139

Woodstock, and passing a reefer. Then Frank, shook his head and wanted to wash said head out with soap.

"I only have pretty things," Jersey said. Too true. Frank liked her wardrobe.

"You are pretty without walking around half-naked," Romeo said. "Do you need some money to buy her some nicer outfits?"

Part of her gambling persona encouraged people to underestimate or slobber over her. Maybe he could buy her a couple dresses for family visits to placate the big shot and Na Na.

"We don't have a problem shopping."

"Listen to me now." Frank smelled the beginning of a Romeo lecture.

"Hit me." Frank jested to lighten everybody up.

"Just listen. We'd like to not see you get hit. We'd like you to do more than hustle balding men with too many dollars in their pockets. You stopped your Ivy League education. You know the new mob, at least the mob I control directly. Each person must be educated. We're heading mostly legit and making even more money, because we're smarter than the average Joes. You had talent, have talent, but you're wasting it. I know you think I'm not tough enough, so I'm only going to tell you this once. Your hero, Al Capone, was an idiot. He brought the feds and locals down on him and the family because he showboated like a politician. One too many politicians. We have to keep a low profile. So you are going back to Princeton and when you demonstrate to me that you cooled your hot head, I'll give you a seat. I'll give you everything."

"But I was an art major."

Na Na answered first. "That doesn't matter. You choose your major, but I think you have art talent."

"It's not the major. It's the process." Romeo said.

"Okay."

"Your na na would love to get a little help from you once in a while," Romeo said.

"So you're saying stop beating people up because it hurts the business?"

"Yes, and get smart. Treat people like *compares*."

"Well, why didn't you say so before?" He wasn't sure it would be easy to keep this promise, but he saw the sense of it.

"We thought you'd grow out of it, but because of Jersey, it's only gotten worse. This brings up another subject."

"Yes, uncle."

"By the way, we have nothing against you, Jersey. We'll get you two a condo off campus if you both want it. You can still visit Atlantic City on the weekends, if all Frank's homework is done."

Na Na interrupted. "But we are all wondering if you two are okay…as a couple. You know what I mean?"

"How come you don't touch her?" Romeo asked.

"You've been spying on us?" Frank stood.

"Sit down. You forget. We're also in the surveillance business. We only do this to protect you." The surveillance business was the mob's new way of selling business people, 'protection.' For all Frank understood, it approached legitimacy. He'd ask Romeo at Sunday dinner to explain the business better.

"Listen, everybody. Jersey and I have an agreement. We aren't attracted to each other."

"Is this true, Jersey?" Na Na asked.

"Can anybody see my rear? Hey, I get gas. I got to air it out." This was no way to impress.

Romeo started laughing. "Nobody's watching your…" Tony and Joe were inspecting ceiling tiles. "We're getting vibes from you two. There are no cameras in your room. We just want to know if everything is okay." Did this mean there are no cameras anywhere? He knew Romeo to be precise in his language, so Frank would stay wary.

"Well, I think he's a doll. But I don't want to mess up what I got with him, only because he has a lumpy dick." Snickering spread like mayonnaise and Frank felt like punching somebody, anybody, just not Jersey.

"Hey, there's nothing wrong with my schlong. I just like money, not sex."

"You could have a girl like me for a dozen dimes over." Never mind.

"No baby, that's not true." He hugged her.

"Frank, I want you to get counseling. Anybody who hangs with Jersey and doesn't get excited at least needs glasses."

"I don't need no freakin' doctor."

"Cut out that stupid talk. You go to a doctor. You go to school. You stop fighting."

"How about one of those sex therapists? The legit kind?" He'd go through the motions, at least. *Who wants to be lumpy anyway?*

"Deal. We'll make the arrangements. Meanwhile, your na na wants you to check out an art exhibition in Manhattan tomorrow and then come home, both of you, for supper. And get this girl some clothes." Tony handed Frank two g-notes.

"Which exhibition?" Frank broke into a sweat. Maybe Na Na was setting him up to be offed on Marciano's turf.

"Slater Bradley. Joe has a flyer, your cell phone, and clothes. We took care of the hospital… So get out of my face."

"Yes, sir. But…"

"I'm going to give you some shadows. You have nothing to worry about. Just don't lose your tails." Yeah sure, nothing to worry about. Something was off, but he had no real choice. Maybe it was a test of his manhood or his newfound kindly nature. He'd be vigilant.

"Say hi to Slater for me," Na Na said.

Who the hell was Slater Bradley? Google search time.

A few key strokes later and Frank understood his na na's attraction to the artist if that was what was really happening. Now Frank pictured his na na running around Woodstock waving a gun, still naked, yuk.

Slater, a renaissance man, had a wicked sense of humor, world famous, had contracted with Disney, his works displayed in a movie "When in Rome." It bombed. Slater created avant-garde videos, one for NASA, photos, and traditional art. The traditional art, drawings or paintings came more from his assistant, due to time constraints, probably. The one day Chelsea show, set for tomorrow, was called Doppelganger or dead ringer, right? The Exhibit seemed more a party of friends than a hard sell. Good. In any case, he'd see. He wouldn't have to stay long.

Chapter 27

Hai ascended the escalator ahead of Troy, leaving him no choice but to drool over her shape and, of course, her lovely dress. Why was it that some women looked fantastic in dresses and not so much in their birthday suit? He'd have to unwrap this one.

Both escalators' sidewalls featured fire-belching and smoke-blowing dragon murals to accompany the guests to and from the banquet hall, today for the wedding feast. Indigestion bathrooms up, indigestion bathrooms down, you choose, mister. He'd probably enjoy the food, hot or mild.

At the top, a sign with two identical Chinese symbols and an arrow pointed the wedding guests to the right.

"Call me, Joy." Hai's grand mom, Joy Lo, offered her arms to Raphael and Troy. She stood about five feet, making her bouffant hairdo of jet-black hair seem too large. For eighty years, her slightly wrinkled face retained a beauty reflected in her four granddaughters.

"What's the symbol on the sign mean?" Raphael asked. Always the first to schmooze.

"It mean double happiness. Shay-shay. Gentlemen, we walk to table now. I'll explain." Joy said.

Not short in terms of words or enthusiasm, she went on to explain to the boys the Taoist tradition of yin-yang as it related to the double happiness of marriage, "man and woman make family—the Tao of marriage." This presented another example of the concept—the sum is greater than its parts—much like his relationship with his brother.

Although Joy, as matriarch, had many duties, she remained laser-focused on the twins, especially Troy. He prepared to steady her; she'd faint from all her head turning. The boys did their duty, being introduced to granddaughter number one, two and four, with Hai being number three, and the prettiest. With number four, the youngest, getting married, hopeful or curious eyes focused on Troy and Hai. Granddaughter number three's complexion became ruddier every moment, rivaling the red carpet. Perhaps Hai was embarrassed, but she also seemed tickled by her grand mom's doting on her date.

Joy rearranged the seating so Raphael and Troy sat on each side of her, with Stella next to Raphael and Hai next to Troy.

Waiters in black tuxedos with red bowties introduced appetizers. Joy told them eight courses would comprise the main meal and one more for dessert, which would really be a montage of tasty delights.

"Eight in Chinese sounds like good luck," Joy said. "First we have cold appetizer, dragon-phoenix plate. It have lobster strips, jellyfish, nuts, meats, chicken feet. In China, Lobster or dragon mean male role in marriage, chicken feet is phoenix. This mean female role."

Adventurous, Troy's mouth watered. He peeked at Raphael listening to Joy ramble on. He could tell Raphael had the same problem. They wanted to dig in, but were afraid to eat while Joy talked. She never stopped talking. Standing it no longer, Troy gave Raphael the secret eye roll and attacked the jellyfish. Surprisingly good, if you like rubber band chewy in a crisped glob.

"Oh, good first choice, jellyfish is health food high in protein," Joy said. "You like?"

Raphael who copied Troy's eating answered, "It picks up the pepper, sesame and soy perfectly." The fuck-head was showing off. The jellyfish had no taste other than the seasonings, but because it was unusual, Troy liked it. He had never slinked away from a challenge or adventure.

"You happy engaged to Stella, right?" Joy peeked by Raphael at Stella and smiled broadly. "Yes," he answered between chews. Troy wondered when he'd be finished chewing this morsel, so he could move on to taste something else. Maybe an hour.

Joy grew more ecstatic with each bite they took, as if chewing jellyfish had some secret significance. Hai was grinning at her date, obviously enjoying his predicament.

"Troy, you like my granddaughter?"

Choking a bit. "Very much. She's wonderful." Actually, whenever Joy looked down at her plate, Troy stole a glance of Stella, and then felt guilty for it. Then he noticed Hai peeking at Raphael, then back at him, then down at her plate. Meanwhile, Stella focused on a strip of lobster. They all, with the exception of Stella perhaps, had to be struggling with the same problem, who loved who more. Even when Stella seemingly focused on food, her mind was always in overdrive and likely somewhere else. This was all good. The four would become closer from hunting for truth and happiness, so say fortune cookie.

"This dish is Shark's Fin Soup. It mean, we have loads of money," she started laughing. "They will serve you Sparrow's Nest Soup if you no like."

"Can I have both?" Troy asked.

"Sure." She summoned the waiter. "But you save room. I get you a small amount." He wouldn't argue, hardly knowing what delights remained. He could eat a ton of food, but the promises of more to come made him save room, just in case.

"You love my Hai?" Joy asked. Hai's mom patted her dad's back.

Troy took a moment, placing his hand on his mouth and then raised one finger, meaning give him just a moment. He downed another glass of plum wine to clear his throat. He had to consider Joy's statement seriously. He felt close to Hai, and Hai claimed to be comfortable with the new him. At this point, they shared the love friends had for each other. They had talked all night while bunked in the living room—had a giddy time. They also confessed their respective crushes on Raphael and Stella. But like Troy, Hai supported Raphael and Stella's reemergence as an engaged couple—as the noble and practical thing to do. This in spite of the confused sexual tension all four suffered, which could supply Con-Edison enough energy to power New York City.

However, Hai and Troy were now *simpatico*. No matter what happened, he couldn't picture a life without her near.

"Yes, Joy, I love your Hai." Hai squeezed his arm, a tad too tight. Joy giggled, "Oh that nice."

"Next course here now, Roast Suckling Pig, very crispy. Groom brings to restaurant. It symbol of virginity and Hai a very good girl." Joy winked at him, but seemed disappointed when she caught Hai's attention. True, they had also kissed through the night although Hai's virginity had been safe with him. Troy stole a glance of a fidgeting Hai, who then elbowed him.

"You like children?" This time, Hai's dad patted Hai's mom on the back. Something contagious was happening. Yeah, Joy. The joy of Joy.

This was an easy one. "Raphael and I intend to field a baseball team."

"No like girls?"

He remembered softball. He didn't mean to suggest he didn't want girls playing sports. He always felt girls, women, could play any sport they wanted and pound for pound, just as good.

"I'd love daughters and sons. Girls are great athletes too, especially with your genes."

Joy let her bouffant touch Troy's shoulder. "Hai win many trophies." The night before Hai had led them on a tour of her old room. Troy hadn't realized she made the U.S. figure skating team while in college.

"Next dish is Peking duck and hot lobster. Red is color for happiness, just like Hai's face." The table erupted in laughter, with Hai leading the way. What a good sport. She remained in good sorts, if not color, through every pronouncement from her headstrong grand mom. Hai's and Joy's broad smiles were addictive.

"Head and legs mean completeness." Whole Maine lobsters stared at them accusingly. He felt certain the duck wouldn't fly off. The duck's succulent rich flavor drove him to consider visiting Chinese restaurants more often. He'd check the closer but smaller Chinatown in Philly with Hai as his guide. Bam, he actually was thinking steady girlfriend. Maybe he'd see a shrink, Stella, well maybe not.

"You two getting engaged soon?" Joy asked. He doubted the Gestapo could sweat more out of him. The comedian within could no longer be held back.

"I proposed to her on Friday at the prestigious Molly Pitcher rest stop, but I am sad to say she said something like 'ney horsee,' in Chinese. She said no?"

Joy fanned herself. "More plum wine." She signaled a waiter, seemingly impatient. Her hard stare bore into Hai, who bit her lip. "You wash your mouth out, granddaughter number three. I sorry Troy, my Hai not mean to say 'go to hell,' but it also sound like 'I love you.' Depends on how you say it... Hai, maybe not ready for love."

Everybody chewed on that for a while. She might have been right about her granddaughter. Before Hai got to know better the notorious Chariote brothers. Before they spent a nearly sleepless night. He vaguely remembered, during the night, Hai saying something about taking off her sports bra and putting on something lacy, saying she stayed focused on career and in college on sports and grades. Joy's verbosity rumbled. Although Hai's parents talked to Troy at length the night before, over a generous late night kitchen snack bordering on dinner, they seemed like spectators to Joy's command of the table, and her attention on him.

"Squab with eggs next, mean fertility." He felt his sperm squirm.

Raphael said, "I love it. The eggs taste a little like honey." The eggs tasted like eggs.

"If you want to have children to make team, your brother must start soon, right?"

"I'm ready to plan a double wedding as soon as Hai says yes to my brother." Raphael said. There was entirely too much cross-smiling going on here among the four lost souls.

Have we four young lovers booked the Titanic?

"Next dish is crab claws. This mean...I don't remember. Maybe pinch each other's bottoms every day." Joy played this crowd like a queen.

"Hai, honey, Hui have four children. Holly have three children. Hanna have wedding, soon she have one child, I hope. Not too soon. This means you must have twins to catch up."

"I hope so too, Nana," Hai said. He finally understood the shades of meaning in Hai's eyes. This gorgeous, exotic woman adored her grand mom.

"Vegetables with sea cucumber here now. Sea cucumber sound like good heart, which mean number three granddaughter not to argue with Troy."

There you go, grams.

"Yes, Nana." Hai answered quickly, which told him of her obedience, perhaps, and, at the very least, her attention to the subject. However, Troy knew from discussions with family, especially his mom, and his innate sense of fairness that both parties to a marriage contract should love and honor each other. Obedience from mates arose from respect and was earned.

The last dish before dessert arrived to a completely stuffed everyone, from babies to Grand mom.

"This last one, fish sound like plentiful in Chinese. Couple to have abundance in life together." Joy smiled first at Raphael and Stella and then as brilliant as the sun at Troy and his lovely date. The waiters had brought large steamed sea bass, each one whole. Its meat melted off the bone and the smells from the ginger seasoning enticed gluttony. Somehow, he made room. The fish appeared hungry, with opened mouths encouraging Troy to eat more.

"I am dying. I not want to leave this world not seeing my number three granddaughter married. You please rectify. More plum wine."

Aside from her fifth glass of wine, she seemed the picture of health. Hai's parents hid smiles. Hai said nothing, bowing her head as if now were the time for a meal prayer. Troy doubted Joy was dying, but all he could think of was lifting Hai's chin and kissing her. Although he admired Stella, Hai's extremely attractive personality and beauty lured him like a siren to the rocks. They had become the closest of friends, not afraid to speak the truth. He repeated to himself: he'd respect, honor and protect Raphael and Stella. Stella seemed to give him the-join-the-real-world look. Besides, there weren't enough life preservers or lifeboats on their Titanic. After all, in life, who really received everything they wanted? Hai of big heart, talent and temperament would be a great mate for any man. He siphoned some strength from his brother who seemed to know what he was thinking.

He did not know whether it was the never ending wine, Hai's gown, her regal, sensual beauty, the luscious kisses she gave the night before, or this adorable little woman beside him; his heart melted, as if ice cream on a stove. He sat with a great family. He'd engage Hai if she'd have him. His heart swelled at the notion of commitment. How odd of him. He peeked at Hai's wonderful eyes once again. Did she see his soul?

"Finally, we have dessert, yummy sweet red bean soup and sweet buns. It mean newlyweds will have a sweet life together…and visit dentist soon."

Troy stood and raised his glass of plum wine to a loving family, his dearest brother and that Stella girl. "Do all you here think that Hai and I are a good match?" He stood straight, with the tiniest of wobbles and then stretched his six-foot-three. Everybody said yes, with the kids at other tables the most vocal. Joy held his hand, a tear in her eye. Joy knew what was coming; she'd planned it, the cute little devil.

"Then I'd like to ask Hai again. I am very serious with this very important question of mine. Okay, I may have tried to keep up with Joy's plum wines, one, two, three, more, but my heart knows what I want."

He pulled out his chair, got down on one knee, took Hai's hand and said, "Will you marry me, Miss Hai Lo?"

After a moment's hesitation. "Yes."

DOUBLE HAPPINESS
ACT 3

Chapter 28

Troy had been close to drunk when he proposed. Hai felt sure he'd knock out, go to sleep right away, but no. They slept in the same positions as the night before, Troy below her on the floor. The only difference, Dad didn't talk of swords, as a bedtime story. Troy kept chattering. Maybe getting him drunk made the loosest tongue at the Comic Freak, looser yet. She decided to test him.

"I'm not going to hold you to your proposal."

Troy sat up, leaned in and wrapped his arms around her. She arched her head. He did things to her.

"The proposal will hold if you'll have me."

"Kiss me, you foolish boy."

Troy found her lips in the dark. They didn't say anything for quite a while. *Some argument, some test.*

"How are we doing, sweetheart?" Troy asked, as if all the world's problems could be solved by kissing.

"I'm amazed you content yourself with kissing me." She reflected on her many years without boys then men, until Raphael kissed her. Kissed her, good. And then Troy carried on. Tally ho.

"Kissing is sex and intimacy."

She pondered this until he spoke again. "It's time for all of us. Think how beautiful life will be for us four. Sweet children, vacations."

"Children aren't candies."

"I know of hard work, Hai. You wouldn't believe the time I put in to help people smile and laugh."

The night whirled on, half-dream, half-reality.

Later and beyond sleepy. "But are our relationships ethical? As you said, Raphael likes me, Stella likes you."

"And you like Raphael."

"And you like Stella?" Troy had already mentioned his attachment to Stella, but now of all times, seemed good for elaboration.

"Let me explain my attachment to her better."

"Okay." She yawned.

"I too, as you all know, am guilty. The moment my brother brought Stella home on Thanksgiving break, I felt he selected the perfect woman. Our tastes are similar, so I pictured Stella as my ideal type of mate. I vowed to find a girl like her someday and you look just like her."

"But I'm not Italian." She had black hair, but Stella's was sandy-blonde. Hai's intellect was took a nosedive as sleepiness toyed with her. Then she got his joke, and laughed.

"It's in the heart not the face or boobs."

"I can't compete with her knockers."

"Being a comedian, I study odd facts. Sixty percent of men prefer big boobs. That leaves me with the forty percent. Just between you and me, one hundred percent of men are just *happy* to be there. The only important feature beyond our outrageous physical attraction is your heart. Maybe Raphael could say this better than me, but I'll try."

"I'm all ears and perky breasts."

"God made people proportional on the average. It's called the golden ratio." Yes, Raphael had something to that effect. She responded with a kiss.

"Just so you know. I think they're perfect, but I won't know for sure until you let me cup your breasts with my hands, kiss them with my lips and do things." He tickled her.

"What things?"

"I'm going to resist saying something like, with a Mafioso maniac killer running loose it might be our last night. So we better make love, for your sake."

"Is it as easy as that?"

He became quiet.

She thought of her rear, but put that thought behind her. Hell, if he got a rise out of her bottom, she'd probably let him get away with a pinch, but not intercourse. She wanted to ask what he thought about her bottom, but thought she'd save it for a time when he was fully awake. She fell into attorney mode and belabored the point.

"When will you be ready to drop your feelings for her, so we can grow as a couple?"

"The same time you drop your feelings for Raphael. Right?" Pretty good sparring on his part.

"Yes. I'd say you're pragmatic. Well, how do you feel exactly about her now?"

"Can I answer that question a little indirectly, counselor?"

"I'll reserve the right to recall the witness."

"Well, I guess that will do for now. I still feel it is more important for both of us to honor Raphael and Stella. If they can't make it, you and I will be tested. I think it is important for us to keep our eyes on the goal. We should grow with each other. Learn to love each other."

"Do you love me?" she asked.

"Do you love me, Hai?" Troy became the lawyer, never answering a direct question and kissing her to stop her rebuttal. "Hold off a moment, Hai." He put his hand gently on her mouth. "Ms. Hai Lo, I'm crazy about you. I love your eyes. They drive me nuts. Your creamy, smooth complexion." He caressed her face.

She returned the favor. "God gave us a beautiful deck of cards. I think we should play the hand."

"My brother's kiss is different, isn't it?"

"Yes. Every moment said he loved me. I'm sorry." She teared, but it was dark and he didn't know.

"Remember these little facts, what I'm about to tell you, my Asian doll."

"Tell me."

"You're a virgin, aren't you?"

"How did you know?"

"It's in your wide eyes. You have little experience, and my wonderful brother is used to loving a woman. He's very expressive.

152

Please give me time to grow." He then whispered. "About loving a woman, I too, am a virgin. Please give me a chance."

They smooched and talked for hours more, somewhere between sleeping and waking. The refrigerator cycled. The dog whimpered, dreaming. The street sounds never ceased in a city that never slept.

His caressing hands, eventually found their way to her body where they belonged. He whispered he wouldn't take her. She didn't resist. They petted, like two teenagers at a drive-in movie. The beginning of young love. Hai promised to kick herself for not trusting any of her many admirers, but then again, she'd also have to thank herself, since now she could share her enrichment course on love with the right man. A man too insistent, too ruggedly handsome to ignore. A man who had opened his soul to her. She was ruined for any other man. If this relationship didn't work out, she'd become a nun, well convert to Catholicism first, and then become a nun.

He so assured her. They had an immediate extended family of four, all of whom would die for each other. All of whom would protect their hearts. She closed her eyes. If things did go whacky, Raphael and Troy could be Troy and Raphael. Probably not bad, assuming the four bought into it, but hardly likely and best forgotten.

Troy cautioned her to focus straight forward, because the road to married life for the four of them would feel like a newly iced-over road. Complete attention needed, final destination wanted, none too soon.

She nudged him to get off the couch. "Please my sweetheart, get a little sleep."

He pulled her off the couch on top of him. She straddled him, fully pajama-ed of course. She wondered when that special day would come when she'd lose her virginity. She bent over and gave him one last goodnight kiss, as if dripping wet sand to make a castle on a beach of a lapping sea, the kiss was destined to be endless.

If it were their last night on this Earth, perhaps it would be smart to see what making love was like. Her sisters made love when they were engaged, so why should she miss out?

She moved her hips suggestively. "Make love to me."

Troy let out a sigh. "Oh sweetie." Then he sat up with her still straddling him and kissed her nose. "We'll save your virginity for marriage, my dearest." Troy who could have any woman he wanted, wanted to wait. How precious. He had to love her to show restraint, by working at, by knowing her needs. She needed his love much more than his body.

"I love where we're going, Troy Chariote."

"Kiss me again."

Chapter 29

Sunday morning, on the sofa, sleepy Hai leaned over and gazed down at Troy's gorgeous face. She couldn't believe she had said yes or that he honestly popped the question, and so soon. No court of law would uphold this engagement.

She cherished a no longer secret attraction to Raphael, which Troy and she had discussed along with every other subject. The way he told it, the four of them were a fine balance of selfless love and carnal desires. They had to live with it. He said, quite brilliantly, they had a family of four, something to treasure and let grow. The family of four would be seated now at the table of life.

Troy was so right. He had a good heart, and he revved hers to a flutter. The two boys were the most spectacular examples of human maledom. Chiseled body, well they had one body. *Strong lines.* Wavy, thick, black hair not too long, didn't matter. Cleft chins a la the Douglas movie family. Dreamy searing eyes, changing color to suit their mood: Something like hazel-blue. Strong eyebrows, a touch of Neanderthal there. Lips—bow and arrow to her heart. Both boys—great kissers. She peeked down at his crotch but the blanket covered it. Her paralegal and girlfriend, Janine, had warned her, never get serious with a guy until you find a way to inspect his equipment, and she didn't mean plumbing at an apartment, or under the hood of his car, or his Weii. Just his Weii Weii.

Janine had said, "When you go to a store, you shop. You make sure you're getting the right thing. You gonna throw this up in the air on whimsy? Come on. His equipment needs a lifetime guarantee." The problem, Hai wasn't sure what to look for. She'd get on it.

Then she worried about something else. She remembered Raphael's behavior last night, couldn't quite get him out of her mind. He peeked at her too often, asked her to dance some Latin number, cha cha. She quietly refused. He looked lovesick. She'd seen mopey interludes on so many boys in college, when all they really wanted was her body. However, the two couples danced and danced, glorious. She always likened dancing to figure skating with the freedom of body movement and expression, pure release.

Also, Raphael hadn't drunk a drop, and at a wedding, truly amazing. Perhaps, she was part of the solution. Really though, he didn't need anybody to be able to stand on his two feet and stop drinking for good. Well, access to his soul would be easy for the three of them.

The foursome bonded as a force to be reckoned with. The boys went everywhere with each other and intended to take their iffy fiancées along. Stella and she didn't seem to mind, not one bit. *Project double-marriage was iffy. Well, we'll see.*

She slipped her arm out of the covers and tweaked Troy's nose. "Time to wake up, baby." He'd buy her a ring before heading to the art exhibition, if the diamond district stores opened on a Sunday morning and if he still wanted her.

"Where's the ring, Mr. Chariote?" She let go of his nose.

He turned toward her, pulled the blanket over his head and then lowered the edge little-by-little until his eyes peeked out. "Did we actually get engaged last night?" he said, sounding like a little boy who had gotten himself in trouble.

"Any regrets?"

"You're not pregnant, are you?"

Miraculous conception.

He leaned up and against the couch, stuck his hand under her blanket, and started rubbing her belly. She drew him to her. Her head spun, and so early. She worried her parents would be up soon and see her goo-goo-eyed. Foo-fighter, her parent's Shiatsu—interrupted Troy's kissing and groping of Hai—with some kissing of his own. Well, at least she squeezed in a little petting of her own, and she didn't have to hide in

156

a dark private place. Check, one more new feeling, nice, very nice but she needed more lessons and more. *Just more.*

"That was so sweet what you did for the children last night." They both petted the dog.

The night before legions of little ones corralled Troy. He told silly kid jokes. Why did the chicken cross the road? Because the crossing guard said it was okay. What did the peanut butter and jelly sandwich say to the baloney sandwich? They say nothing, my little sillies, they're just sandwiches. He performed one magic trick. He left the room talking to them but appeared in their midst in mid-sentence. Of course, Raphael had a hand in the illusion. The twins repeated the trick and not a kid could figure it out. They gave up and then Raphael walked into the room and stood by his brother. Troy had said diversion and the fact that kids don't study adult faces had a lot to do with the illusion. Both men were great with kids, another quality and an absolute must, *for this woman.*

Time to get up, buy a ring and then on to the Slater Bradley exhibit. Later, she'd ask Stella to elaborate on how the boys' equipment functioned. She already knew they were big according to Stella, and had really no idea why that mattered, except it might hurt. She didn't need to follow Janine's advice and get hands on knowledge. She was far too conservative a girl to do that anyway. Although she had been tempted last night. Why hadn't she pressed the point after his refusal to take her?

What if the mafia guy, Frank, found out where they were? All she knew, Troy drove her out of her mind and that was all she needed, until they married. If they lived that long.

Chapter 30

After a late breakfast insisted upon by Hai's mom and dad, the teams, Stella and Raphael and Troy and Hai, had no time for ring shopping.

So Mrs. Joy Lo gave her granddaughter a pretty loaner ring, a brilliant nearly one carat round cut white diamond set in antique gold. Hai and Troy seemed the happy couple. Raphael wondered if it would be this easy, if either of their engagements would hold. He'd invest every available moment into finding out and helping make it work in spite of his darkest desires to have and hold Hai.

Now he guessed it would be two couples at Father Brian's engagement encounter, a tough-love weekend retreat. Even though Stella was the only Catholic aboard, her church had graciously allowed this. They had the foresight to ground couples in reality before they chose marriage or a break-up.

Or to switch partners?

Today they'd enjoy a simpler task. Art was Raphael's life. Slater Bradley was his buddy. What could be more fun than to visit and participate? Hai had an esthetic sensibility. He'd wait and see how she took to the great artist.

Troy hadn't been immediately available when Romeo called this morning to tell them about his experiment, sending Frank to the exhibition. It was the only way to release the four of them from constant worrying. Frank would be watched and likely would drop his grudge if

158

he wanted to live. Now that was brutally honest. Raphael agreed. It was better to put it all behind them then live every day in fear.

Raphael would not allow Frank to hurt his brother.

They headed over to the Chelsea neighborhood on a warm and cloudy day to visit an art gallery where Slater awaited them. The sign read, *Doppelgangers: the foolishness begins, a one-day show.*

Slater's more serious effort, *The Doppelganger Trilogy,* ran at Guggenheim for three years. Raphael worried Frank might somehow ruin the show. Romeo had already sat down with the young man for a serious talk.

If Frank isn't a complete idiot…

Troy and he would join another set of identical twins plus Slater's look-a-like associate artist and whoever else wondered in from the mailer, or walked in the door from the sign, or from flyers stapled or tied to poles and scant trees. Slater promised zany, so zany it would be.

Slater, his girlfriend and associate required everybody visiting the gallery today to sign a release for all videoing. Then don a white night cap, a long white nightshirt, glass-less glasses, paste on a black mustache and eyebrows, and chomp on a rubber cigar. Slater and his lovely girlfriend were both allergic to real cigars, at least when lit. She was a first class artist in her own right, MFA from NYU and independent film director.

The interior of the art studio mixed gray tones with stark black and whites appropriate for a black and white movie they'd be making.

High up on the far wall of a long rectangular room, the Marx brothers' famous mirror scene from "Duck Soup" looped on two fifty-five-inch video monitors siding double mirror-image bedrooms with a floor to ceiling imaginary mirror between them. The magic mirror was the walk through for the actors. A precision job, as always.

Slater encouraged any and all to ham it up by experimenting with the Marx brothers' set and scene. After they were satiated watching it and got over laughing hysterically, they engaged in a little organized lunacy.

The real identical twins, although everybody looked alike, took turns hiding behind opposite sides of the wall next to the pass through mirror. Raphael played Troy's mirror image and had to guess what face

Troy would put on as they peeked out. Then they'd see if they matched. Raphael had to figure out how high Troy's head would pop out, what angle, when, and with what expression. They started by mimicking the Marx brothers' antics for practice and then Troy tried to fool him with moves of his own. Raphael always believed, partially due to Stella's studies that he and his brother were a touch telepathic or had some sort of strange twin magic. However, he could only guess Troy's moves at maybe ten percent better than random, so said an enthusiastic Stella. Meaningful, but not impressive, just fun. Although one time, Troy jumped out backwards, his head facing away from Raphael and Raphael did the same.

He knew Stella loved the shenanigans not only as a scientific observer, but also as a cigar-chomping participant. She said she'd submit her identical twins psychology thesis in weeks now, finishing with a flair, by showcasing the video Slater would put together.

They didn't worry much about possible violence from Frank when he arrived, for two reasons: Romeo's assurances and one set of New York City police identical twins who accepted Slater's invite. Today they were literally under cover or nightshirts. Julia and Elizabeth Pratt tucked their red ponytails into the nightcaps, but their femininity couldn't be hidden, nor their cop-like ways as they blustered in typical New York-ease. The cop twins did much better at guessing each other's moves, on the mirror set, than Troy and Raphael. Stella couldn't wipe that silly grin off her face if she wanted to. She had impressive research.

At precisely 1:30 p.m. Frank, looking a little frazzled by humidity, pushed through both glass doors into the air-conditioned studio with Jersey trailing behind him. Jersey sported a fetching, pleated, aquamarine, knee-length, spring dress and white heels. Nothing like what he had heard she normally wore. Troy had joked: sight of her caused sore eyes. Yes, she was pretty for a bleached-blonde with a kind of a wholesome Taylor Swift sort of face and figure to match.

Frank and Jersey signed in along with a couple of walk-ins. They all dressed up to be Grouchos, and seemed excited from all the chatter. Frank appeared relaxed and happy, if a little street smart looking, eyes shifting. Frank spotted the Chariote brothers, and trekked over to the set and looping videos. Slater, also a Groucho, everybody was Groucho today, interrupted Frank's walk to introduce himself and talk a moment about another passion. Slater loved all-things chess and the Greco family history included Gioacchino Greco an unofficial world champion from the sixteen hundreds. Frank claimed he couldn't offer a good game, but suggested Slater try his uncle Romeo someday. Raphael had to hand it to Slater for a nice touch but wondered what would happen to him if he met and then beat Romeo Greco. Artist flavored cat food?

"I heard you came to the hospital to check on me." Frank raised his hand to shake, but didn't know which Groucho was Troy or Raphael.

"I'm Troy." Troy employed a roman handshake right out of *The Gladiator*. They shook and then Troy told him Raphael was the one who visited the hospital on his behalf, which—of course—wasn't true since the twins had swapped, but saying anything else would be confusing information and waste valuable time. There was the small matter of today's festivities.

"That was cool, Troy," Frank said, referring to the handshake, and then raising his eyes to the ceiling. "Picture us under the coliseum with the lions, the Emperor."

Troy and Frank raised their arms to the ceiling. Raphael, feeling it, could almost hear the Roman crowd roar and taste the grit falling through the wooden rafters.

"We're both going up. One will live, one will die." Thank God, Frank delivered these words with an earnest smile. Still, Raphael clenching his right fist hoped this was merely guy talk—but good imagery.

"Are you the doctor who pinched my ass?" Jersey asked, revealing her whacky side. Would this start world war three?

"Hey Jersey. This is Jersey." He spun her into his chest. "You didn't pinch her ass did you?" Frank steadied her by his side, then leaving the imaginary coliseum and Troy behind invaded Raphael's space, and stretched on his toes to about an inch from his face.

Frank reeked of garlic, not kidding.

"Never," Raphael said, his breath clipped.

"What's wrong with my ass?"

He said nothing. He knew nothing. Actually, nothing was wrong with Jersey's ass.

161

Frank jumped in. "I'm trying to change some bad habits I got, have." He pointed his cigar at Jersey. "Sometimes I got to bite my lip, you know." He grabbed her again and lowered his voice, gritting his teeth. "What did you mean by saying these things about this fine gentleman? You know what Romeo told you."

"Well this guy, Doctor Chariote," she curtsied, "sat so close, my ass felt pinched, is all." She pondered for a moment. "Like suddenly my panties were too tight."

That was close. All pinchy, yep that was the Chariote scourge. The twins gorged women without touching them.

Frank diverted Jersey by starting to play peek-a-boo at the non-mirror with her. Somehow, she matched his every move from sticking out his tongue, to lowering glasses down his nose, to every hop or gyration across the face of the mirror. How did she do it? They were warned she was different. This in itself should excite the psychologist in Stella, who was scribbling feverishly.

Troy spoke up. "Frank, I wanted to tell you, I was afraid to catch you the day you fell because you were leading with a roundhouse punch." This was another subject Romeo and Troy had discussed and the main reason for Frank's anger.

"That's okay." Jersey stole his cigar while his attention was diverted, but stuck hers in his mouth.

"No it's not. I quickly thought while watching you fall, you'd land harmlessly on the pavement on your chest with your arms breaking the fall. By the time I saw the concrete abutment, it was too late."

"You considered helping me. Not many people would do that." He poked Troy with his cigar. "Let's do that handshake again here at the mirror."

The cop twins approached. "You look like a young Al Pacino," one said, of Frank. Considering his gladiator theatrics and rough Italian features, yes, he did indeed look a little like Pacino.

"Yeah...thank you." He waved his cigar and shook his head admiring the too cute mustachioed cops. He had been informed of their true identity, Slater's idea, to help with the catharsis, and perhaps save the gallery or Chariotes from destruction. "Yes, except I'm taller than Pacino by an inch." Of course he was.

"We're here to arrest you if you start beating up anybody."

"And we're here to have some fun," said the other twin cop. Raphael couldn't tell who was Julia or Elizabeth. Hell, today they all looked, well, Groucho.

"Maybe you two would like to handcuff me, rough me up." Frank said, raising an eyebrow, and obviously in a good mood.

"Please, Frank." Jersey said.

Oh. She seemed to love him. Raphael could tell Frank—maybe nineteen, or twenty—still had a lot to learn about a young lady's heart. The difference between two more mature twenty-seven year old twins, the Chariotes, and one youngster trying to be cool-headed, wasn't much on this day.

"Up against the mirror. You are under arrest for being, younger, more handsome, and an inch taller than Al Pacino. This is against New York City ordinance 107B17 dash 69," twin cop said. Frank leaned against the imaginary mirror. The cuffs jangled.

"Yeah, no one should be allowed to look this good," said twin cop number two, applying real handcuffs but not clasping them.

Surprise. Surprise. That's when Jersey went berserk. She had no trouble knocking off the twin's nightcaps since it was obvious the cops focused on, hell, fancied Frank. She grabbed their ponytails and pulled the girls off her man. Who knew such a delicate thing could gather the strength to handle two police officers. Perhaps her biting their nightshirt-protected arms went a little too far. Troy and Raphael tried to pull Jersey off the flustered cops, who no doubt refused to use their fight training. You had to know when force was necessary and how much to use, he surmised. Anyway, the cops were laughing off the catfight. Nothing would come of it.

Wrong again. "Hey, don't touch my girl." Frank pushed Troy and then Raphael on their backs and ploughed forward. Maybe Frank would get too rough, but his smile and laughing suggested otherwise. This bunch up of six people caused them to pitter-patter forward to Slater and the walk-in patrons. Someone tripped. The whole group crashed into the set causing it to collapse. The monitors stayed anchored to the real wall, so no harm. They all fell like a group who tackled the guy carrying the football. That would be skinny, five-foot-eleven Slater. He'd survive.

Slater's associate continued videoing, but had trouble holding the camera straight from hiccups he developed when they fell. Slater seemed okay.

Slater's girlfriend ran over from the front desk and jumped on the pile. "Hey, get off my Slater." Her cigar went flying.

"Hey, off my man," Stella said, and jumped on.

"Hey, me too," Hai said, and did the same. Raphael felt like the cheerleaders joined the football team on a gang tackle, ah one of his all-time best fantasies. What a mangle of femininity.

After a little while of Groucho-like comments, the pile heard Slater whimper from somewhere way below. "Help. I can't breathe." Raphael's friend and art colleague was asthmatic and getting squashed. Everybody stopped, untangled the mix of arms and legs they had become and profusely cross-apologized for grabbing breasts and other body parts through teary giggles, grunts, and smudged make-up. This reminded Raphael of another Marx brothers' scene in which everybody had fallen out of a closet-sized stateroom. Two men, presumably Romeo's guys, gawked from the double doors at the street in disbelief. They probably thought better about interfering.

"Please don't tell my uncle. He'd kill me."

"Hell, it was all in fun." Slater said, regaining his breath, while his girlfriend unpeeled an errant eyebrow off his nose. The disheveled bunch meandered over to a snack table for juice and chips, slapping each other on their backs.

"You don't have to worry. I'll just call Romeo or his secretary and tell him we set the whole thing up for Slater's video." Troy said, coming to the rescue with a good idea.

"This could go Guggenheim." Slater said, suppressing a smile, and hugging his gal.

Speaking about hugging. Although Raphael felt Hai was a better match for him, by how much, he didn't know. He didn't know her well enough. He did know she made his brother happy. He did know Stella was so comfortable and he loved her. He did know he wanted Troy to make that next step, marriage. Troy engaged Hai. Stella and he happily supported this new love. Stella. Stella. The last they spoke she felt the same way as he. "Four people loving each other is greater than two loving and two wondering what happened," Stella had said while falling asleep in his arms.

Chapter 31

The sun blared on the wet road to Hai's office, but this didn't distract her. The blooming spring wild flowers didn't make her mind wonder, much. Hai's developing love life only made her want to drive more safely. The twins and Stella first pointed out her inattentive driving, and then instructed her on how to stay focused on the mundane but critical task of driving within the speed limits and on the road. Now aware, she'd avoid accidents, hopefully.

Today however, she could hardly slow down. This Monday morning, at the office, excited her like no other. She'd crow to Janine about her engagement. The others in the office needed to wait, because the whole affair might blow-up and some couldn't keep secrets.

Engagement ring hidden in her business suit pocket, Hai pushed through the glass door, picked up her pace, gave quick hellos and hand waves and nearly slammed her office door behind her. Janine was doing crunches on the floor.

"Hi Hai, I really have to lose my tummy." Janine looked perfectly fine and healthy.

"You're lovely the way you are. Life is beautiful."

"Life is beautiful, huh. What happened this weekend?"

Hai sipped coffee, waved and pointed at the seat next to her desk. She quickly slipped on the engagement ring and grinned like a watermelon slice.

"This happened." She held out her hand and wagged it back and forth to catch the light.

"Not Troy?"

"Yes, the one and only."

"You weren't listening to me. This is too soon. What did you do? What did he do to you?"

"Well it, ah…"

Mr. Furgensen stuck his nose in the door, "I'm very proud of you, Hai." The boss backed out the door. Silent, they waited for him to trek down the hallway. This place had to be bugged.

"Did you do it?" Janine did something nasty with her finger and cupped hand.

"Of course not."

"Was he drunk?"

"Well, he ah."

"So he was drunk. Girl-l-l-l. Hear me. Just because I told you to go after him, *last week,* I didn't mean… You've got to date first, to see if you're at least compatible." At least, Janine spared her 'the contract to marry could be nullified' argument—so first-year law school.

"Let me explain."

"This ought to be good. Don't spare any detail." Janine's eyes bulged.

Hai filled her in on every step taken, but neglected to mention her confusion and entanglements with Raphael. She finished with, "Troy has changed, just as you predicted. He's focused on family now. He, no we, also want to help keep Stella and Raphael together, and what better way than to travel through the coming months together. We're going to a take-no-prisoners retreat next month and intend to test this new love. Troy and I know it's too soon, but we're happy. We know our chances of the engagement falling apart are maybe fifty-fifty, but we're happy. Get it?"

"How do you know he loves you?"

"You know Janine, life is complicated. We both see this as an opportunity to grow, not as something that will tie us down. If the engagement fails, we'll still be friends, because we're an awesome foursome."

"Foursome? You don't know what life will serve up to your *foursome*, Troy might have to move to Los Angeles or New York and you two won't have Raphael and Stella nearby. Besides, those two are a crutch. Think about that."

"Maybe? We are taking this one, a baby step at a time. One thing I do know is, you are and always will be my best friend and if luck and hard work holds Troy and me together, I want you to be my maid of honor."

Janine squirmed in her seat. "I need to tell you, I went to the jail to get court papers signed and kind-of made a pass at him. I mean, he's so gorgeous. I just could not help myself. I'm so sorry."

"No worries. Last week he was a free man. I'm not the jealous type, anyway. You told me if I find my soul mate, he'd never cheat on me. I intend to find out if he is my one true love."

"You know, I didn't start out to do anything. I only wanted to see what he was like in person, so I could help you." The Chariote brothers made normal women crazy. She wasn't going to blame Janine for falling into their abyss.

"I know. Either way, it's okay." She didn't shout, *He's mine and you can't have him,* toss coffee at her pretty houndstooth dress and roll on the plush blue rug, pulling Janine's hair. Besides, her nosey boss would show up again and the too good to ruin carpet would be stained. A little decorum here would be highly recommended.

Hai neglected to tell Janine she had actually tried to seduce Raphael who was playing the part of Troy, who on her second visit was Troy as Troy, who later switched again to Raphael, etc, etc. Did she get the swapping right? Her head spun. Both men, bless their hearts, had resisted Janine. Did they resist her because she was too short for them, or a tad too heavy, or maybe not as pretty as Stella or *moi*? *Maybe Stella and I could hire some knockout actress to tempt them, and see what happens, or would that be too much for any man?*

Hai never went negative. Why start?

Chapter 32

Joe and Lisa Chariote had lobbied for dinner at their place in Medford Lakes, to grill, well meet Hai. Joe and Lisa were gentle souls, just different, like their boys. Stella felt loved unconditionally like a daughter.

They'd even supported her when she kicked Raphael out of his own home. Joe had thought this was hilarious. She remembered him saying he wanted Raphael to attend his funeral, not the other way around. It was all a far off haze now. So much had happened. Hai took Troy off the market, quite a coup. They destroyed Slater Bradley's work; made friends with a killer and his strange girlfriend. Stella had made love to Raphael, nothing strange there, except she had thought he was Troy. She got over it. The boys really were the same in so many ways. Stella now had a fantastic new best friend, Hai. End and beginning of the story.

Dinner at six, about an hour from now, and various tours of the home the boys grew up in, would fill the evening. A ton of trophies and memorabilia awaited their review. Hai would freak out when she saw what Joe had in his small den.

When walking by the downstairs closet under the oak steps, which led upstairs, Stella heard a 'pssst' sound. The door opened, a hand came out, grabbed her and pulled her in. She had to get to the kitchen to help Lisa as promised. She pulled against an irresistible force.

169

"You drive me crazy," he said. The door closed, pitch black, and she found herself in the clinch by either Troy or Raphael.

"Is this you, Raphael?" She patted his crotch.

"Of course it is. Kiss me you fool." He kissed her with urgent passion, as if starved. After patting him on his crotch, he showed how hungry he really was. She had fed him regularly.

Perhaps, Troy and Raphael swapped again, or Troy sneaked a swap, or maybe it was just good 'ole Raphael. She did not care. Kissing in the dark exploded within her like the fourth of July. Maybe for this once, she could pretend it was Troy, like eating Hai's chocolate.

She had to get out of this place. Her last closet interview was in sixth grade. At a party, kids took turns kissing, to see who could kiss the longest. The only timer stopping her was the one about to go off over the oven in the kitchen. She had to help. She loved to help Lisa. She had to help herself, too.

After a while of coat pushing, vacuum cleaner kicking, and full on two-way ass grabbing—oh my—she broke loose. She had been very polite in sixth-grade, only kissed a boy's cheek, facial of course.

"Later, honey," she said, flustered. "I have to help your mom in the kitchen."

All she could hear was his heavy breathing for a while. He released her.

"We have to do this more often," she said. She tiptoed up for a kiss, missed his mouth but caught a salty tear. Interesting, very interesting.

She put on her impish face with no one to see. "You know me as dessert will spoil your dinner."

"Closet sex." He said in a gurgly whisper. Silly boy.

"Closet sex, whoa baby," she whispered back while squeezing his ass again. "Later—in your closet—on the rug. Take me."

"Closet sex." He pinched her rear. Oh how she loved that, and spankings too. Maybe she deserved one today.

Never a dull moment with closet man lurking, his identity never to be known. Maybe undercover work would solve this mystery. She didn't want to know. The boys shared almost everything, so she'd still not know for sure. Walking into or by a closet would never be the same again.

Stella peeked out the door, slipped out, composed her hair at the hallway mirror, reapplied make up and headed for the kitchen. She thought she heard a low and gravelly voice say, "closet sex." After the four married, she'd insist on glow in the dark tattoos for both boys.

* * *

Troy removed a panel from inside the closet, stepped into the garage and replaced the secret door he and his brother had made years ago. They had both made love to Patricia Sweetwater, who had a thing for closets, something she had said started at a sixth-grade party at the kissing level. They'd sold their dad on the extra door, with a lame excuse; it would give them an escape in case of an armed robbery, which never happened out in the woods of Medford. Dad loved the idea and invested in a seamless door and soundproofing and a few extra baseball bats strategically hidden in closet and garage. The soundproofing was a windfall with the way Patricia carried on.

Troy reflected on the wonder of Stella's lips. He had decided he had to taste her before it was too late, before the wedding.

He had arm-twisted Raphael to get these kisses and only paid the price of one tear. He was happy for his brother, and that happiness completed him, as a man, as a brother. He loved no one better, embarrassing as it sounded. Come on, they were silly putty separated from the can.

He played over their conversation.

"You owe me one... You kissed Hai," Troy had said.

"I thought you owed me two."

"Who's counting?"

"I don't think it would be right, we're both engaged now."

Raphael had a point there. He was also getting more conservative with age. He was either ahead or behind Troy, depending on viewpoint.

"It will be the last time we'll swap. You can have one more go at Hai."

"Listen to you." Raphael shook his head no.

"Alright, I'll go it alone."

"I didn't say yes."

"I'll tell her I'm you. I'll finally exorcise her from my fantasy life, and then I'll be able to focus on Hai." Stella wasn't the devil, so exorcism would not be necessary. Troy would treasure her kisses, and ribald moxie.

"Do you love Hai?" Raphael asked.

"Yes."

"Then you're a scoundrel." Surprise.

"Wait a minute. You too have feelings for Hai. In fact, you know we're all a little haywired."

"Yeah."

"So don't blame me. This is good for us and the last time," Troy said.

"Don't let your lips head south."

Troy wished Raphael hadn't said that. Now, he'd have to avoid his own wicked imagination, which played like a broken record, 'what's so different, so special about down there on Stella?' How tasty were Northern Italian dishes? How rich a presentation?

"And this is our last swap forever," Raphael added.

"Forever." Troy couldn't think of any excuse to swap one more time, to do what he knew would earn him a beating if he mentioned the subject of velvet thrones or any kind of sex. Besides, Hai was off limits, period.

Swapping with abandon had worked in high school, but...

He doubted this would be the last time, he had a feeling there'd be a need, perhaps on a separate issue, but why confuse his brother, with speculation at this point. He truly would honor Raphael's specific wish. One kissing session and then off to marriage. They'd all march happily ever after. All would have known all, in a sexy personal way, and put it behind them if Troy had his way. Likely, he had planted doubt in Stella's sharp mind, which would after she thought it through, produce closure in her mind too. Okay, maybe his thinking was a little convoluted.

In hindsight, Troy should have known better. Her lusty kisses seared his brain, not that Hai's weren't wonderful and sweet. He'd get over it, for the love of his brother, if nothing else. Hai would make a fantastic wife and mother and nothing beats the fabulous four traveling life together. If only he, the weak link, could keep his mind focused on one simple concept, two plus two equals four.

* * *

The Chariotes kept their home impeccably. Hai didn't know for sure whether Joe or Lisa was responsible. They both claimed credit for the neatness on the tour. They'd discuss in married-couple half-words with secret meanings. Were friendly, full of laughter, as if psychically poking each other in good fun. They made a handsome couple. Joe was almost winning the battle of his small paunch and Lisa couldn't be prettier. The boys got their curly thick black hair from her and their athletic bodies from their father. Joe's solid brown hair and rugged face mixed well with Lisa and her dimpled chin to make the twins incredibly desirable.

Dinner for six was served on china designed with a wisp of translucent carnations circling the plates, making a pretty picture. The dining room had cherry wood wainscoting matching the table. Joe had crafted the table in his spare time. He banked a lot of extra time from his football-coaching job at Gloucester State to work on hobby and home. Hai enjoyed the boys' parents very much and so would her family when the time came.

"So Hai, what is it you see in our two devils?"

"Mom," Raphael said.

"I should tell you all the things they did, while growing up."

"I'd love to hear your stories, Mrs. Chariote."

"I'll join you, Hai, just to refresh my memory. Besides, it can be pretty scary," Stella said.

"So Hai, I hear you were on the gymnastics team. I was on my gymnastics team in high school and college," Joe said.

"I was too tall to be very good, but I loved the sport and team. What did you do on the team?" Hai asked. Joe looked too big for anything other than weight lifting.

"I somehow managed the rings, bars, horse and floor exercises."

"He was impressive," Lisa said.

"Still am."

"All the time."

"Mr. Chariote, do you think Raphael or Troy was the better football player?" Stella asked.

"Well, Raphael will be the first to tell you that the quarterback is the most important player on any football team and his brother played the position better than anybody. But I bet they never told you about the quarterfinals senior year, state championship."

"I don't know, Dad," Troy said. "They might rip us out of the record books, and take our medals and trophies."

"Hai and Stella will never say a word, because they love you. So keep loving them and you won't get in trouble," Joe said. He went on to tell how Troy injured his throwing arm and swapped with Raphael who threw a record breaking five touchdown passes. Troy ran for one hundred and fifty-six yards on the ground, and caught two of the touchdown passes for another sixty-two yards. Medford High honored both boys as outstanding athlete of the year, awarding for the first time, co-champion dual trophies.

"I could tell I freaked you out with my insects, Hai."

In little more than a closet, Joe had hung floor to ceiling mahogany and glass cases with rare insects displayed within. At least to Hai, they were unusual looking. Some had horns a couple inches long. Some resembled tanks. All were intriguing. She had felt sad though at their unfortunate plight.

"No, I only wish they were alive."

"Me, too. I'm hoping their odd beauty will cultivate a lessening of fear and more respect for these exotic species. You wouldn't believe all the converts I get on bridge night."

"After a while, people came to parties, loaded with bug trivia," Lisa said. "Say they bought a rare one for their wall or the like."

"I've always wanted to know, since tarantulas bite, why they don't bite their human owners?" Hai asked.

"Well, I don't know directly, but it has a little bit to do with survival and food source, a little with familiarity. Any arachnid is no match for a hard swat."

"How do you feel about Troy?" Lisa asked.

"He doesn't bite," Hai answered.

"A hard swat will keep him in line," Lisa said.

"Raphael bites." Stella said.

"I could bite," Troy said.

After dinner and a fine cherry pie with decaf coffee, Lisa asked the girls to come with her up to Troy's old room. Hai expected trophies, but they were all down in the basement where the family would gather to watch the Eagles play or conduct small make-out parties, back when.

"Come over here, both of you," Lisa said, standing before the closet. The girls left gazing at the kick-knacks on the chest of drawers and complied.

Lisa opened the door and flicked on the light to Troy's walk-in closet. Most of the clothes were gone, which left abandoned posters visible.

"You see Hai?" There before both girls were sports, movie posters and one playboy centerfold. Hai was drawn to Kristi Yamaguchi spinning on ice. The movie or TV posters included classic films and newer releases, from Nancy Kwan in *The World of Susie Wong,* the more recent *Charlie's Angels* starring Lucy Liu posed with her Caucasian costars Diaz and Barrymore, and Grace Park of *Hawaii Five-O* and *Battlestar Galactica* fame. The playboy centerfold of an anatomically perfect Asian, probably Thai, had a bikini painted on her. The centerfold's favorite things included hayrides and espresso machines. On it went, a nearly all-Asian review of lovely ladies. The boy had extremely good taste.

"What do you see, Hai, aside from girls almost as pretty as you?" Lisa asked.

"He's got a thing for Cameron Diaz or Drew Barrymore?" That produced giggles and guffaws. Good, she too could make a funny.

"Troy went through a phase in college," Stella said.

"He's more balanced now, but I can see one reason my boy loves you."

"Mrs. Chariote?"

"Please call me Lisa. No better yet, let's try on Mom." Lisa's face flushed red with pride.

"Mom, when I was in college, I had a poster of a shirtless model on my bathroom door," Hai said.

175

Stella crinkled her eyes and broke into a smile. Perhaps Hai had said too much, since she was turning guilt red.

"Did he look anything like my boy?"

"Well, he was Caucasian, but your boys are better looking than any model I've ever seen. Oh, and that poster was my roommate's doing."

"Oh sure," Stella said. The three girls in a jovial mood hugged and headed back downstairs.

* * *

Hai left the girls to catch one more glimpse at the bug room before they left. Perhaps Joe was right. By preserving these creatures, he had called attention to the diversity of planet Earth. She wanted to find some creature in that room to help her focus on the issue.

When she passed the hallway closet, she heard a 'pssst' sound, something similar to a bug. Hai froze, wondering if Joe kept live bugs as well, and one broke loose. The closet door opened, a hand came out, grabbed her and pulled her in.

"How'd you like my posters?" The door closed, pitch black now, and she found herself in Troy's embrace with the top of the vacuum cleaner making advances on her butt. Her fear disappeared and she surrendered to the nasty boy.

"Kiss me, darling," Troy said. She could kiss until someone wanted the vacuum cleaner or a coat. They smooched like two kids hiding from their parents. Perhaps, Troy hadn't had enough dessert tonight, although she fed him kisses regularly.

It was getting a tad hot in the closet. She felt like tearing off all his clothes. No. She'd wait for the honeymoon. His kisses were different, more tender tonight. He cupped her face…just as Raphael did in jail. So was closet cuddler really Raphael or had Troy stumbled on a new style? Or had Raphael shared his technique with Troy? She didn't know. She was too dizzy being loved to figure it out, to want to figure it out. He ravished her.

If it was Raphael, then why? She fell against the back wall pulling a wool coat off its hanger. Troy didn't stop to pick it up. He pressed his body urgently against hers. She didn't know how she could wait for the honeymoon. Somehow, she had to. She stepped into what must have been an empty shoebox, which stuck to her shoe, but she didn't care. It made her giggle through kissed lips. Then she steadied herself by grabbing what felt like a broom, which slipped to the floor. Bang. She shot upright by grabbing Troy's something. Whoops, his bottom. Oh good. She had lusted after a squeeze of this hard-assed man, the moment she figured out women relished ass-squeezing. She enjoyed, no loved it very much. Breathless.

"Excuse me," she cried.

"No problem," he whispered.

Tongue, now there's tongue. She really didn't know what to do with this invasion, but she liked this too. With a little coaching of unused muscles, she tangled her tongue with his. This seemed right. What a time for a lesson.

"I'm hot, so hot," she whispered.

"We'll wait, my darling."

"Yes, we have to. My ancestors would haunt me."

"I love you."

"I love you, too."

Eventually, she shooed herself out of the closet and hurried into the bug room before she lost her mind.

The oddest bug, a walking stick, *Phamacia Serratipes*, according to Joe's engraved plaque, became her empathy experiment, but it was hard getting her mind off closet cuddler and those wonderful kisses, and that ass. She felt so wet, wondered if it showed. Wearing black slacks helped. Anyway, the walking stick highlighted all of nature's interwoven themes, like legs hoisted high and feet caressing Troy's face. *Theoretical, of course.* Alright, she had peeked at a sex book, correction, the witness isn't being forthright—had bought a book on sexual positions.

Oh my God, no wonder the girls at the office were all so crazy.

* * *

Raphael picked up the wool coat and the broom, and straightened the rack. He exited into the garage through the trick backdoor of the closet. In the light now, he wiped a tear away from his eye. He was fond of Hai, too fond, but he'd never get in the way of his brother's happiness, and he did care deeply for Stella.

"I thought you said you weren't going to reciprocate." Troy said, surprising Raphael by stepping from behind Mom and Dad's Lexus SUV. All the noise, the broom, the shoebox, the coat and the pushing of hangers, must have given them away.

"Well, here's another nice mess you've got me into." He tried levity and their favorite line, but Troy looked not at all amused. He stared. Raphael tried, "I know. I thought you'd feel guilty if today was one-sided."

"Did you enjoy it?"

"Did you?"

"Of course."

"Of course." Apparently, Troy didn't want to find out how much he enjoyed it. Her kiss was like heaven. Hai's were sensual. Stella's were hot and sexy. *Hard to choose all other things being equal.*

"Was that a tear you wiped away? A tear?" Troy said with animation and a little bad acting.

"Nope," he gulped.

"Don't lie to me." Troy pointed a finger from a straight arm. Neither of them could lie to the other, but Raphael would have to try.

"I must have been caught up in the emotion of your Hai. And, she is your Hai. I didn't complain about you kissing Stella."

"Why not? Don't you love her?"

"Of course I do. Come on brother, let's admit it," Raphael said.

"Admit what?" Troy leaned against the Lexus.

"Admit that you care about Stella in the same way I care about Hai, and now that we've satisfied our curiosity it's time to move on," Raphael said it and he meant it, he hoped. Or, at least, he convinced himself that he meant it.

"Alright, the most important thing to remember is that we love each other."

"Forever."

"Forever, of course." They hugged. All was forgiven. No knock-down drag-out this time. Good, because there were way too many things in the garage to become impaled upon.

Nothing would ever shake their faith in each other now, right?

We are so done switching, bro.

Double Happiness by RW Richard

Nevermore, quoth the raven-haired boys.

Chapter 33

Troy drove the loves of his life into the countryside about seven miles north of McGuire Air Force Base, New Jersey, to a Catholic engagement encounter. He loved his brother as if himself, and through so many of life's little travels, they were one. He loved the fantastically beautiful, alluring and talented Hai, for putting up with him as a fiancée. He loved Stella, because she loved his brother. Yes, and oh well, he still crushed on her. Ironic, considering, she cultivated her crush on him and to a lesser degree his brother, when she was unripe fruit at Medford High School.

This weekend would give them all a chance to make sure they were on the right path, to make sure they'd have two successful marriages. Marriage for Troy and his brother was a life commitment, period. They'd make every moment count, and work every day to keep their women happy and their children levelheaded and precocious, of course.

The pre-marriage retreat turned out to be a getaway from the world. Nestled amidst slight rolling hills, far away from any big city, lay an estate bequeathed to the Church, with a going apple orchard. The apples called George Cave were pale green-yellow with a red flush if ripe and being big seemed ready for the picking.

Each engagement encounter participant had a cookie cutter, spar, but clean room with a full bath and windows focused on the orchard.

"No cell phones, no TV, just the truth," read the banner over the entrance to the estate. They might have added no sleepovers.

Outside the front entrance at a welcoming table, the monks issued all the couples' nameplates. This mid-morning on a crisp late July day, eighteen couples and eight Franciscan Monks trekked out to the orchard for some picking and a casual meet and greet. Everybody except the monks wore long jeans of various colors. The monks sported simple black frocks with white waist chords, probably wearing blue or rather black jeans underneath.

"I can't reach it," Hai said.

"But there are plenty of trees here that have reachable fruit," Troy said. Most of the trees had lower branches that would bop anyone preoccupied with watching the other fruit in the garden—the opposite sex.

"But look at that apple. It's perfect." The apple was huge and if they waited under it any longer, they'd be clunked on the head.

Troy bent over and Hai scampered up his back and saddled his neck, but that didn't quite do it. He started to walk to some lower branches.

"Whoa, horsey. I want that apple, in this tree."

"Yes, ma'am."

"Besides, I love tall challenges."

"Are you a tall challenge, Mr. Troy?" Brother Angelo asked, while squinting at Troy's breast pocket nameplate. Monks and priests, and any other holy person, were first and forever—philosophers. Since this was a retreat, they were *forever* on the point of why the couples came here. Troy knew himself to be a reformed tall challenge.

"Maybe so, Brother Angelo."

"He's worth it."

"Lift me too," Stella said, who was then hoisted by Raphael, but they weren't close enough to Hai's favorite apple. Hai and Stella feigned chicken fighting, locking arms, for a little fun. Stella broke-off in search for easier pickins' in apples and probably opponents. All this drew some of the other couples closer.

"Only pick the ones that want to be picked or the healthy ones that have fallen already," Brother Angelo said, seeming a bit exasperated. He went on to explain that the couples shouldn't pull too hard on an attached apple. If the apple was ready, and loved you, it would easily come off the tree by giving it a small tug.

"Which one of you ladies is Eve?" Troy asked, trying to start a riot. Banter and hilarity were his game, and they bit, as usual.

"Steady yourself, sweetheart," Hai said. She deftly used Troy's thick curly black hair and head as balance and came to a standing position. Just a feather on his developed shoulders.

"Don't try this unless you were once upon a time trained," Hai said. She had gymnastics and of course ice skating in her past. She was as much a jock as the twins were. Nobody else tried standing, but a couple of chicken fights were going on under two of the nearest trees.

Raphael steadied Hai's ankles.

"I'm okay, thank you."

"Don't touch her ankles," Troy said. It was obvious Raphael had not gotten over her.

"She's okay," said Stella.

"Listen, brother of mine. Remember the time you caught Stella when she fell from the rafters?" Raphael asked.

"Alright, okay," Troy answered.

"No, it's not okay. I'm only worried about Hai's safety." Troy doubted his brother, but then why should his brother be any different from himself. Troy vowed to use this retreat to dig deeper into his own psyche.

She looped a sturdy branch with her arms and lifted herself up onto the tree to about twelve feet off the ground. The birds shot out of the tree in all directions, no doubt insulted by the big bird, but unlike in a yellow Big Bird, Hai adorned in skin-tight black jeans and a red and white-checked cotton shirt.

"I'm your Eve, and you'll have to come up here if you want a kiss or this fine apple," Hai said, giving her best impression of a temptress without portfolio or snake.

Some of the other couples pointed and asked Hai to pick this one or that one. They made a game of catch out of it. Troy loved the camaraderie, his meat. His livelihood depended on it. He'd never miss a chance to practice at making people feel happier.

Troy glanced over at Brother Angelo, who smiled back.

"Is it okay, this climbing?" Everybody else except the apple catchers were picking from easy trees. Easy trees were like prostitutes, giving freely and often.

Surely, the little girl in Hai refused to grow-up. She exuded happiness with every come-hither laugh. He'd have to find a way up to her, if he wanted to sin.

"Well, if anybody here falls and breaks their necks, please don't hesitate to sue the Creator of this tree, of this fruit, of all of us, but leave the monastery out of it." The monk was also a comedian. Troy thought about the similarities between the priesthood and stand-up comedians, and vowed to develop a sketch someday. Regarding the obvious, all the couples signed release of liability papers at the front desk check-in, *but could you sue them if you left without your sweetheart, or you took somebody else's gal?*

The riper apples tasted sweet, tart and juicy. The summer wildflowers, nearby honeysuckle, and the smell of the orchard, including rotting, fallen apples gave an exhilarating feeling, as if Saint Peter had opened the gates. The sun streamed through the branches, his cell phone app read seventy-three degrees. The breeze wafted through the orchard gently swaying the trees and their guests. Troy wondered how Raphael felt about this place. He'd be in rapture, most likely.

Hai's apple throwing to the others, now over, she stretched out on the branch like a jaguar wanting a nap. Her glistening long raven hair fell in a beguiling pose, with favorite apple in hand, all dangling down amidst the smaller branches and leaves. Striking sensuality.

Troy wondered how much longer he could hold off seducing her, taking her completely, ravaging her, maybe in this tree. He'd climb up to purchase a kiss for the price of her tease and one apple. She smiled and kissed the apple, widening her mouth. For a girl with little to no experience, she knew how to get a guy's attention. At first, he tried jumping to grab the apple. He had played basketball and could jump to ten feet for a dunk, but she swooped her hand up out of his reach. He'd climb. He loved tomboys, this tomboy. He loved the whole idea of his girl treed and waiting for a kiss.

Raphael and Stella were comparing fallen apples to the ones they picked off the trees and gossiped with two of the monks about the ripeness and the subject of true love. Stella had a calico shirt tucked into her body-tight jeans, just perfect for a morning's jaunt in the Garden of Eden. My God, were her apples huge.

"We believe in organic farming. The apples are ready to eat, but you might want to rub the dust off before you eat," Brother Angelo said.

"Give me a boost, buddy," Troy said, to the nearest strong looking guy.

"Name's Jonathan and this is Suzie. We're from Brooklyn." He looked like a dockworker.

"Troy and Hai, Cherry Hill, New Jersey." They shook hands. Jonathan cupped his hands. Troy purchased the hold and grabbed the lowest branch. "And over there is my identical twin Raphael with Stella, also Cherry Hill."

After a few pecks in the tree between the lovers, which raised the temperature of the orchard, the crowd started back for lunch of a different sort, carrying their apple stashes.

"See you two later," Raphael said, barely hiding his amusement. As Raphael and Stella waved bye-bye, perhaps he and Hai were stuck up here, and everybody else seemed to anticipate their pending predicament.

"Wait, catch the bag," Hai said, hanging upside down, swinging by her knees. Raphael ran back and caught the bag full of apples as if he had just won an egg toss contest. The toss wasn't more than two feet. "You can leave them on the orchard floor. We can get down easily; your brother just doesn't know it yet."

"Okay." Stella and Raphael waved and skipped off arm-in-arm, singing about Johnny Appleseed, bagged apples slung over their backs, like a scene from Tom Sawyer. "See you later, much later."

"Don't eat all the bread," Troy said. The smell of fresh baked bread had had everybody's stomach growling earlier.

Troy cupped Hai's face. "We're alone now, up an apple tree, with nothing but kissin' to do, my Asian beauty."

"Don't climb into the apple tree with anybody else but me, anybody else but me."

"Oh I'll climb into the apple tree with nobody else but you, nobody else but you...I love that song. My grandma and grandpa danced to it. But don't try out for American Idol, kid." Hai's singing voice sounded something like a monkey in a peanut grinder. Hai let her body slowly slip down, easily holding onto the branch with both arms extended.

"If you add my arms to my height, it's at most a four-foot drop. Plus all that moss, the flowers, and forest-cover, makes dropping out of an apple tree, a piece of cake."

"If the apples can do it, why not us?"

With that, she fell to the orchard's floor and raised her arms into a gymnast's 'I've stuck the landing' pose. Troy followed, but faltered and landed on his can, more weight, less practice.

"Need your booboo kissed?" Tempting, very tempting, but there'd be no gossamer moon out today.

They ran to the monastery hungry, happy and free and with no booboos.

Chapter 34

Troy's stomach did back flips in anticipation of the rolls. Lunch was served in a long skinny hall. Its ceiling was two stories high with plenty of natural light streaming through endless abutting windows on both sides of the long narrow peak. They sat at a pine table at least sixty feet long. Troy and Hai's seats had been saved. They sat across from the couple from Brooklyn, and next to Stella and Raphael. The monks attended, first serving some fragrant fresh-cooked sourdough rolls. The crowd was loud, and happy, but everybody was on the same Titanic with only so many lifeboats. Catching up, Troy and Hai dug into lima bean soup and choice aplenty of sandwiches: crab cake, veggie or ham with cheddar.

"So how do you two tell each other apart?" Jonathan, from Brooklyn said with mouth full.

"Every morning I call Raphael to check if I'm still me."

"He means, you two get people confused," Suzie, Jonathan's partner in crime said, while wiping off her face and a silly grin with a napkin.

"I think we've confused our fiancées."

"I think you two are perpetually confused," Stella said.

"They love us. I'm just not sure who loves whom more," Hai said.

"Personally, I love my brother most of all," Raphael said, pursing his lips, and squeezing his thumb and finger.

"Same here, bro." Troy said, while stuffing an entire roll and displaying a big grin.

"They've always been like this," Stella said turning to Hai. "This is very true of identical twins. Sometimes when one dies, the other one kicks the bucket shortly thereafter."

"Here's to the thereafter…with you, bro," Troy raised his Merlot and sipped through the dough. Yum.

A strolling monk stopped. "Don't worry about love. Love is infinite. You can't run out of the stuff unless you stop working the presses."

"Is it possible to love two women?" Troy asked.

"Ask my mom and sister," The brother, of quick wit, answered.

"But…"

"If you have to ask that question, you are not ready for marriage." The monk raised his voice. "Who here hasn't looked, even for a moment, at an attractive new acquaintance in this room?"

The monk started a firestorm.

"When you understand the difference between love and devotion to your partner and lust, let me know."

"I don't look at anybody but my fiancé, Brother," a young lady across the room said.

"Stand up, Raphael Chariote, please. What do you see, Patricia. Is he handsome?"

Patricia turned red.

"You cannot deny the way the Lord made you, Patricia. God gave us all a driving, almost insatiable need to survive by mating. Your jobs today, and for always is to transcend survival and become love."

* * *

Hai was very impressed with the monks. It wasn't long ago she had fixed what was obviously wrong with her life: no life except the law. Oddly enough, well not so oddly, her practice flourished now more than ever. Mr. Furgensen had broached the subject of becoming a partner soon…but the only important change came to her heart.

"I understand, you, Miss Hai Lo, have won the intercollegiate ice, figure-skating championship and made the U.S. Olympic team. You worked hard to bring out your best. Marriage is no different with the

187

award coming in the form of love. Which is more important, a sports title or a loving husband?" Brother Angelo asked.

"Life is meant to be lived. I played and worked hard and by doing so honored my parents and family with my talents. I promise to love with my whole heart."

"Well put, young lady. For those of you who are Catholic, you have undoubtedly heard from the pulpit on numerous occasions about using the talents God gave you to the best of your ability. Loving thy neighbor as yourself, means growing, being productive, so one may share. Love is doing. Love is action. Sorry if that doesn't sound romantic."

"But it is, Brother Angelo," Troy said.

"Well enough talking for now. Anybody here, fancy some monastery-made tart apple and tart cherry pies? One per customer." Everybody smiled. Hai couldn't eat a whole pie, but she could down the whole idea. She felt at home with the Catholic way of looking at things. She understood the delicate balance between the needs of a group and an individual, or in this case, couples. What was true for the awesome foursome, also applied to the law. Attorneys for defense and prosecution ensured a trial where the truth and individual rights remained in balance.

* * *

Stella couldn't be happier with the way Troy, Hai, and Raphael were enjoying Catholic philosophy and theology. Later that evening, as had been promised for tonight or Sunday night, Father Brian stopped by to corral anyone interested in a good conversation by one of four huge open hearths. A little red wine, Christian Brothers' varieties, Vermont cheddar cheese and crackers were laid out on pine coffee tables. A little later only his two couples remained at their chosen hearth.

"Now that I have the four of you alone, I want to ask if after all the monks put you through today, are we still on for the double wedding?"

"They were wonderful, Father," Stella said.

"I feel like converting," Hai added. Stella's new best friend warmed her heart.

"We too." Raphael said.

Troy added, "Yes Father, we're ready. Raphael and I must have some Catholic blood, because once we marry, we marry for life or until one of them kills us."

"I think that's death do us part, not part the head until dead," Father Brian said. The joke didn't quite work, but Stella laughed. She had laughed at mostly anything Father Brian came up with.

"Yep, the saying doesn't include a catalogue of the means of death," Father added.

"I hope never to drive my wife crazy enough to kill me, because surely she's an angel." Troy leaned toward Hai and gave her a peck.

"I know of you, Troy. Besides, both of you boys being great football players, I've been to the Comic Freak when you were on stage. You can't possibly get my goat."

"Sometimes I'm a little blue, Father."

"No worries, the kids say. I'm hip, my father was fond of saying. I'll tell you four what's bothering me… It is well known you boys have a history with most of the young ladies in High School and for a while at Villanova University. If half the stories are true, you'd think the end of the world was coming."

"Go ahead, Father," Stella said, hoping he didn't go on a tirade about her obsession.

"You two are so close to each other, and look so much alike, I'm afraid there might be some shenanigans. I want to know, you both will honor not only your wives to be, but make to me a pledge."

"Raphael, I'm the worse one, let me speak to this," bad boy Troy said.

"Amen, brother."

"Father, it took me a little longer to grow up than Raphael, because he fell in love with Stella in college. I admit that we had to resort to swapping places in our adult years a couple times…"

Raphael cupped his mouth. Troy staggered a tad at his brother's lack of faith, it seemed.

Stella recalled with elation the many times Raphael drove home from University to sit in the football stands with her on cool autumn Saturday mornings. Her entire high school senior class had envied her, and anybody else who knew of the gorgeous legend sitting with her holding her hand. Finally, she had become pretty enough, smart enough for a Chariote brother to notice and love her. Something the boys had never done before, love, that is.

The hell with Troy, she had thought. Raphael was perfect. Some of the jealous ones said, although she doubted they thought it, she was shallow in picking a football jock. She wasn't about to deny the way God made her. Besides, the boys were not only beautiful and talented, Raphael had an empathetic heart and it seemed now, Troy had one as well. Her classmates were so wrong.

"…We switched a couple times, to fix problems with my false arrest and imprisonment. We believe in soul mates and we've found ours."

Father Brian frowned. "And what do you mean by soul mates?" Apparently, Father was not interested in their jail swap.

"I know mysticism is frowned upon, Father," Stella said, "but sometimes you just know."

"I hate to tell you this, kids—nobody is perfectly matched. Science will tell you that. Only through eternal love and embracing its concept, can you hope to work at happiness in this imperfect world."

They mulled over the meaning of life for a while. Their conversation made sparks fly like flipping logs in the hearth. Stella's heart was strong. She knew the unspoken and unresolved question. Is it better to serve the needs of the many and gain happiness by a circuitous route, or be selfish and possibly ruin four lives? She focused on Raphael's face, glimmering by fireside, and knew he'd make her happy, give her babies and be a great father.

Father Brian seemed tuned in to Stella's thoughts. "I can see you all have stars in your eyes. Youth is a wonderful thing. I see trials ahead for you all. I want to leave you with a question to ponder. Is it better to serve others or serve yourself? Be aware, I may have offered you a false choice. Come to the altar with the answer to this question in each of your hearts and I'll not doubt you'll be happy and have blessed marriages and, of course, my blessing."

Still, Stella's heart ached. The four of them had traveled an intricate path for months now. All four psyches were more and more repressing libidinous desires. Beyond sexual attraction, all four might have sublimated their natural preferences for a mate in order to honor the group dynamic. The wedding in Chinatown had been a good start as were their attempts afterward. But they drifted now, getting ever closer to the waterfall of a double wedding.

The fab four needed one or more cathartic sessions where they spoke honestly of their feelings.

What is right and what is wrong here, Father Brian?

Chapter 35

Hai felt comfortable in the low-lit Comic Freak, munching Snyder's Sourdough pretzel nuggets, sipping ginger ale, waiting for the little surprise Raphael and Troy had planned. Although Stella and Hai both extracted under pain of death a promise from the boys never to swap again, both girls felt tonight's surprise would be harmless enough. Troy had laid out the plan, and it seemed very funny. Hai was no stick in the mud, but she had never been to a comedy club before.

The Comic Freak filled, great for a Tuesday night. Candle flickers highlighted the intimate black and white room. However, intimacy was an illusion. The girls would have to share their talented men with the world, tonight.

The MC stepped from behind a maroon curtain. After warming up the crowd with silly jokes about the Philadelphia water supply and why everybody had to order drinks, he introduced Troy.

"Please welcome the man Jay Leno refused to let on his show, the man everybody refused to let on their show, the man every mother and father hid their daughters from, our very own Troy Chariote."

Raphael masquerading as Troy trotted out in Troy's signature black cargo pants, and tight black T-shirt. Hai couldn't help knot up and worry for Raphael. She had three inseparable best friends now. One, of course being her fiancé, Troy. She had to keep getting that right. She had never been happier in her life. As a woman, she felt fulfilled, and soon her virginity would go by the wayside. Troy was such a gentleman.

The audience went wild, especially the women. Yep, there was his raw magnetism. Weren't comics supposed to look, well not so gorgeous?

"How 'bout those Phillies." A lame start but what did she know? More cheers.

"They should trade Jones for a chimp with long arms after last night's boner."

"You suck." A voice from the back of the room interrupted. It was Troy, playing Raphael. Troy, in the dark, squeezed Hai's hand and patted Stella's shoulder.

"Thank God somebody finally after all these years has heckled me. The problem is I've forgotten what to do." The crowd laughed.

"You suck."

"Okay, Joe, can you get a spotlight on that guy. You there, think you can do better, come on up here and try."

"You suck."

"Do you know more than two words?"

"You suck."

"This ought to be easy folks, let's encourage him." The crowd egged the heckler to the front. Troy had a strip-away outfit under which he wore the same clothes as Raphael. He also had pulled his Phillies cap down low, and sported their favorite fake mustache.

Troy ripped the mike from his brother's hand. "Is there an officer in the house? Somebody should arrest this man, my identical twin brother, for thinking he can imitate me."

Deputy Bronkowski walked up and cuffed Raphael.

"Nobody does Phillies' jokes, especially about Jones… *He really does suck.*" Troy stripped off his fake tux and even the more inebriated patrons understood the switch.

"I've had trouble with my brother ever since he kicked me on the way out the womb. Please give my identical twin brother a hand, *out of here.*" But he'd stay. "Did you like our little routine? Would you like us to repeat it sometime?"

The crowd shouted yes. They were getting into it. Warming them up, Troy had said. Brilliant Troy had pulled it off, with the help of his brother. Raphael stood up at their table and bowed to his brother giving

193

him the swirling hand of a thousand kudos, Johnny Carson's signature move, Troy had explained. The spotlight jumped back to the stage and Hai relaxed. Raphael planted a kiss on Stella, which caused Hai to scratch her nose. She'd get over it.

"He kicked, I punched back, but somehow we got out of the womb without the bell sounding."

Chuckles.

"Now he leaves me confused. Sometimes I think I'm him and he's me."

Hoots.

"We went to a Catholic Retreat for engaged couples." The spotlight fell on Stella, Hai and Raphael.

"There's my lovely fiancées. Okay, I said fiancées, on account that the retreat confused us. Hai is the gorgeous Chinese woman who could have taught Kristi Yamaguchi how to do it right…and don't mess with her in a court of law. And Stella the Italian with daggers. What?" He pointed at her while looking at the Greco gang.

"Stella has just gotten her doctorate in psychology. She studies identical twins." Applause.

"Convenient.

"Stella stalked both of us in high school. Only because she was confused which one she wanted…and still is." The women gasped, the men laughed.

"You know what a retreat is, right?"

"That's where you retreat back in time to the Spanish inquisition. Why do you love her? What is love? Do you covet your neighbor's fiancée? *Not today.*" He said conspiratorially. Then he held up his hands.

"I had an urge to leave the great hall and long wooden table with its loaves and fish and wine, leave the questions and lame answers…

"Priests are sworn to chastity and at a retreat you'd need a passport, stamped by the Pope himself if you wanted to sleep over with your fiancée. It's not a retreat. It's no treat.

"First of all, I want you to know, only Stella is Catholic. That will tell you something about this strong Dego." The crowd rumbled. "What? Goomba. WOP. What?" He panned the Mafioso in the front row and showed them to the rest of the crowd, with an arm sweep.

194

"However, we might convert to Italianism."

The crowd guffawed. He gestured again to the Greco family and their friends. He bent down in front of Romeo Greco, Don of Dons, and said to his face. "Mackerel snappers. Madonna." Troy bit his hand, giving an Italian salute. Romeo and his bodyguards rose, as planned, thank God, and put their hands on the outside of the suits at chest level. This could have been scary, if FBI lurked in the crowd. A clean-shaven man sitting with another, both in cheap business suits, late twenties, seemed unduly nervous.

Romeo reached into his breast pocket, pulled out an expanding bouquet of flowers, handed to Troy, and then issued an Italian salute of his own. He bowed and the Mafioso all sat at once like synchronized soldiers.

"My brother, for those who don't know, is an acclaimed artist. Recently he won the paint by numbers contest at McDonalds."

The crowd was his.

"Back at the retreat. We learned to strip away all our feelings and build a truer love. A love based on mutual respect and working hard at it every day."

Ahhs.

"That ought to buy us six-months of wedded bliss...

"Hai, how are you feeling, darling?"

"Okay." she shouted.

"You love me?"

"I'm thinking, I'm thinking."

"Jack Benny said that." He looked at Romeo.

"I've got a question for all the men here. You don't have to answer out loud. Has anybody here, while engaged, looked at another woman and fantasized?

"Believe it or not, the priests tell you, this is normal for men and women. It's the way God made us. So if you are a nun and married to Christ who do you look at?"

The crowd liked this one as it started many side conversations.

Troy patted the air before him to shush everybody. "I'm not saying I'm coveting any of you beautiful ladies, especially not Jersey over here, with the too short squirt...skirt."

Jersey stood up and pushed down her skirt. "We're all fray-nds and I'm a Catholic, already," she said.

The crowd exploded, probably over her accent and discomfort at trying to hide very long legs and a panty line.

"I have a confession. Hai, Stella, Raphael and me, we might be confused, the retreat might have left us worse off but we love each other like soul mates. I think soul mates don't fantasize about others outside their soul community, unlike most couples… The trouble is we haven't figured out who's whose soul mate.

"Thank you, folks.

"How 'bout those Phillies?"

Hai hadn't realized Troy would dig in this deep, but she was glad he did. She loved him and his brother. This identical twin madness had overwhelmed her. But she was a one-man gal and once she said "I do" she would never look back.

That's the way God made this woman. She suspected the same applied to all women or at least one other lovely lady named Stella.

Chapter 36

About 10:30 p.m., six nights before the wedding, Hai called Stella, contracting a bad case of eight cold feet, so empathetic was she.

"I've been getting quite a lot of text messages from Troy. How about you?" Hai asked.

"From Troy?" They snickered, but they both knew the truth. Deep within each harbored a passion and not necessarily for the right person or reason. All four of them were entwined like a bowl of lo mein or in Stella's world, linguini.

"No sweetie."

"Raphael has been mothering me, texting me, wondering about every detail. He wanted to be at our measuring, claiming an artist's right to see his creations, but I didn't want bad luck."

"Troy too. He only wanted to admire us," Hai said.

"Is Troy admiring me, okay with you, Hai?"

"I understand it. What about us?"

"I admire you," Stella said. "Troy's sense of humor has rubbed off on all of us. They look alike, how could we not notice both of them?"

"Excellent point," Hai said. "They're the most gorgeous males on the planet."

"And we do them justice."

"Absolutely."

"And almost as smart as us."

"We need to sit down with them, only the four of us, and make sure everything is okay." Hai decided against digging any deeper with Stella. She loved Stella like a sister, but tomorrow would be a better time for answering questions.

"Agreed. No matter our tangled hearts. We have a winning team." Stella said with little energy.

"The fab four."

Hai had arranged breakfast for four at Ponzio's Diner, now five days before the wedding. They wanted to avoid all the relatives and friends who were in town and chasing them, trying to monopolize their time. Only gossip would result and little work would get done. The boys' friends especially, since they had been razzing the twins with endless swapping jokes, had been doing this since high school. Why stop now?

7:55 a.m., a bit early, she waited alone in a cushy booth next to a window overlooking Route 70.

Her cell rang. Janine, her maid of honor, paralegal par excellence, and other best friend was mothering her lately.

"Hi, Janine."

"I've wrapped up Champsky versus Miller." This wasn't why she called.

"Janine. Come on, they'll be here soon."

"You love Raphael." Janine said, as if she summed up before the Supreme Court.

Damn good prosecutor without a shred of evidence.

The proper amount of silence, ten seconds, seemed right.

"What makes you think that?" True, she was attracted to Raphael's sensibilities, thought he was a better match, but she was very happy with the zany Troy. He thrilled her. Besides, they had an agreement and it would be tested one last time today.

"I can tell from the last few times I saw your face. Your body language tells, like a juror leaning one way or the other," Janine said.

"My face is that of a woman in love."

"Yeah, but with whom?"

"Listen, my dear Janine... I see them. They're coming. Don't worry. The four of us are all aware of cross-feelings to coin a word, and we're comfortable, we're okay. It is all for the best."

"Just dig a little deeper, make sure. You know I love you," Janine said.

"I love you too. I'll be in the office before lunch. I need to meet with Judge Marquart again, 3:00 p.m."

"I'll have the file freshened-up and ready to go." Janine hung up.

Hai scooted over. Troy kissed her. Stella scooted over and Raphael kissed Stella as if he was following some sort of protocol set by his brother.

Troy and Stella ordered scrapple and eggs, Raphael and Hai ordered buckwheat pancakes. When the food arrived, Hai seized the moment.

"You all notice that Raphael and I have ordered the same, and you two have ordered that pork mush, ah scrapple." Scrapple, in its defense, was a scrumptious mix of seasoned grains and piggy parts. What parts, God only knows.

"The pancakes are healthier," Raphael added, ignoring her real point about who should be marrying whom.

"I need the energy, nothing gives me more energy than scrabble and eggs," Troy said.

"It's spelled, S-c-r-a-p-p-l-e." Raphael's mind must have been floating elsewhere. By now, you'd think all present knew of Troy's romance with the English language and his insatiable joking.

"It tastes better, pass the ketchup," Stella said. "Not the wood letters, too much varnish."

As exhibit one, I offer Stella's type-A personality. Her attempt to joke, shows the defendant is leaning Troy.

"That's my point: Five days to our double wedding and are we sure we will be happy?" Hai asked.

"Of course we will, we're doing what's best for each other," Troy said.

"Consider the dynamic we have. Opposites attract," Raphael offered while dribbling maple syrup on his pancakes in an attempt to

199

draw a face. *Now he and his inner artist is awake.* She felt like kicking him, but that was Stella's job.

"The school girl crush I had was based on Troy being quarterback. You guys are both loving and gorgeous. We'd be trivializing it." Stella's words weren't convincing. Hai felt everybody understood this. She also feared pushing Stella and Raphael too far. Both Troy and she had agreed to protect what Stella and Raphael had grown over the years.

The right thing to do.

"I...I don't know what to say," Hai said. She forked one pancake from her plate and put it on Raphael's stack. Stella's eyes followed the transfer. Raphael seemed oblivious, then waved his fork, raised an eyebrow, and dug in. Troy just chowed down.

"We don't have to say anything, we all love each other. It will work out," Stella said.

"Okay, let's just spit it out one more time," Troy said. "I, Troy Chariote, have always felt since the day Raphael brought Stella home that I'd like to meet a girl like her someday. Raphael, on the outs with Stella, was smitten by Hai, when he pretended to be me for my sake, and after kissing her, I can see why. Stella had or has a crush on me. And, Hai will never forget the kiss Raphael planted on her. Her first serious kiss. So what else is new?" Aside from Troy trivializing the situation, it was a fair summary.

After a round of rumbling yeses, Troy continued, "I'm okay with this as well. I know I've joked about it at the Comic Freak and..."

Stella interrupted, "You two boys are really not that different. True Raphael is a neatnic, and you, Troy, are the opposite," everybody but Troy snickered, "but listen to me. That's not important. Both of you are artists working different mediums. Both of you have true hearts. And both of you will not covet thy brother's wife or the two of us will leave you, the Church be damned."

"I'm not into coveting," Troy said.

"Me neither," Raphael said, displaying a hint of sadness in his eyes, from an angle only Hai could see, it seemed.

It was then, Hai realized the marriages had to proceed. Somehow, the relationships worked, and upsetting the balance could ruin both weddings. Besides, she was so excited about Troy's promise to teach her lovemaking secrets. She'd stand no further delays or she'd burst.

Raphael had stopped drinking, and as long as the two couples stayed together, she'd influence him to stay sober. They all helped each other. Their unusual dynamics would ensure a loving future for them and their children. Case closed. Wrapped up, neatly. Really. Really?

"Raphael has stopped drinking. This to me means he's a happy man," Hai said.

"I am."

It stung a little to absorb these two abrupt words, but she'd get over it. She squeezed Troy's hand. Who studied her hard, but not in an adversarial way. He probably admired her sleek cheeks, his endearing term for her facial lines. Sleek cheeks, slinky eyes and inscrutable, but she thought for a moment she hadn't done a good enough job of displaying her feelings in a way easier for Raphael to read.

Time was called. They were all so busy. Nothing was resolved except that they would marry.

They said their alohas, because they'd never part. The fab four forever, and by the end of the week, two plus two, married. Besides, Stella, Raphael and Troy had been a team for years; they had to know what was best. She was raised to respect and honor social structure and besides she loved Troy and she loved the life all four were excited to start.

Chapter 37

Under a tent over grass, on abutting card tables, rested two wedding cakes. Troy noticed Raphael the perfectionist fiddling with one of Raphael's creations.

Troy came up to the back of the cake, peeking at his watch. The ceremony would begin promptly at twelve noon. There remained twelve minutes left to get in place for Hai and Stella. Everybody else had already seated themselves on the other side of the rolled-down white canvas.

"I'm amazed at the loving attention you gave to the little statues on our cakes," Troy razzed who he felt was sometimes too fastidious. Granted, great artists needed this mindset. Still.

Raphael had carved a little Troy, Raphael, Stella and Hai. At present, Raphael straightened Hai, who leaned like the Tower of Pisa.

"How are you feeling?" Raphael asked. "I mean, are you one hundred percent sure this is right for the four of us?"

These identical twins harbored no secrets. It was no secret; Raphael had tried to bury his initial crush on Hai. He shouldn't have pretended to be Troy and surreptitiously land Hai for Troy, because Raphael became ensnared by the tenderness of Hai's kisses. Troy had forgiven him long ago, because Raphael was on the rocks with Stella. True, Troy had had a thing for Asian women, but he left that preference behind in college, unknown to his brother. Troy had once upon a time obsessed over Asians almost as badly as Stella had over "her" identical twins, with the stronger crush on Troy. *What a mess.*

Troy moved-on his senior year to appreciate all women as individuals. *It's called growing up.* Ms. Hai Lo was about to become Mrs. Troy Chariote, because of his commitment to her as an individual, not to some stereotype. Beautiful, of warm heart, brilliant and most importantly a full-fledged member of the gang of four.

"We've always been honest with each other, right?" Troy asked.

"I read your mind half the time, so yes, tell me."

"Okay Mr. Mind Reader, you tell me what I'm thinking."

Raphael lowered his voice and responded. "You're worried I still have a crush on Hai and since you have always liked Stella, you think it would be great fun to swap places—after we're married. After you broke Hai in, naturally. Well, knowing you, we'd maybe even swap on the honeymoon, but not the first night. You'd think of this as fulfilling our fantasies. Right?" He practically spit out his last words. Poor Raphael looked like he was going to have a stroke.

"So who would be the father of our children?" Troy wasn't really thinking about swapping, he wasn't thinking, except to lower his brother's temperature with a joke.

"Don't you see it, Troy?" Raphael said, exasperated. "It's a juvenile fantasy."

Okay, maybe Troy stood guilty of unrealistic and whimsical thinking, even if he didn't think it consciously. The four of them were so intertwined and always would be. The twins had lived lives dedicated to crazy shenanigans. He couldn't feel guilty for what was most likely the past. Fingers crossed. How dare his brother bust him for a crime he hadn't gotten the bright idea for, yet. *If ever.* But he knew his brother knew he knew and might.

"Well actually…" Troy mumbled.

"Actually, my ass. First of all, Hai seems to be able to tell us apart, somehow. Maybe Mom taught her a trick. No, then Stella would know it too. We need to grow up."

Hai wouldn't know for sure who was who in the dark, probably. No, Troy had to stop thinking this way. He was wild and everybody else had sticks up their bottoms.

"Stop right there, bro," Troy decided to test his brother for said stick. Raphael held his tongue for once. Waiting for his brother's gems of wisdom? "It is you who are fingering Hai's figurine as if she were some sort of Barbie or hula girl for your dashboard."

"She was leaning. That's all."

"Leaning to me or you?"

"You're out of line and we're out of time." Raphael narrowed his lips, obviously getting angry. Troy would have to break him of this false umbrage.

Troy pulled the Hai figurine out of the cake and switched it with Stella atop the other cake.

"Damnit Troy, do you know how hard it is to keep icing looking good? Every swirl a perfect French curve.— Don't stop me." Raphael switched the two girls back and started smoothing the icing with an artist's wooden spatula, which had been lying by the cake to keep his creations, perfect, just perfect.

"Don't you dare touch the cakes again, Troy."

Unheeded, Troy removed the little Troy and Raphael and swapped them.

"Okay, you win, Troy. Of course I had, no, I still harbor a crush on Hai and, let me remind you, you have always crushed on Stella."

Troy interrupted. "But hear me, bro. I love you too much to ever take anything of yours let alone your sweetheart and about to be wife and okay we won't swap anymore.— I mean it."

Raphael still seemed upset. It had to be the mussed cake. What the hell was his too too devine brother getting married for, anyhow?

"It's really old ground, isn't it?" Raphael muttered. "We're just going round and round. Time for me and you to hop off this merry-go-round."

Yep. This came up every time the gang called a meeting, starting with the retreat weekend, and lastly, the breakfast at Ponzio's. He could tell by Raphael's tone he was still disturbed about the figurines being switched and the infinitesimal mess he had made.

"Listen, maybe me and you should get married." Troy deadpanned.

"Our children wouldn't turn out right."

"Damn. Raphael, that's funny."

"We already are in so many ways, *married.* Let's not worry. Everything will go happily ever after," Raphael said. He continued smoothing the cake; the little couples now back in their correct positions. Raphael's face relaxed, his inner artist's harmony was right with the world now, no doubt.

Troy noticed that the figurine of Raphael was taller than his figurine.

Now I'm pissed.

He knew his brother to be the measure three times, sculpt once type. There had to be an explanation.

"You're taller than me." Troy politely pointed at the Raphael figurine.

"Oh come on. I swear. No, you're kidding. Well—maybe." Raphael leaned over to inspect. "I'll be damned, Troy, I didn't mean this." He glanced at his watch. "We only have four minutes to slip around this tent and present ourselves to the crowd. I just can't fix it now."

The devil on Troy's left shoulder had a bright idea. "It's no big deal. I can fix it," Troy leaned over and pushed the Raphael figurine a little too deeply into the cake.

Raphael grabbed Troy's pushing hand. "Stop, you're making it worse, making a mess." Little waves of cake icing had formed around the base of the figurine. Troy pulled away but Raphael kept a hand lock on his brother's arm. This caused Raphael to lean forward over the table. One of the legs must have been over a gopher hole because the cake started sliding toward Troy. Raphael noticed, let go of his brother's hand but couldn't keep his balance. He began falling with the cake and gimpy table onto his brother. He managed to push the table aside to save his brother and hugged the cake the rest of the way down.

Splat, squish, blblublubl.

"This really pisses me off. You've worked *days* on this cake." Troy mocked, voice still lowered. He smashed a good-sized portion of the top layer into Raphael's face. Raphael stuffed the Troy figurine into Troy's breast pocket and laughed.

"You horny pig. Stay away from my Stella." Raphael took a chunk of another layer and smashed it on Troy's cummerbund and then crotch. They rolled around making the mess worse. That's when they both tried to outdo each other until covered head to toe. The people at Men's Warehouse were not going to be pleased with this. The hired staff stood back snickering so as not to alarm the guests and likely not wanting to be caked by two berserk grooms. Troy laughed so loudly, Father Brian ran into the tent. Unashamed and having more fun than they did at age six in the pig pen, the boys continued rolling on the new mown and caked lawn.

"Boys, boys, we have no time left. Get up immediately."

"Sorry, Father."

"Sorry, Father."

"We're on this earth together, boys, if you would be brothers; fight not on your own behalf, but for the sake of others."

"Exactly what we were doing, Father," Raphael said.

"And well worth the caking, Father," Troy said.

The priest lowered his voice. "Well then, are we going through with this ceremony or not?"

"Give us some time to change," Troy said.

"Absolutely not, or I'll go on without you." Raphael said. Surprise—time trumped neatness. Hell neatness, they looked like two alligators flopping in white and pink mud. Perhaps he worried that too much time would cause doubt. Troy formed a tear over the comic possibilities. He knew his brother as he knew himself. He'd marry now looking the fool rather than chance the alternatives.

"Okay, we go, exactly the way we are now, or *my* wedding is off." Troy said, picturing the absurd look they'd present to the gathering crowd. The truth—removing jackets wouldn't change much. *Might as well go formal.*

"Fine." Raphael said, with a smile marred by an icing scar.

Troy guessed there'd be two marriages and a side order of cake. "Keep smiling. You're so ugly when you do that."

"Let's go get our girls." Raphael patted his brother's shoulder and then looked at his hand.

"Another nice mess?" Troy asked, imploring.

"And tasty too."

The boys hugged, squished, and laughed some more. Tears weren't visible, too much cake make-up.

"Follow me, boys." Father Brian led them around the corner. The mostly seated audience gasped and chuckled. Cameras of all kinds and shapes were focused and snapping away. Then applause, as if they were a vaudeville act. They were maybe thirty seconds early. Nice timing. Father Brian used one of the many white linens, on the makeshift altar to wipe his hands. Somehow, he acquired a touch of cake. He then offered the linen to the twins who were beyond help.

"Let's do this," Troy said, and his brother wiped his eye so he could see better. They hugged again, squishing for the wedding party. Troy fingered the icing out of his ear. They slid apart and awaited two very special ladies.

Chapter 38

The brides wore white silk sparely beaded, with a hint of taffeta business jacket. The grooms wore cake and grass stains.

Stella hovered excitedly next to Hai in the alcove of Raphael's back door. They stepped out into the brilliant noon sun on a perfect mid-August Saturday.

Stella couldn't believe the sight down the long walk to wedded bliss. Setting up this double wedding with Hai's help and the full support of three sets of loving families could not have gone more easily. She peeked at Hai, so stunning, so beaming, for just the hint of doubt. Hai had to be dreaming of luscious kisses, or the squint caused by the sun riffling through the willow branches blinded her to the boys' condition. Who knew marrying identical twins could be so much fun and so exasperating at the same time. Yes, Stella loved Raphael and Hai loved Troy. It had become no secret, they all loved each other like minestrone soup—meant to be inseparable physically and by heart and soul. Since they did everything together, Stella didn't have to let go of her old crush on Troy, as nasty as it seemed. Hai still harbored similar feelings for Raphael, which started when Raphael, in jail, awakened her with a kiss. No problem. All four had addressed these crossed feelings, multitudinous times.

No problem.

Stella decided to awaken Sleeping Beauty.

"They look good enough to eat," Stella said. Okay, this was corny, but to be more precise, cakey. Both boys had expensive Italian rum wedding cake, damn, and grass stains all over their rented black tuxes and frilly white shirts.

When everybody is looking at her, she'll be looking at you and thinking about dessert.

Yet they stood there as if nothing had happened. Sure the crowd seated dutifully in lawn chairs chattered, snapped a ton of pictures, yet the double piece de-resistance—the gorgeous brides—had not yet made it completely around the weeping willow tree.

Hai cupped her mouth, the unflappable attorney just flapped. Stella squeezed Hai's other hand. They'd walk up hand-in-hand, dads on both sides. Both dads tried to suppress snickers, to keep a little decorum.

Hai's maid of honor, Janine, had a ridiculous grin on her face and seemed to be laughing tears. Janine, on seeing Hai, hand-signaled, I love you and followed it with thumbs up. What were friends for?

Hai let out like a deflating tire, "Oh my God."

"Dad, do you know what the boys were up to this time?" Stella asked, of either father, her eyes seeking sympathy more than answers.

Her dad cleared his throat, and with authority said, "We still have one cake intact, and everybody is on a diet." Daddy lived at the gym, for him a squashed cake was a good thing in his never-ending battle against the fat cell terrorists.

Hai said something whimsical sounding in Chinese, and her dad responded in English. "Not to worry girls, the boys had an accident, and they are very excited to see the most beautiful and special girls in the whole wide world." His eyes and mouth cornered upward like crescent moons. He holstered the flip phone he had palmed.

Accident my foot, the boys were covered in cake from their curly blacks to the shiny patent leather shoes with not much on their backs. They looked like the cardboard target-practice figures at a shooting range.

"So let's go get them." Stella's dad said.

Two flower girls and two ring bearers stepped in front of them. The two girls, both five-years old, Stella's little sister and Hai's niece wore the same design as the brides, except for pink bows and yellow trim at the bottom of their dresses, once again from Raphael's sketches. True, he was a paint and sketch artist, not a clothes designer, but he extracted a favor with a clothes designer friend and managed to create unique designs. Brilliantly conceived and executed. However, executing one or both boys was not an option.

Standing there, the boys looked like pie-eating contestants. Their unabashed stance had to be Raphael's idea. The time freak within him trumped his neat freak. He must have said 'no time to change,' to his brother and all who attended to the Pillsbury doughboys. He would rationalize, let Hai and Stella walk to heaven, they'd notice but wouldn't care, because they knew Troy and Raphael were incurable Peter Pans and they'd wash up nice. Not tossing the jackets must have been Troy's idea, anything for a joke. Although the rest was a mess, and in spots a very lick-able mess.

The six bridesmaids, six groomsmen and two maids of honor all seemed satisfied, nicely flanking the cake boys. Six and six, a quarter of them from Stella, quarter Hai's, half the boys and all stunning. Raphael had used his bucolic backyard for inspiration. He sketched and oversaw the making of the bridesmaids' pastel pink and tan peasant dresses. Stella supposed brides couldn't be outclassed anyway, because they beamed with joy.

Her veneer felt the smallest of cracks, and not from their beauty.

Hai squeezed Stella's hand back. They took their first step to "*Here* Comes *the Bride*," well brides, but who's counting?

Would Stella, by the time she stood next to the handsome twins, run and make it, 'there goes one bride,' dum-dum, da-da? Quite a different song. Raphael's place had the acreage. She could kick-off the highest of high heels. Those she selected to come close to the model perfect five foot nine of Hai. She'd hike her willowy gown and run. Oh, but where? She had loved the Chariote brothers for so long she ached for completion, for children.

The problem was she loved both Chariote brothers. "Practicality over foolish old teenage crushes," her mother had said crying, implying drop one boy and move on. Nonetheless, her crush remained very much alive and maybe a tad foolish.

They took another rose-petalled step. Really, all four of them reached the joint conclusion: All this would be good. But were they all lying to each other more or less? Hai, now her best friend was first to agree. They would raise babies together. Moms and dads could babysit. The four of them could go anywhere. They played bridge and no one was the dummy. They played normal scrabble, and no one had to strip. Oh so comfortable and loving they had become, since the day Hai helped save Troy from unjust charges, by the Grecos. Frank, Romeo, Jersey and other Mafioso sat, quietly enjoying the scene. What now, five whole months was it? These two marriages would last five years easy, with the kind of mess the four of them have gotten themselves into. *All for the happiness of each other.*

No problem.

Why would Stella want to mess up the best foursome since the Beatles?

They took another step on the red rose petal path. People ceased staring at the boys. Then all turned.

Damn it, she was Catholic. She laid a great foundation. Their marriages would last a lifetime. They just needed the right beginning. Hai Lo, of Chinese heritage was just as conservative. Hell, she was still a virgin.

They had taken a few more steps.

Daddy, hold me up.

God, give me the strength.

Oh Jesus, they did look good and edible. Not only were they the most striking men she had ever laid eyes on, their hearts were pure. Yes, they acted very impish and boyish. So why would today—a woman's greatest day—be any exception?

The dads kissed and handed over their daughters. Stella's maid of honor, her sister Lucia, signaled, using her wide eyes to show loving approval and support. Troy wiped his hand on his pant leg, which only made the situation worse and took Hai's hand. She peered down with a twisted closed-lipped smile at the creeping cake blob, now part of her. Stella swiped a piece off Raphael's collar and tasted it, giving him the come-hither look and thumbs up to the audience, who responded with polite giggles.

"As yummy as you, baby." Then under her breath, she said leaning into him, "What happened?"

He leaned down, "Troy and I had a mishap. Tangled, we fell into one of the cakes. Everybody is on a diet." She had heard that before. Had he called Hai's dad?

Father Brian said. "We are gathered together," but Stella raised her hand.

"Just a moment, Father."

She whispered to Raphael. "Why did it happen?"

"I swear, I was helping him straighten his bowtie when Jerry slinked by. Troy, surprised, afraid he'd squash the ferret, lost our balance. That's all." Knowing both of them, she called for a four-way huddle, but Troy could add nothing more. At least their stories meshed.

She could run away and let Hai marry Troy and then just kill herself. She could stay part of the fab foursome, and have a fantastically exciting and beautiful life.

"Does anybody here today know of any reason why these two couples should not be married?"

"A moment, Father." Stella remembered Joe and Lisa Chariote, before they went to their seats, had chased down, Jerry, who had been stealing various items from the guests' windbreakers and pocketbooks. She looked over her shoulder at the kitchen bay window. Jerry was jailed and peered forlornly out at the wedding from his wire cage. Duh. She was now certain she understood the problem all four of them were having, especially the boys. The twins so loved each other, they wanted what was best for each other. They both felt more strongly than either would let on, because of their love for each other. Simply twisted, the four, like a bowl of spaghetti.

Troy loved her, crazy loved her.

Raphael magically gave up drinking. Which was Hai's doing.

Raphael loved Hai, crazy loved her.

With a little luck Hai felt the same, because Stella couldn't get Troy out of her head. Hai always had that look, maybe a small sadness, when peering at Raphael. She'd take a chance. The odds were good for that dreamy happily ever after.

Resolute. Shaking.

She peeked back at her mom, raised her eyebrows, shrugged her shoulders and slapped her thighs in frustration. Something her mom had seen her do countless times as a little girl, when the little girl was about to put her foot down. Had she regressed under stress? No one was speaking up. Hai seemed somewhere else, likely wondering what it would be like naked making love in a honeymoon suite.

Would it hurt?

Although Raphael was big and identical twins are identical, she remembered her first sweet moment of surrender to Raphael. He had a way, a gentle way, every movement like falling, held by a bungee cord. Hai would be in for the treat and ride of her life with Troy, no Raphael, the man she really loved.

God, I hope so.

Stella raised her hand with fingers crossed.

Troy said, "The bathroom is down the hall and to the left." The professional comedian played the crowd and they responded.

Silly boy. Oh, she knew Troy, irascible, spontaneous, irrepressible. Exactly what she needed, wanted. Not that Raphael, the loving artist, with his more quiet ways, wasn't wonderful. She needed Troy's craziness to mix and keep up with her type-A personality. Worse yet, she knew Troy wanted her too. Maybe her personality, which matched Troy better than Raphael, had something to do with the way she grew up. She scanned her six siblings, remembered the general mayhem that pressed a working class Catholic family and produced its greatest joy. Her big brother gave a nod as if to say, 'I'm with you no matter what you do.' His eyes said, 'Go ahead, my dear little one.' His kindness always gave her strength and God did she need it now.

"I object to this marriage." Stella said, with enough force to knock over the other cake.

"But—on what—ah, why, tell me why, young lady?" asked Father Brian who probably being flustered forgot her name. They had known each other her whole life, for Christ's sake. She crossed herself in her mind, what was left of it.

Raphael raised his hand.

"You too?" asked the priest, flabbergasted.

Troy got in his brother's face, jaw to gooey jaw. He said in a low threatening voice, "I thought we had this settled." She had seen Troy do this a couple times when Troy as quarterback berated his brother for messing up a handoff. On the next play, Troy handed off to Raphael and Raphael ran more from his brother's criticism than his opponents' slipped tackles. Raphael scored a touchdown and the school paper wouldn't stop writing about them. Possibly since Stella was the reporter.

Please, please, please don't obey your brother.

Hai also heard these stern words. Soon everybody heard by the grapevine. Bits of gossip filled the air like the gossamers floating about.

"Something happened between the boys," someone said.

"They fought over the girls," another said.

"I knew this would happen," Hai's Janine said, beaming brighter than the confused brides. Good, Hai had to be on board. *Come on, Hai. Come on.*

Raphael came close to his brother, whispered something in his ear. They hugged, making a squishing sound similar to ketchup in a hurry to leave the plastic bottle. They both shook their heads no. Separated now, Troy raised his hand. Maybe there'd be no handoff today, no new brilliant play, maybe not.

"I object," Troy said and then started laughing uncontrollably.

Father Brian grabbed his chest in mock horror, and then crossed himself for real. His long dormant Irish brogue returned to full blush. "Be there anybody here might explain what on God's green earth, Mother Mary." He looked skyward. "What be goin' on?"

Hai raised her hand. The priest grasping for straws said, "Yes, child, you be the most careful of the group." He got that right. "You shall speak for the group lass. Won't you?"

"I will and I object."

"Yes, yes, I know everybody is objecting. Have you not something mor-re to add? Go on, lass."

Yes, go on, lass.

"The boys now stand in the wrong places, Father." Simply put. Yes. Yes. Yes. And yes. With tears in her eyes, she met Stella's watery gaze. They understood what this could mean. Be it total disaster or a fairy tale finish, there was no turning back.

"Go on, boys. Do it." Stella encouraged.

They switched places. Troy fingered off a piece of cake, which had invaded his brother's eye.

The priest pulled out his notes, flustered. Then he had an inspiration, call it a miracle. He called out for the boys' mother Lisa to come forward. The diviner of truth approached, somberly. Not giving away a thing.

Then Romeo Greco stood, cell phone to ear, "I'm not objecting, but…"

"Oh no, what now, sir?" Father asked.

Romeo calmed everybody by waving his hand downward. "With all due respect, Father, you can't have a wedding without wedding cake… There will be two Italian rum cakes here in less than two hours. We can't object to that." He slipped his cell phone back in its holster, smiled broadly, and sat down to applause. Troy and Raphael sign-languaged hugs for him. That made three cakes but who's counting, calories today, aside from Daddy?

The ceremony continued. "Do you certify before me and God, oh God, that this one be Troy and this one Raphael?"

"I do." Their mom said. Sampling some cake from both boys, she sat back down beaming because she loved the cake or the idea or both. She had asked her daughter months ago to seek the truth, to dig deeper when Raphael and she were on the rocks. *Yes, Mom.*

The priest had fixated on Lisa when she tasted the cake. They had better finish the ceremony before Father Brian's stomach started to grumble.

"Do you Troy Chariote take Stella Riccardi, and do you Raphael Chariote take Hai Lo as your lawfully wedded…and *separate* wives?" He stumbled but improvised correctly. "That is Troy takes Raphael, no I mean takes ah Stella, right?"

Well, Father, no wine yet or rum cake?

Troy gathered Stella's hands. The sun played with his exquisite bad boy and frosted face. "I do," he said beaming like a pregnant woman. Something Stella had on her agenda.

If not now?

"And you there, Raphael, do take Hai?" Both Raphael and Hai were taken by Troy's emotion.

"I do, with all my heart." Raphael gave Hai the most incredible of looks, tears pooling. Both boys had finally become men, *this day of our Lord, right before our eyes.*

"I too, take Stella with all my heart." Troy added.

"I take Troy without reservations and of my whole heart," Stella said not waiting for Father Brian's prompt. Besides, he could throw his wedding service book away on this one.

"Me too, and forever," Hai said, with so tender a smile and so red a face. That girl did blush often. "I mean I take Raphael and only Raphael forever." Okay, that worked. Thank God, they all finally got it right, and no one would be hurt. The fab four became even more fabulous.

* * *

After the wedding, they hosed down the boys.

Troy said, "Whatdaya say we all go on our honeymoon together by upgrading to one two bedroom hotel room to save money?" The two couples were booked for the Caribbean island of Saint Thomas in separate hotels, different sides of the island, just as Hai and Stella had planned.

"Not if you want to live another day," Stella said to her husband. He laughed.

"I think we'll have to give up swapping," he said to Raphael.

"Gladly."

"My ancestors are pleased," Hai said, bursting with happiness. "See you guys on the beaches maybe, I have a lot of homework. It'll require me to stay indoors mostly. Raphael is going to teach me the art of love." No secret here. She nestled Raphael with her head on his shoulder and hand over his heart. Stella and Troy, and Raphael all beamed.

Everything straightened out, the way destiny dictated and desires enforced, now of true hearts all. Hai noticed pink-bottomed white puffs bumping each other across the blue sky. She closed her eyes for a moment of thanks.

Just a little miracle.

Epilogue

Lelanie and Pauline Chariote celebrated their tenth birthday in their dad and mom's really huge backyard with Uncle Troy and Aunt Stella's kids and a whole bunch more kids and their parents.

Lelanie didn't see it coming, when Bobby Fielding ran up to her, whipping around the willow tree, then put his lips on hers, and ran away right away, laughing. Not knowing what to do, she found her sister sitting next to Uncle Troy, who always told the funniest stories. She asked her sister to come to their—way back in the corner—secret tree house for a special meeting.

After the latch was locked, and she could see nobody coming near them, she said, "I just got my first kiss from a boy."

"Was it Joey? He likes you." Pauline said.

"No, this is a big surprise to you. It's Bobby."

"Wow, he's so cute." Bobby was cute. He had curly blonde hair and green eyes and he liked snakes.

"He didn't ask me. He kissed me here and ran away laughing."

"Oh, boys do that."

"How do you know?"

"Jamie told me. The same thing happened to her."

"Do I have a bruise?"

"No silly, your lips are like cushions. They can take a beating."

Lelanie looked in their secret mirror at big lips.

"Well, what did it feel like?"

"I like it." She touched her lips. "But it was too short."

"Do you think he'll do it again?"

"No, because I'll be looking for him. If he's running near me, I'm going to knock him out." Mom taught the girls to defend themselves from boys. She peeked over the bottom of the window and saw their beautiful China doll mom leaning on Daddy. Uncle Troy, and Mom and Daddy were laughing with Aunt Stella.

"Don't hurt him."

"He has to ask next time."

"How come he kissed you not me? We are identified like Uncle Troy and Daddy."

"Identical."

"Identical. Do you want him to kiss you?"

"Maybe not. What did he taste like?"

"Pizza."

"Macaroni and cheese could be better even better, but I'd still wish I could get a kiss."

"You can't. He told me in school he liked me not you, because he sits right behind me, and likes the way I push my hair straight up. He thinks he can hide pencils in here." She knocked the top of her head.

"I got an idea."

"Tell me, piece of my heart, soul sister, mirror mirror, forever yours." They did the secret sister hug, hand shake, and rubbed noses.

"Piece of my heart, soul sister, mirror mirror, forever yours, listen to this. We will switch dresses and fix our hairs…"

"And you go stand next to the willow tree…"

"And you run and tell him that that's you over there wanting another kiss."

"Okay, deal."

"But tell him to slow down and then tell me how it felt and does he still tastes like pizza."

"Deal."

"And then we'll swap again."

"Forever yours."

"Forever."

* * * * * *

You have just read *Double Happiness* and the author wants to thank you. The Author needs your support to succeed. Please correspond if you have questions or write a review if you have the time. I'm at rwrichard@ymail.com or visit http://romancetheguyspov.blogspot.com.

If you enjoyed this story, you may enjoy the author's other works:

The Wolves of Sherwood Forest - a novella in e-book format only. Wolves…is a lighthearted romp through Sherwood Forest with a young-adult Robin, Marian and real wolves (as opposed to werewolves). The couple banded together to save the recently returned to England, King Richard. If you like your politics really dusty-old (before the Magna Carta), try this flashback to a time when people could just walk into your home for no particular reason (oh, you say, they're relatives and neighbors, nevermind).

Neanderthals and the Garden of Eden: Running with Wolves - a novel in e-book and paperback. This, the author's first story, is different from anything else you will have read, because multi-protagonist stories have been out of style for 120 years. But that's the way life was back 100,000 years ago when we, through this story, witness the intermingling of tribes and wolf packs and how they lived. Although not a romance in the traditional sense, this story includes a man traveling back in time to find his one true love. The pace is fairly quick because the tribe members usually demonstrated their thoughts with action. You may think of this novel as a scientist's rejoinder to so many well-written but scientifically incorrect pre-history stories.

The Carlos series in chronological order:

Autumn Breeze: I am a New Yorker - a novel in e-book and paperback. **Amazon's editors' pick for best books of 2015.**

On the morning of 9/11, a fourteen-year-old genius's mother disappears. Her beloved father had been murdered years before. She's now without parents. She resolves to get a new mom and dad and have them adopt her, before she is deported to Trinidad. For new mom, she selects her BFF (best friend forever), a New York City detective. For new dad, she selects the handsome spy who is investigating her BFF. The investigation was the girl's fault. She had predicted the terrorist attack to her BFF. Her BFF, in turn, won't give up her source, which makes the spy investigating her consider the detective as the possible predictor. Unbeknownst to the girl, a terrorist is also trying to find out who the predictor was, so he can silence him or her forever. Now, the girl is fighting to stay in the country, trying to make two people who hardly know each other, fall in love, get married and adopt her, while she is playing a most dangerous game of hide and seek with the terrorist to not only protect her life but also the life of her best friend.

The story, as it progresses, delves into how the City of New York responded to 9/11 by establishing an anti-terrorism taskforce, in which the girl's BFF and the spy play important roles.

On the journey, the girl learns that love is earned, sometimes with a heavy price.

Angel's Eyes- a novel. Will be out mid-2015. An Army Colonel loses her sight in battle and discovers she has an unusual talent, blindsight, a documented but little understood human condition. Out of the Army, she copes with a world in which she must rely on others, specifically one other.

A More Perfect Union - a novel in e-book and paperback. **Finalist: San Diego Book Awards.**
Former Miss Cherokee Nation, present Virginia Senator, Ayita Starblanket, is running against a former MLB slugger and present Florida Governor, Arturo Arnez. After circumstances force the unlikely pair together, she suspects her opponent is falling for her.